THE ORIENTAL WIFE

THE
ORIENTAL WIFE

A Novel

EVELYN TOYNTON

OTHER PRESS

New York

Production Editor: *Yvonne E. Cárdenas*
Book design: *Simon M. Sullivan*
This book was set in 12.5 pt Fournier by Alpha Design &
Composition of Pittsfield, NH.

10 9 8 7 6 5 4 3 2 1

LIBRARY OF CONGRESS CATALOGING-IN-PUBLICATION DATA

Toynton, Evelyn, 1950-
The Oriental wife : a novel / Evelyn Toynton.
p. cm.
ISBN 978-1-59051-441-2 — ISBN 978-1-59051-442-9 (ebk.)
1. Jewish children—Fiction. 2. Immigrants—New York (State)—
New York—Fiction. 3. Jews—New York (State)—New York—
Fiction. 4. Parent and child—Fiction. 5. Conflict of generations—
Fiction. 6. Love stories. 7. Domestic fiction. I. Title.
PS3570.O97O75 2011
813'.54—dc22
2010054143

For RJT

THE ORIENTAL WIFE

PART I

CHAPTER ONE

*A*lready, in what passed for their childhood, they had banded together: three only children, their fathers away at the war, their mothers variously distracted and harassed. All the maids in the neighborhood had rolled up their hair and absconded to the munitions factories, where the wages were higher. The cooks, being too old for a new life, had remained, but as there was less and less food to be had, they no longer commanded the same respect. They hid themselves in their kitchens, brewing up slimy messes with chicory and turnips. Having been coddled and spied on for all their short lives, the three children had finally achieved the freedom of young slum dwellers.

Otto was the linchpin: Rolf was his best friend from school, Louisa his shy cousin who lived next door. The two boys were feverish with excitement much of the time, partly brought on, though they did not realize this, by hunger. They chased each other, shrieking, around the garden behind Otto's parents' house. They rushed at each other with toy guns and fell down writhing. Then Louisa had to play nurse, fetching cups of water from the house and wrapping their heads in old dish towels. But sometimes she turned mischievous, pouring the water on their faces as they lay there.

Rolf would have smacked her for that, or pulled her hair, but Otto would never permit it. Nobody was allowed to hurt her while he was around; she had a bad enough time of it at home, he said, with her crazy mother, who locked her in wardrobes and beat her with a strap. He, Otto, had pledged always to protect her. Rolf, though he remained skeptical, was impressed by the grave, adult voice in which Otto told him this. Usually Rolf was the commanding one; it was the basis of their friendship.

And sometimes Louisa had a fit of inspiration that redeemed her even in his eyes. When two shops on a nearby street were bombed one night (by mistake—a British Sopwith had flown off course on its way to Munich), it was Louisa's idea to bring the charred wood from the bomb site and use it to make a fire. Fire-building became their great passion in that last, coldest winter of the war, though it was the two boys who had the job of dragging the planks back to Otto's garden and making the pyres. Otto said it was because Louisa could not risk soiling her clothes, her mother would beat her, but Rolf thought she was just being a girl.

The streets he traveled to get to Otto's house were full of the Kaiser's soldiers returned from the front, men who had marched out as heroes of the Fatherland and come back with wooden legs, or iron noses, or arms made of faded cloth stuffed with rags. There were others, their bodies intact, who staggered and grimaced and argued with themselves out loud. In the beginning Rolf had saluted them, every one, but as their numbers increased, he could not look them in the eye any longer; sometimes he ran away when he saw one approaching, ducking down an alleyway until the man had passed by.

On the night they got the news that his father had been wounded in Russia and might lose his arm, his mother told him, pressing her hands to her cheeks, that really it was nothing to mourn for, they should be grateful instead: now he would be safe behind the front lines. Then she shut herself into the parlor, and Rolf went into his bedroom and read a whole book for the first time in his life. It was about a fearless young German, with a heart pure as fire, who traveled through America and saved the life of a noble red man he recognized as his spiritual twin. Together, inseparable, they performed many heroic feats among the mountains of the Wild West, overthrowing evil and restoring justice. Rolf fell asleep with the light still on and woke, a few hours later, to the sound of his mother crying in the next room. For a moment he could not place the sound; he lay there in confusion, thinking it must be an animal, or a branch scratching at his window, before he remembered. His father would come back like those cripples he could not look at in the street, and it was his fault, a punishment for all the times he had ducked down an alley to avoid them. His throat constricted, the pressure in his chest was mounting until he thought he might burst.

And then a vision came into his head, of the prairies, and the buffalo, and the sunlit rivers full of trout; a space opened inside him, radiant, cleansed of grief. He picked up the book where it had fallen on the floor and clutched it to him as he drifted off again.

When the war ended, and his father came home with two arms after all, but one of them held stiffly, at all times, by his side; when bands of men were fighting each other in the city; when the police fired shots at the Communists in the Hauptmarkt, and the German Fatherland party attacked the Socialists with truncheons; when the cobbled squares were smeared with blood, and there were more women than ever sobbing in the streets, he shut his eyes and conjured up the wheatfields, the white foam on the rivers, the iron horse, with its red caboose, crossing the prairie.

Some day, he knew, he would live in America. He told no one of his plan, not even his mother, until the afternoon Louisa came into Otto's garden—Otto was off gathering kindling for another of their fires—in a blue dress with a lace collar and a matching blue coat, her red hair released from its braids and tumbling over her shoulders. She stood there expectantly, swishing her skirts from side to side.

"Why are you dressed like that?" he asked.

"I'm going to Munich. To visit my aunt. And we're going to the ballet. Have you ever been to Munich?"

"No," he said, and then, because she looked so triumphant, "I'm going to live in America when I grow up."

She stopped moving, though her hands kept their grip on the dress. "What are you going to do there?"

"Be a cowboy," he said.

She tossed her head. "No, you're not."

"I am so. Like Old Shatterhand."

"Who's that?"

"A German who went to live with the Indians."

"A real one? Or someone in a book?"

"In a book. You look stupid in that dress."

She looked so stricken he wished he could take it back, he almost told her it wasn't true. But just then Otto appeared, with an armful of branches. "Don't you look pretty," he said in his kindly way.

"Rolf says I look stupid."

"Then it's Rolf who's stupid."

Immediately she was flushed and excited again, telling him breathlessly about the ballet they were going to, with swans in it, showing him the cameo her grandmother had given her, fishing her kid gloves out of her pocket so he could admire them. As soon as she had gone, Rolf hurled himself at Otto and knocked him to the ground. Twigs went flying everywhere. Otto writhed and bucked with surprising ferocity. Rolf had to sit on his chest to restrain him, and even then Otto went on throwing wild punches. Finally, though, Otto was drained of rage and lay there panting.

"What's wrong with you today? What was that about?"

"I'm sick of fires," Rolf said. He stood up, brushing off his clothes, and pulled Otto to his feet. He tried to shake hands, but Otto withheld his. "Don't be childish," Rolf said sternly. "I'm going home now. You can build the fire yourself."

Just when things were normal again—the streets were peaceful, the women had stopped crying and stood in line at the butcher's for kidneys and offal—Rolf came home from school to find his father striding up and down the library in a rage. The French, it seemed, had marched into the Ruhr on the dubious pretext of some missing reparations. Sigmund's one good arm swung energetically back and forth as he called them damn swine, greedy duplicitous swine. Meanwhile Rolf's mother said "Now now now," in a briskly soothing voice, as though calming a flock of excited chickens. Nevertheless, Sigmund said, glaring, it was mad of the government to permit this talk of a general strike. Rolf sat at the far end of the sofa, where his cat Hansel used to doze in the sun. In the last year of the war, Hansel had gone out the window one day in search of mice and never come back. Sold for food, Rolf's cousin Hans had told him, when he visited with his mother: "He'll be all trussed up now, hanging in some butcher's shop with his thing cut off."

"And how are they going to pay the strikers' wages?" Sigmund demanded, wheeling around to face his wife. "Have they even considered that? They are leading us straight into catastrophe." Doggedly, Rolf tried to picture the waterfalls, the deer racing up a mountain; he shut his eyes and pretended he was talking Apache to himself.

His father was right; within a month, catastrophe had struck. The mark fell and fell—twenty thousand to the dollar, forty thousand, a million, a hundred million. People rushed to the market with all their money as soon as they were paid, trundling the paper notes in wheelbarrows. The headmaster at Rolf's and Otto's school, a moist-eyed, wheezing man who had only ever made vague speeches about duty and Fatherland, called an assembly and urged the boys to tell their parents they must buy shares: with any luck, he said, stocks could be counted on to rise at the rate of the mark. It was typical of him that he should be offering this advice long after everyone was buying shares already. The Latin teacher, formerly so punctilious about time—a boy who was one minute late would feel the crack of the ruler on his palm—went rushing out of the classroom at all hours to check with his broker. The baker's assistant grabbed his paycheck and ran to the stock exchange. Even the seamstress who came to Otto's house each Thursday morning to replace collars and sew the old sheets sides to middle took the money Otto's mother gave her and went to buy shares in steel.

When a pint of milk was fifty million marks, and the papers no longer reported the suicides in the city, Louisa's father began taking her with him on those trips to the countryside where he bartered the contents of her mother's trousseau for food. It was her mother's idea that Franz should bring

Louisa with him: she had called Louisa into the living room and yanked up her blouse to show him Louisa's ribs jutting out through her flesh. Louisa grabbed the hem and tried to tug it down, but Jeannette slapped her hand away. "Look at that, Franz, look at her. And her legs are like sticks. Somebody will take pity on her. Nobody is going to pity you." It was true that Franz had not had much luck so far, though he had worn his colonel's uniform, with the Iron Cross on the breast pocket. But there were too many others making the same journey. Half the burghers of Nuremberg, it seemed, were emptying their china cupboards and their wives' closets and going in search of bacon and turnips. The farmers' wives appeared in town in velvet dresses, with garnets dangling from their ears.

It was wrong, what she was suggesting, Franz said: he couldn't use his own daughter like that. Jeannette flew at him, hissing. "Then we must all starve, your daughter too. You will kill her with your principles." So he took her along, holding her hand as they walked together out of the city.

The farmers had high, hard bellies and leathery hands. Some of them called Louisa over in their guttural German while her father was talking to them. Sometimes they said, "The poor child," which was a good sign. With her father tensing beside her, they pinched her thin cheeks or stroked her long hair. She could not tell if the painful, churning feeling she had then was because she liked it or because she was frightened. Certainly she did not like their smell, or the calluses on their fingers. She stared at the flowers growing around the steps of their houses and wondered if people ever ate them. Mrs. Müller, the cook, who stayed with them despite being paid in useless money—for Louisa's sake, she said—boiled dandelions for breakfast when there was nothing else.

Then the bargaining began: so many cabbages, so many moldy potatoes, for the Meissen serving platter with the latticed border; a chicken and a bunch of beetroot for the pale pink tureen with the gold handles. Once a farmer's wife, a black shawl wrapped tightly around her shoulders, came out of the shed with a jug of milk still warm from the cow, which she handed silently to Louisa. Another time, a harelipped boy who had been watching from the kitchen window came hobbling down the steps to present Louisa with an egg. When she got home, Mrs. Müller took it from her reverently, in both hands, and boiled it for Louisa's supper.

By the time the Ruhr war was over and the New Mark could be counted on to keep its value, the boys' voices had deepened; the toy soldiers they had played with when the war began—Louisa had made them swords out of darning needles swaddled in silver paper—lay discarded in the attic, gathering dust. With the return of prosperity, Rolf became football-mad, even forgetting about America, and Louisa was sent to dancing classes presided over by a humpbacked Frenchwoman. Then she graduated to tea dances at the homes of her classmates. The dressmaker made her a floaty green chiffon dress with a silk underskirt that rustled against her legs as she moved. Some of the boys she danced with also wanted to stroke her hair—it was a deep chestnut color—but now it was up to her whether to let them or not. She could duck away if she wanted, or slap their hands, or laugh in their faces; she watched their cheeks turn red and noted the sudden stammer in their voices.

A sort of dizziness seized her at those moments, a heady sense of power that she could not allow herself to name. Sometimes she let them kiss her in the street as they walked her home, to see how it would feel; sometimes she gave them a push and walked ahead, waiting for them to catch up. Once one of the braver ones grazed her breasts with his hands, and a little shock went through her, not pleasure exactly but an inkling of what pleasure might feel like some day.

Meanwhile Jeannette was spending more and more time in the blue sitting room at the front of the house, reading the letters her brother had written from the University of Freiburg. His name was Adolf; he had shot himself, aged twenty, after failing an exam in his second year. (It was a time when many young men, brought up on legends of burning lakes and swords, were firing pistols through their temples. Those Jews who prided themselves so on their Germanness were not immune.) For as long as Louisa could remember, his portrait had hung over the marble fireplace in the little parlor; his desk was there too, with his letters tied with ribbon and propped up in the cubbyholes; his leather-bound books were neatly arranged in a locked mahogany bookcase with doors of etched glass. In the year that Louisa turned nineteen, Jeannette had the portrait cleaned and reframed; she unlocked the bookcase and seemed to be working her way through the volumes it contained, though often, when Louisa passed the door, her mother was simply sitting there, twisting her hands in her lap, the book she had been reading open on the sofa beside her.

At the sound of Louisa's footsteps in the hall, her mother would get up and slam the door, or rush out of the room to accost her. Where was she going, where had she been, didn't she know what those boys really wanted? She was heartless, a hussy, she had always been an unnatural child. Trapped in the narrow vestibule by the front door, watching her mother's lips move, Louisa conjured up the image of the green velvet beret in the window of Bamberger's department store, or a three-legged dog she'd seen on the street. Sometimes Franz emerged from his study, if he was at home, and told Jeannette sharply to leave the child alone, while Louisa escaped out the door or up to her room. "My mother hates me," she told a boy who had brought her a plate of supper at a dance, and laughed.

"I don't believe that," he said. "Nobody could hate you. You're so beautiful." But in the dark it was her mother's words she remembered, not the boy's.

One Sunday morning her father summoned her into his study and announced that he was sending her to a ladies' academy in Switzerland for a year. It wasn't just her mother's nerves, he said—Jeannette's condition was always referred to as nerves—though perhaps it would be best for everyone if Louisa got out of the house for a while. But he hoped too that she would apply herself to her language studies; languages, he said, clearing his throat, would be useful if she ever wanted to live abroad.

For several years, gangs of Brownshirts had been roaming the streets of the city, shouting of the great cleansing that was to come. The men who came to sit with Franz in his study—members of the veterans' committees and the board of the charity homes—told each other that soon those young men would settle down; the worst of the hard times was over; unemployment was down; there would be decent jobs for them all, and then they would come to their senses. They recognized, among the marchers, the man who delivered beer from house to house, the man who cleaned the chimneys, the boy who swept up in the Frauenplatz on market day. They were good fellows, they said, ordinary fellows, they only needed to be given a chance. Otto's mother told Louisa how she made a point of speaking to them kindly when she saw them on their own—the delivery man, for example; she always gave him an extra tip, she said, and had bought a gift for his baby daughter.

Only Jeannette insisted shrilly that this was just the beginning. The country was going mad, one day those men would be shooting them in broad daylight, and nobody would lift a finger. She could see it in people's eyes, she told Franz as he peeled the figs Mrs. Müller had brought for his *Nachtisch*: the eyes of the laundress who came and hung out the sheets in the attic, and the dressmaker's, and the maid's, and Mrs. Müller's too. "All the women are in love with the little corporal." Nonsense, Franz told her, with unaccustomed firmness. She should be ashamed even to suggest such a thing. He leaned across and patted Louisa's hand. "A nation that gave birth to the Enlightenment will never consent to be ruled by a gang of thugs."

Louisa never told them, but she had a Nazi admirer—a skinny, rawboned Brownshirt who had materialized on the street one night when she was walking home alone and asked if he could escort her. She remembered him from the marketplace, where his cart had tipped over; apples were rolling everywhere, and she helped him pick them up. The next week, when she was alone again, he appeared in the same place, stepping out of the shadows as she passed. His face, illuminated by the streetlamps, was pale and splotchy, with one tuft of hair protruding from the cleft in his chin; his walk was stiff and shambling, but something about him impressed her, a painful dignity lacking in her dancing partners. Mostly, on those nights they walked together, he was silent, but sometimes, with a kind of clumsy grandeur, he pointed out Orion or the Great Bear. "Imagine how far it is, in what pure air it lives. Up there you have the one true greatness." "I would have liked to be an astronomer, but it was not possible for me," he said once. "My parents are very simple people. Good folk, but ignorant. They have no sense of any higher destiny. So I have had to make my own way."

Another time, as they turned into her street, she asked, "Did you know that I am Jewish?" and felt him grow wary.

Yes, he said, he knew it.

"So aren't you supposed to hate me?"

He stopped walking. "All that is foolishness. I have no hatred for anyone, I only want to see my country restored to its honor. To take its rightful place among the great nations."

After that they did not speak again until they arrived at her door, when he took her hand and kissed it, like an old-style knight. He was the only National Socialist she had met, and she could not imagine him shooting her in broad daylight. She felt embarrassed, for his sake, about the things her mother said; she knew he would feel hurt, he would flush bright red if he could hear.

CHAPTER TWO

*A*t the school in Lausanne, the Italian boarders wore silk underwear and high-heeled sandals, and painted each other's toenails after tea, but they crossed themselves a lot and were strict about their purity. They were saving themselves for the men they would marry. The English, they said, rolling their eyes, had no morals whatsoever. "Is due to their climate. Everybody go to bed with everybody there to become warm."

But Louisa did not believe that. The English girls, with their light scornful voices and careless grace, were so clearly a higher order of being than anyone else. At dinner they commandeered the best table, as though by right, and afterward took possession of the red parlor next door, where there was a fire laid every night, and a vase of silk peonies was reflected in an ornate gilt mirror. If a Greek or German or Italian wandered in to retrieve a book or a handkerchief left behind during the day, the English girls would fall silent, watching her through narrowed eyes, until she retreated again. Everyone grumbled about them behind their backs—it was a bond among all the other nations—but was nonetheless anxious to curry favor. The Swiss girls seemed grateful to be asked about local dressmakers or the best cafés; the French girls, approached to explain the rules of the subjunctive in their language, were almost pitifully eager to oblige.

The most glittering of the English boarders was Celia, who could often be heard on the telephone under the stairs, expressing disdain: "Tell me you didn't. You really are too ridiculous . . . surely not, poppet . . . not even the Caitfords are that stupid." She had once stopped Louisa on the landing and asked her if she happened to have seen a pink kid glove anywhere. Louisa wished passionately that she could produce it, but she couldn't, and Celia carried on up the stairs.

Apart from that, there had been no contact between them until the morning she came bursting into the common room, where Louisa, in preparation for her English class, was going over "The Highwayman" with a girl from Stuttgart. Something too horrible had happened, Celia said, brandishing one of the yellow slips the secretary left in their cubbyholes when they got a phone call. Her fiend of a brother was stopping off that afternoon on his way from Zermatt, having given her no warning, just when she had a date with the most divine creature, who happened, only happened, to be the ninth richest man in Switzerland. Or at least his father was. Not that it even mattered. He was so dishy that money was beside the point. But her English chums had absconded to Geneva for the day, to visit some doddering governess person, which meant there was no one to entertain Julian for her until she got back.

"It's too shattering." She looked assessingly at the two Germans and then seized on Louisa. "I don't suppose you'd be a brick and keep him occupied for me for a couple of hours."

"I cannot," Louisa said in alarm. "My English is never yet good enough. It could not be understood to him."

"What nonsense! You speak marvelous English . . . Anyway, you can always take him for a walk if you can't understand each other. Maybe tell him I had to visit an old friend with TB. He can't be cross if I'm off comforting the sick." And then, when Louisa expressed doubt, "Honestly, what's an hour or two in a person's life? Nothing to make a fuss about really." So Louisa capitulated, and Celia called her a perfect angel. "I should warn you, petal," she said briskly, as she was leaving, "he can be a bit difficult . . . Actually, he's a perfect brute. But I'm sure you'll manage him beautifully."

By four o'clock, Louisa had washed her hair and changed into her new, square-necked green dress with the scalloped hem; she waited on the sofa in the red parlor, rehearsing to herself the explanation about the ill friend she had composed with the help of a German–English dictionary. But the brother, when the maid showed him in, interrupted her just as she was beginning. "Oh, Christ," he said savagely. "She's ditched me for some bloke."

"No, no," Louisa protested, as he stomped the snow from his shoes and blew into his hands. "Your sister is so much looking forward to again seeing you. She will as soon as possible come back."

"Well, it's damned inconsiderate of her, is all I can say. To you too. How did she bribe you into it?" He blew noisily into his very large hands. His hair was the same honey blond as Celia's, and like her he had an air of commanding deference, but his air of dissatisfaction—and in this too he was not unlike his sister—seemed pervasive, more than the mood of an hour. There was a sense that the world had failed to arrange itself for his convenience.

"Since you're stuck with me," he said, stripping off the checked scarf that was wound several times around his neck, "could I ask you to requisition a cup of tea?"

So she headed for the pantry, to place a request with Birgitta, the Swedish maid. On her return he was seated on the couch she had just vacated, his legs stretched out toward the empty grate. She wasn't sure if he was really extraordinarily tall or if he just occupied space more emphatically than other people. When Birgitta had set down the tray, and Louisa was handing him a cup of tea, she noticed that his hands trembled slightly, which was curiously thrilling.

"So, Ulian," she said, feeling bolder. "How long is it you are traveling today?"

"Not Ulian. Julian. Like Jew."

"I am myself a Jew," she said stiffly, before he could say something worse.

"Oh, Christ, are you? Sorry. I was only correcting your English."

There was a pause. Perhaps he would like to see the lake, she said with dignity, when he had finished his tea.

"Actually I've seen enough bloody lakes since I came to this country. It's not exactly short of bodies of water. But thanks anyway. Are you a big chum of Celia's?"

Not really, she said.

"Wise girl. No one should get too matey with my sister, she's dangerous." He leaned back, shutting his eyes. She was about to tiptoe out when he sat up and asked if she could scare up some wood; he would build a fire for them, he said.

By the time Celia returned, two hours later, Louisa's knowledge of colloquial English had improved exponentially: she managed to grasp that Julian had left Oxford in disgrace, having missed his tutorial once too often, and that his tutor had been a sexually suspect man who lacked all sense of humor. Since leaving university, two years before, he had had a bit of a disaster with a City firm and now had a job in advertising, writing ghastly slogans about hair oil and beef tea. "It's vile work, I can tell you. But I don't mean to stick it out much longer."

"Oh, no, you must leave there," she said fervently.

"I can't chuck it all in for poetry or anything like that, because I don't write the stuff."

"But you will find something else. Something better for you yourself."

He looked gratified. "What about you? Do you have any plans?"

"I am hoping very much to pursue further studies," she said, so he wouldn't think she only wanted to get married. She was most interested in art history, she told him.

"Why not study in London? You could practice your English."

It was at this point that Celia arrived, full of breathless apologies, and swooped down to kiss him on the cheek. Louisa stood to leave.

"You're not deserting me, are you?" Celia asked, in mock alarm. "I was counting on you to make him behave himself."

"You can't keep the girl against her will," Julian said. "Maybe she's dying to escape."

"Not at all. It is only that you may wish to be alone together."

"Would you wish to be alone with your brother?"

She bowed her head. "Alas, I have no brother. I am a lone child."

"Well, if you did you'd know that brothers and sisters don't generally want to be alone together. In fact, just the opposite."

He was as horrid as ever, Celia said. She would just run upstairs to change for dinner, she'd leave him in Louisa's capable hands.

"I meant it, you know," he said, when she had gone. Louisa could still smell her perfume in the air.

"What is it you were meaning?"

"About your coming to London. I think it's rather a good idea."

In the end, he extended his visit to four days. His air of dissatisfaction never entirely left him, but that only made him more compelling. He reminded her of the Englishmen in the novels the girls read under the covers at night, moody, restless young men who always seemed to come to a bad end somewhere far from home, though surely that wasn't true in life. At times his impatience was turned on her—he would go and stare out the window while she was talking to him, or interrupt with some irritable comment on the stuffiness of the room or the beastliness of the Swiss. Once, when she reached over tentatively to push his hair out of his eyes, he shooed her hand away as though it were a fly. But his very crossness seemed proprietary; if she did not spend every minute with him that she wasn't in class he became crosser still.

He decided he wanted to see the lake after all, and grabbed and kissed her on the far side, also in the red parlor, which the English girls had ceded to them from his first evening, and twice, more lingeringly, behind an orange tree in the conservatory. "It'll be smashing when you come to London, you'll see," he said on his last evening, and then launched into a description of the white Triumph his friend Rupert was going to sell him if he could raise the money. She could not lure him into mentioning love, however many stratagems she tried; with him, unlike the boys she had danced with back home, the power had been taken from her. The air thickened when he was there, robbing her of will.

As soon as he left she wrote to him, quoting English poetry and describing the snow on the mountains; the letter she got in return was taken up with complaints about the London weather and his vile toad of a boss, who was browbeating him more than ever. "I don't know how much longer I can stick this. I'm thinking of chucking it in and emigrating to Australia." But in his next letter he told her about a room to let in Marylebone, quite near the house of his aunt, where he was living. "It's in a boardinghouse for young ladies. Very respectable."

She wrote to her father, asking if she could take courses at a new institute of art history that had opened in London. Two other girls from the school were enrolling for the term beginning in January, she said; they would find a place together. It was the first big lie she had ever told him, and she was almost ready to confess when he wrote back approving her plan. The situation in Germany remained unsettled, he said; much though he missed her, it would be wise for her to become fluent in English.

Celia had long since ceased to be charming to her ("Never mind," Julian said, "some day I'll tell you the real story of why she was packed off to Switzerland"), but the rest of the school was thrilled with her romance. Ayako, the one Japanese pupil, much admired for her pretty ways and her boredom with lessons, came and sat on Louisa's bed one night while she was brushing her hair, sighing wistfully and telling her how lucky she was. "I wish I could marry Westerner," she said, brushing aside Louisa's protest that she was not engaged to Julian. "If my parents would not disown me I would go right now and find European to marry. Anyone. Big Swiss shepherd, I don't care." She came up beside Louisa and examined her face in the mirror, smoothing down her eyebrows. "Do you think some Westerner would marry me?"

"Of course," Louisa said.

"I think so too. But is hopeless. My papa has already found husband for me. Another diplomat, like him. He is in Portugal now."

"But then you can live in Europe, if that's what you want."

"Yes, yes, I can live there for time being, but even so, my husband will expect me to be Oriental wife. Always meek, docile, my eyes cast down. Never making my own destiny."

"Perhaps your husband will be more enlightened than you think," Louisa said, at a loss.

Ayako turned her head, eyeing her profile in the mirror. "No, he will only pretend to be enlightened. I know what such boys are like." She knotted her hair at the back of her neck, frowning. "I would love to be actress. Or singer. Something not mundane. Don't you think that's best?"

But Louisa could not remember ever having such yearnings; all her daydreams had only been of romance, and now it was upon her. Soon she would escape to London, Julian, happiness.

"Oh, look," Ayako said, brightening. She snatched up Louisa's malachite ring from the dresser and put it on her finger, where it slid around until it was facing her palm. She laughed merrily. "What hands you all have! So large hands and feet. Mine are very elegant, don't you think?" And Louisa agreed, sincerely, that they were.

In mid-January she arrived in London on the boat train, with three matching pigskin suitcases. It was early afternoon, and as she pressed her face to the window of the taxi on the way to the address Julian had given her, the rows of brick houses, the sodden-looking trees, the marble pillars, all seemed dense with some heightened meaning she felt herself just on the point of grasping. Even the air, so freighted with damp it was a presence in itself, felt pregnant with richness and mystery. People had warned her about the grayness, but nobody had mentioned the constant, otherworldly changes of light.

But Julian was in one of his fed-up moods when he came to fetch her that evening; now his boss was blaming him for losing a client whom, according to Julian, the man himself had alienated with his swinish behavior; worst of all, Julian's father was on the boss's side, he being an old classmate from Radley. "That tears it. It's Australia for me. I'm going to the consulate tomorrow." Not until they arrived at their destination, an oak-paneled pub with a coal fire opposite the bar, where they joined a group of his rugger mates at a square table, was she able to share her revelation about English damp, which the friends immediately drank to. Wait until she got chilblains, they said. She could hear herself imitating Celia's laugh, she was reproducing Celia's inflections as she described the deportment mistress in Switzerland ("You must float, float into the room, girls; never be defeated by anything so banal as gravity"). All this arduous performance was for Julian's benefit, to tie him to her with silken threads; if all his friends found her enchanting enough, he would forget about Australia. Afterward, walking her back to her lodging house, he told her that when she was in the loo Clive had said he never thought a German could be so amusing. "Well done you," he said, but absently, still preoccupied with other things.

Three nights later his aunt went out to a concert at the Albert Hall. First they sat and kissed on the chintz love seat in the sitting room, until Louisa pressed her breasts urgently against him, straining through her blouse. Ever since her arrival in London she'd been waiting for their happiness to start, for the connection between them to be carried onto a different plane. She was no longer sure she could trust him to make it happen.

Breathing hard, he pulled her to her feet and guided her up two flights of dark stairs. His room on the third floor was cluttered with old birdcages and fringed lamps and chairs with broken seats, things his aunt must have wanted banished from public view. But the bed was neatly made, with a white chenille spread—Louisa found herself wondering distractedly if he had made it himself or if his aunt had a maid.

Then he was yanking at her clothes, fumbling with buttons. Jesus, he muttered, when he got to her belt, so that she felt she ought to help him, and did. He kissed her fiercely on the mouth and tumbled her back on the bed, moaning, and wriggled out of his trousers. She lay there in a state of confusion, but felt she must show enthusiasm, and made encouraging noises, until she gasped with the pain, and he stopped. "I'm sorry—am I hurting you?" he asked, and she said he wasn't, and bit her lip. Shortly after that, just as she was beginning to feel some stirrings of pleasure, it seemed to be over. He lay panting on top of her, before kissing her on the mouth again; then he rested his head on her breasts. She felt a great relief that they had managed it. When he rolled off her, sighing, she propped herself on one elbow and stroked his hair, feeling tender and womanly, while he told her about the red leather seats in the Triumph and his ongoing quarrel with his father, who continued to side with his boss. She was just getting nicely sleepy when he said they'd better get dressed and he'd take her back to Mrs. Webster's, his aunt would be returning soon.

And so the pattern of her London life was established: her evenings spent with Julian at the pub or the cinema; her mornings taken up with lectures at the Courtauld, couched in a special, German English clotted with compound words; in the afternoons, solitary excursions to Westminster Abbey and the Tower of London and the National Gallery, or solitary wanderings through the streets.

She had imagined that Mrs. Webster's house would be like school, with the girls running in and out of each other's rooms, but her fellow lodgers only seemed to communicate through the notes they left for each other in the big drafty bathroom on the second floor. "Personally, I find it extremely offensive to be surrounded by dripping undergarments while I bathe." "To the girl who's been using my Floris bath oil: do you think I can't smell who you are?" It was disturbing to think that all the pink-and-white young Englishwomen who said good morning so politely in the hall should be harboring those secret reservoirs of ill will. She made a running joke of it for Julian and his friends at the pub, saying how very warlike Englishwomen were, how they terrified her. But it was a little bit true.

There were moments of pure elation, when everything she saw—an old red tugboat on the river, a frilled plaid umbrella—seemed redolent with promise, but the euphoria could not be trusted to last, and for whole days she longed to be elsewhere. While she was dressing to go to the pub, leaning toward the mirror to apply her lipstick, her hopes were always high, but the talk about rugger and MGs and the Prince of Wales could not occupy her mind fully, and the unoccupied parts kept wondering what exactly she was doing there.

On the evenings when Aunt Jilly absented herself, things in the upstairs room always seemed to go too quickly, leaving her agitated in a way she could not bring herself to mention. Sometimes she buried her head in the pillow afterward and responded in monosyllables to the saga of his boss's and his father's latest piece of perfidy. But the moment he grew offended, the moment he said *Bloody hell* and flung off the covers, she lost her nerve and started asking lots of questions, until he settled back down and began kissing her, and they started over.

Then, when she had been in London for just six weeks, she got a letter from her father, warning her not to come back. It was an unseasonably warm day in March; the sun had broken through for the first time since she'd come to England, and her period had arrived that morning, after three days of terror and garbled prayers. She was on her way to lunch with a girl from her Neo-Baroque class, a Parisian with short, dyed red hair who had sat beside her in the lecture hall one day and whispered that the professor was all wrong about Poussin. Since then they had spoken together in French several times.

She started reading the letter as she waited at the bus stop; all the women in the queue were commenting on the fineness of the weather for that time of year. Then she read it again, more slowly.

"I wish I could be sanguine," her father had written, "but the German people show no sign of rebelling against these measures. The German people seem very happy indeed. And the more I see of their Führer, the more I am convinced that on the matter of the Jews we must take him at his word . . . Practice your English, *Liebling*. You are always in my thoughts. Your mother, too, sends her love." At the bottom he had added a postscript: "Do you remember Rolf Furchgott, Otto's friend? He left for America this week, a cousin of his mother's found him a job with a pencil manufacturer in New York."

She remembered, for the first time in years, the boy who had told her, in Otto's garden, that he was going to be a cowboy. Then the bus arrived, and she climbed the steps with the others, clutching the blue air letter. In the unfamiliar sunlight the city seemed to have lost its romance. Buildings she had thought of as stately in their grayness were shown up as covered with grime; the people on the street looked down at heel; the conductor's voice, when he asked for her fare, was harsh and toneless.

Huddling in her seat, she shoved the letter into her handbag and smiled timidly at two straight-backed elderly women across the aisle, but they looked away without smiling back. She felt they knew, or suspected, that she needed more from them than was decent. She pressed her face against the window. The bus was traveling down a street of neat identical houses, with scrubbed steps and solid brick facades, each with its own brass knocker and high, fan-shaped window. The doors were red or blue or gray or black, their glossy paint shone in the sunlight; she could not imagine any of them opening to let her in. The only English home she had ever entered was Aunt Jilly's, and that was when its owner was out. She took the letter from her bag and read it again.

CHAPTER THREE

By May it was already harder to send money out of Germany, especially for Jews. Her father managed to smuggle her grandmother's jewelry to her, in a round tin of Lebkuchen with a picture of the Frauenkirche on the lid. There were two square-cut diamond brooches, a small emerald pendant shaped like a lily, and a pair of sapphire earrings that dangled pearls. She took them to a pawnbroker in Whitechapel, an *Ostjude*, as her mother would have called him; coming out from behind the counter at her entrance, he fingered the stuff of her dress, complimenting her on the quality of the fabric. But when she brought the jewelry from her handbag, he assumed his professional manner, turning each item over and clucking his tongue. Then he told her, shaking his head and sighing, that they were all too old-fashioned to fetch much; it was a pity, but that sort of piece just wasn't attractive to people any more. He offered what she knew must be a very low price, but still it was enough for her to get by for three months if she was careful.

She was still going to the pub on most evenings, though it had become harder to strike the right note. For the first time in her life she was reading newspapers. Then there were the stories whispered by the refugees who'd started trickling across the Channel—accounts of a Jewish baby being snatched from her mother and hurled into a dustbin, an old woman set upon and knifed in the street.

Two sisters she'd gone to school with, sent to London to learn to type, brought a letter from her father folded around her grandmother's wedding ring. She invited them to meet her at the King's Head one evening, where she introduced them around, but they were not a great success. Julian was telling a story about climbing into his own window at Christchurch after curfew: how the beadle had called out to him, and then he'd bumped his head as he tried to extricate himself, which made him stagger, so the man had thought he was much drunker than he was. The girls from Nuremberg hadn't laughed; they only smiled politely, in unmistakable puzzlement, their hands folded primly in the laps of their unfashionably wide skirts.

"They're a bit heavy going, aren't they?" Julian said sotto voce. "Thank God you're not like that." Later she tried to defend them by telling him they'd been having a very hard time in Germany. He wasn't surprised, he said with a shrug. Everyone knew the Hun was a beast.

Since she'd been in England she'd come to understand that he was not after all a figure of romance but a recognizable type—that there were many young Englishmen as restless, derisive, even sulky, as he was. If she shut her eyes, in those evenings at the pub, she could not always be sure who was speaking. But such knowledge did not free her; it only made her afraid. She needed to go on loving him no matter what; she needed to believe she was there because of love, or she would only be another refugee, like the two sisters, someone whose country didn't want her any more.

At the Aliens Registration Office in Lambs Conduit Street, a stocky man in a bright blue suit looked her over suspiciously and told her the only work permit available to foreigners was for domestic service.

"And what does that mean?" she asked timidly.

"It means a maid."

She thought of Ilse, her mother's housemaid from the mountains, whom she'd courted with bread and jam and almond pretzels when she was a child. Ilse could carry a bucket filled with coal up three flights of stairs without pausing for breath, or push the heavy sideboard away from the wall single-handedly when she wanted to clean behind it. Louisa got dizzy just scrubbing the bathtub after her bath; often she could not get the front door of the lodging house open, even when she hurled her shoulder at it while turning the key. She had to ring the doorbell instead. The other lodgers, who presumably had not lived through a famine, rolled their eyes; the landlady grumbled. Nevertheless, she asked the man humbly for an application and sat at a long high counter, filling it out in her best handwriting. She was the only person there in a hat with a feather on it, or a coat that was not sagging at the seams.

She had stopped attending the lectures at the Courtauld. The bus fares were too high, and such interest as she'd had in Baroque art was waning. On the other hand, she could not spend all day in her room, either; the landlady didn't like it, and the gas fire ate up sixpences at a terrifying rate. She wandered around the department stores on Oxford Street, avoiding the salesladies' eyes; she sought comfort in the dingy splendor of the Paddington Library, where she sat reading books about medieval queens, but finally, stammering with embarrassment, she had to explain to Mrs. Webster that she had only one week's rent to give her; she would need to look for a cheaper place.

"I known something like that was happening, dear," the woman said. "I can always tell with my young ladies."

Louisa hung her head, ashamed to have been so transparent —one in a long line of impecunious lodgers.

"You're best off going back to your own country, if you don't mind me saying so."

"But I can't," she said wildly, and then stopped. "I can't," she said again.

Mrs. Webster gave her a shrewd look. "It's that way, is it, dearie?"

"I'd get a job," Louisa said in a rush, "but they'll only let me go into service. And I'm not strong enough."

The woman looked her up and down, pursing her lips. "I tell you what," she said. "I got a sister, see, who does sewing for some very fine ladies, and just today she was telling me about one of them, Mrs. Grenville I think her name is, what's just had to fire her lady's maid on account she was stealing from her. Robbing her blind, she was. Anyone can be a lady's maid, I'm sure. There's nothing to it, is there? Just hanging up her clothes and keeping the dressing table tidy, as far as I can make out. Cleaning up the spilled powder. You can do that much, can't you?"

Louisa nodded uncertainly. It did not seem possible that anyone got paid for doing so little, but at that point she was ready to try anything.

"I'll get my sister to put in a word, shall I? This Mrs. Grenville might take quite a fancy to you, you being so ladylike and all. And then you can stay here. You'd like that, wouldn't you?"

And so, on a rainy morning in May, Louisa found herself entering a russet-painted gate in Blomfield Road, just opposite the canal, where a row of shabby-looking houseboats squatted in the water. When she rang the bell, a roly-poly little maid appeared and showed her into a blue-and-gold morning room. Louisa looked at the beautiful pale masses of Mrs. Grenville's hair, piled and twisted and coiled around her face, and wondered if she could possibly create such a coiffure. But when she explained haltingly that she was most anxious to obtain a position and, inexperienced though she was, would do her conscientious best, the other woman looked at her in distress. Louisa realized that Mrs. Grenville was only a few years older than she was, twenty-four maybe, or twenty-five, and not completely mistress of her facial expressions.

"Oh, but I couldn't," she cried in an agitated voice, and then more firmly, "I'm sorry, but it's out of the question." She leaned toward Louisa as though she were about to clasp her hands in sympathy. "It would be too awkward, don't you see? You're so obviously not a maid."

"But what am I going to do?" Louisa blurted. "I have to get a job, and they won't give me a permit for anything but domestic work. I can't be a proper maid—I'm not strong enough—and I don't know how to cook. What would you do?" Then she blushed, because of course it was presumptuous to suggest that Mrs. Grenville would ever find herself in that situation.

Mrs. Grenville frowned, shifting her hands in her lap. The rain lashed harder against the window. Louisa was sure she would say, *What business is it of mine?* But no. "Let me think," she said, and Louisa waited tensely while she thought. Then her face cleared. "Hang on a moment. Isn't a governess domestic help?"

Louisa had no idea, but it seemed a moot point: she could not possibly be a governess, what with everything she didn't know.

When she said that, though, Mrs. Grenville laughed in delight, dislodging one of the coils of hair. She tucked it behind her ear. "My dear, you can't imagine the ignorance of the average English governess. Mine had barely mastered the times table. The only thing I learnt from her were the Latin names of flowers. Can you play the piano?"

"A little. Not very well."

"As long as you can thump out a tune or two. How's your French?"

"Not too bad. I went to school in Lausanne."

She clapped her hands like a child. "Splendid. And fluent German, of course. You'd be perfect. I know it's a rotten sort of job, but better than a lady's maid, don't you think? And if you have a decent employer . . . Let me see."

Louisa sat there expectantly, as though Mrs. Grenville might come up with a job on the spot. Instead, she picked up the gold-and-white telephone and rang her mother to find out the name of the governesses' agency she had used. Then she wrote, on beautiful cream-colored letterhead, a character reference stating that Louisa was known to her personally; she could vouch for her good character, as well as her exquisite German and French. She blotted it and put it into an embossed envelope. For a moment it almost seemed as though she might invite Louisa to stay for coffee, as though they would even become friends, but of course that didn't happen. Louisa never saw her again, though Mrs. Grenville stood as she was leaving and kissed her impulsively on the cheek, wishing her luck.

Two weeks later, just when the money from the jewelry had run out—she had one pair of stockings left, and had to choose between bus fare and breakfast—the woman at the agency sent her to a tall whitewashed house in South Kensington, where she was hired on the spot to teach a precocious, lame little boy not strong enough to go to boarding school. She never became as fond of him as she had hoped—he mocked her accent and was skeptical about her grasp of geometry—but she had no trouble feeling romantic about his parents. His mother looked like a nun, always dressed in gray, with her dark hair pulled back into a chignon and her pale forehead always slightly puckered with the weight of conscience. She was the daughter of a rich industrialist in the Midlands who had converted to Catholicism after his wife's death and given away a large part of his fortune. Now she was writing his biography, with the help of a Jesuit priest. Her husband too seemed burdened with some undisclosed worry; he was a Balkans expert at the Foreign Office, and seemed to understand better than most why Louisa could not return to Germany. Occasionally he even sought her out to discuss the situation there. She reported what the refugees had told her, and what her father had written about the massive rearmament going on. It was plain, Franz said, that sooner or later Germany would be going to war. When Louisa repeated this to her employer, he nodded grimly. She hoped, though she did not place much faith in it, that maybe he was taking the news back to the Foreign Office.

But most of her fears were about Julian. She no longer asked herself what she felt for him, or didn't feel; it only mattered that he should feel something for her, that she should not lose him entirely. More and more, she was nervous and clumsy around him, which made him irritable with her, and then she grew clumsier still. There always seemed to be a bit of food dangling from her mouth, or a sneeze coming on, at the very moment he glanced over at her.

She tried harder than ever to be entertaining, she even told funny stories she had read in books, pretending such things had happened to her, but her voice sounded false and strained, and anyway he wasn't willing to be charmed. It had been three weeks since they'd gone back to his aunt's house. Even his friends at the pub no longer addressed her so often; sometimes whole evenings passed when all she could do was to laugh appreciatively, from the sidelines, at their jokes.

With the warmer weather, they had moved from their table by the fire into the back garden, where rickety tables were set up under the trees and the air was scented with the wisteria growing up the wall. People brought their dogs, Labradors and chows and Pekingese who wandered panting from one group to another, to beg for scraps. The sky was a fresher blue, surely, than it had ever been in Nuremberg.

Sometimes people at the other tables would call to Julian by name; jokes would be exchanged about the Test match or the scandalous behavior of a politician's wife, but he never introduced her to them. After smiling at him in vain, then at her hands, then at whatever dog was closest, she would stand and announce that she was going. He stood, as the others did, to wish her good night. But he never made a move to follow her.

In August she was to accompany her employers to their house on the Norfolk coast. Julian, it seemed, was going to his parents' place in Suffolk, something she only learned when he mentioned it to a couple at the next table. She was always nerving herself to speak to him, rehearsing impassioned speeches as she went over French verbs or the geography of Africa with her charge. But he seemed to know, every time, when she had summoned the courage to ask to talk to him alone. Just as she was going to touch his hand, he would turn away and call out a remark about the rugger to someone at another table, or push back his chair and ask who was ready for the next round of drinks.

So she went to Norfolk and walked up and down in the garden between lessons, still making up things to say. She wrote him pleading letters—*At least talk to me, at least tell me how things went wrong between us, surely you can do that much*—and furious ones—*How dare you behave like this? What kind of coward are you?* In the end, they all landed in the wastebasket, but then she could not sleep.

He did not write to her. She had known he wouldn't, even as she gave him the little slip of paper with her address in the country. But still, every morning, sitting on the terrace with her coffee, watching her charge being led around the sloping lawn on his pony, she strained her ears for the sound of the mail landing on the mat inside the front door, the bronze flap banging shut. Then the maid would bring it through to her employer in his study. On those few occasions when there was a letter for her—it was always, only, from her father—he would bring it to her on the terrace, handing it over with a small flourish; then he would call out encouragement to his son, who was attempting small jumps over a low hurdle they had erected on the grass.

On her return to London, she stayed away from the King's Head, and from every other place where she had gone with

Julian. There were whole streets she had to avoid walking down, perfectly innocent buildings from which she averted her eyes. In her room at the top of the house, with the housekeeper snoring next door, she lay on the bed, trying to conjure up a future, or switched on the light and examined her face in the mirror, appraising her chances of happiness. At four in the morning, she was full of defiant plans—she would be a spy, or a chorus girl, or a kept woman—and wild energy surged through her. With daylight, though, it always sputtered out again.

On some nights, she remembered people she had not thought of in years: the French mistress in her first school, the boy from her dancing class who had trembled as he kissed her. When she wrote to her father she sometimes asked what those people were doing now, but he rarely told her. More and more, his letters were devoid of real news; they were filled with silly jokes, as though she were twelve years old.

The sisters from Nuremberg, who had moved on to Holland, had told her about a café in South Kensington where refugees from Munich, Berlin, Frankfurt, Vienna went to drink wine and coffee and carry on running arguments. The first time she went there, she drank her coffee in silence and left quickly, meaning never to go back; she was shocked by their flippancy about the English. "It's astonishing how they all still believe in their schoolboy code." "That's because they never really cease being schoolboys. No proper Englishman ever outgrows his childhood." But a week later she returned, to eavesdrop further. She was the youngest person there. The women were mostly in black, and waved their cigarettes as they talked, and interrupted each other. The men, so much darker and shorter than Julian, wore shabby suits and highly polished shoes. As in the pub, conversations spread from table to table. Mockery was the order of the day, even running to jokes about Hitler: "It's because he's an artist, you see, that he hates the Jews so much. He wants to get rid of the competition."

There came a day when she felt impelled to speak out, to register a protest; they had been laughing about J. B. Priestley: "He is too nice a man," they said, "to be a novelist. So sweet and nice, so adorable, one wants to strangle him."

"That's not fair," she said. "He really loves his characters, their goodness is real," a statement that amused them greatly. Another time she defended English cooking: "It's because they don't really mind what they eat; they're indifferent to material comfort." Her romance with England became a running joke with them; they made up grand love affairs for her: "Our little Louisa," they said, "will wind up a duchess." She bought a silver-gray dress with flowing sleeves and black satin cuffs, a dark gray hat with a rakish brim, long jet earrings; she took to wearing her hair in a chignon at the nape of her neck, like her employer's, thinking it made her look older, until they insisted she unpin it again. It was comforting to be petted and teased like that, though it did not solve the great question of what would become of her.

It took her months to figure out that many of her new friends were Communists. Her own political activity was confined to giving sixpences to canvassers for the Independent Labour Party—because they were anti-Fascist—and signing a petition for relief for the unemployed miners. She was more affected by the sight of the whey-faced little girl who stood begging at the entrance to the Tube on certain winter nights; to her she gave whole shillings, and sometimes rolls, wrapped in napkins, that she took from the baskets at the café.

Not everyone who frequented the place was a refugee. There were also painters from Chelsea who rolled their own cigarettes and consumed vast quantities of cheap wine; there were bearded Oxford graduates in scruffy tweed jackets and stained ties who wrote for the left-wing journals and carried on tremendous political arguments, though they were all ostensibly on the same side. Sometimes the more erudite of the refugees were called on to settle a question about collectivization, or Rosa Luxemburg, or the peregrinations of Trotsky, always referred to fondly as the Old Man.

One of the café's English denizens was a backer of the *New Examiner*, a quarterly that had recently published an account of the Nazi persecutions. But he was also a poet, he told her, on the night he first sat down at her table, in fact primarily a poet, only he could no longer turn his back on what was happening in the world. Even poets had to get their hands dirty now, he said, somewhat incongruously, since his own looked very soft and clean, with pale stubby fingers. He had been noticing her, he said, for some time: what would she like to drink?

His name was Phillip Hallowell. He had a house in Bloomsbury and manufacturing relations up north who wanted him to go into the business, an idea he referred to with scorn; he had studied law at Cambridge, but quit in disgust. Disgust and scorn were things he expressed very often, but not when it came to her. She was delicious, he told her, the first time he took her out to dinner—they were on their way to an Italian place in Soho, which he assured her she would love, and she was telling him about a Goya show at the National Gallery that she'd been to the previous Sunday. "How did I ever find someone so delicious?" he cried, interrupting her, and said how marvelous it was to be around people who weren't English, how irredeemably boring he found Englishwomen in particular. "The very sound of their damn voices makes me wince." After their third dinner, when he was taking her home, and the cab was stopped at a red light in Torrington Square, he gestured at a handsome brick house opposite. "Would you like to live there? Shall we buy it when we're married?"

She never really knew why he had decided to love her; there was much in her character he seemed to object to. When she was feeling high-spirited, talkative, when she made fun of anything, or imitated someone she'd met, he sat there tapping his foot, a frown of disapproval on his face. Flippancy didn't suit her, he declared. "You mustn't try to be sophisticated in that awful way; it's nothing but a pose." She was one of nature's innocents, he told her. "My little waif," he called her sometimes, or "my poor wee lamb," in a mock-Scottish accent.

If she rebelled then, if she told him she wasn't his poor wee lamb, would he please stop saying that, he only laughed. He seemed to enjoy her little bursts of defiance, knowing they would not flare into anything serious. And it was true that she could not bring herself to walk away. She felt heavy and torpid in his presence, yet oddly comforted. The stillness in his dusty house, with its shabby Turkish rugs and piles of books on the narrow stairs leading to the bedrooms, blotted out the pervasive sense of dread that she had carried for so long. The hungry way he looked at her when he'd had too much to drink, the way his voice went husky then, restored to her something she thought Julian had taken away for good, though it made her uneasy too. If she did not desire him exactly, she was excited, nevertheless, by his desire.

When they became lovers she could never stay with him overnight, she had to get back to her employers' house. So he would take her home in a taxi, holding her hand in the back seat, explaining things to her, as he liked to do (the class struggle, the proper way to tie a fly, the use of the broken-backed line in Renaissance poetry). She felt perfectly peaceful during those journeys through the darkened streets, lighter and freer than in bed with him, and content just to listen, or half-listen, without speaking, as she looked out the window.

One June evening when she arrived at his house—she always timed her arrivals to avoid seeing Nellie, his daily woman, who had taken a dislike to her, based, according to Phillip, on nothing more than her red hair: Nellie's wicked husband had had red hair—he was standing on the steps, a tumbler full of Scotch in his hand, looking out for her. "We're going to America," he announced, as she climbed toward him. And when she only stared, bewildered, he laughed with delight. "Yes, we're going to join the vast migration, the huddled masses . . . though only temporarily, of course. I'll tell you all about it."

It seemed that the *New Examiner* wanted an article about a Collective Security Congress due to take place in Chicago, which the antiwar socialists threatened to boycott. But the journalist they'd commissioned had left for Spain abruptly, to cover the war that was brewing there. Phillip and his editor had been talking about whom else they could get when Phillip suddenly decided—had the inspiration, he said—to go himself. "It's not my kind of story, of course, but perhaps it's time I made it my kind of story." They would stay in New York for a few days, he said, before heading for Chicago. "And we may as well keep forging on and visit my brother." (His younger brother lived in California with his wife and small daughter, and taught geology at a university there.) "Though of course there's his cow of a wife. But I really ought to meet the infant."

She couldn't go, she said; she could never ask her employers for leave to go traveling in America with a man.

"It's time you gave your notice anyway. We might even stay a bit longer. I'll say you're my secretary and get you a proper work permit. And then I had a rather good idea: why don't we get married over there? The Yanks are much less strict about that, you know. There's no nonsense about special licenses for foreigners."

It was the first time in months—the first time since the night in the cab—that he had mentioned marriage. They had reached his study; he was watching her intently, waiting, and she felt the panic rising. She groped for the right words, a way to say no while blaming herself alone: she was so confused, she'd tell him, she didn't know what she wanted. Then he said, "We'll get your parents out too. When we get back, and we're married. I'll start looking into it."

He said it in the same casually kindly tone he might have used to offer her a ride to the bus stop. That was what made her want to cry: that he should be doing this enormous thing for her without even making her ask, without demanding gratitude. She imagined the letter she would write to her father: *You don't have to worry any more. I'm getting married, Phillip is going to get you out.* Because of course she would marry Phillip; at that moment she was weak with love, her whole body was flooded with it.

"Thank you," she whispered, taking his hand. She turned it over and kissed it.

"Don't," he said in a thickened voice. "Don't be humble."

"It's just I didn't know how frightened I've been until you said that."

"Of course you were. Are. It's hardly surprising."

Now she could not stop the tears. "Ssshhhh," he said. "It's all right, everything is going to be all right." He had his hand under her elbow; he was steering her upstairs. In the doorway to his bedroom he kissed her ears, her throat. "Yum," he said, making smacking noises. "My own little Jewess." She felt the echo along her spine; a small cold space opened in her brain, like a third eye, and the panic returned. But then she shut her eyes and kissed him back.

CHAPTER FOUR

*S*he had forgotten, when she dialed Otto's number in New York, that he was living with Rolf. When a man answered the phone she began babbling excitedly: "We're here," she said, "I can't believe it, you have to come down to the hotel right now."

"I believe you want to speak to Otto," the man said stiffly.

"Oh my God, is that Rolf? This is Louisa. How are you?"

He was well, thanks, he said, in the same stilted voice. Should he ask Otto to phone her when he came in?

"Of course," she said brightly, still trying to strike a spark. "But tell me how you are, really. Do you love it here? You always wanted to come, remember?"

Yes, he said, he did remember. That was a very long time ago now.

"Well, it would be lovely to see you," she said, in her best English voice. She had felt luxuriantly English since arriving in America. Here she could finally be what in England was out of her reach.

A few minutes later Otto phoned, and she gave him the address of their hotel. "You might have consulted me first," Phillip said peevishly. "I'm not really in the mood for this."

"But Otto is like my brother. And I haven't seen him in four years."

"Well, I haven't seen my brother in five years, but I wouldn't have invited him round on our first night in New York." Phillip's mood had been curdling ever since they boarded the ship, where their fellow passengers had never heard of the *New Examiner*, and the men at their table ignored him, preferring to flirt with Louisa. They despised him for betraying his class, he said, the poisonous smug bastards; they were all Fascists at heart, he insisted, secret anti-Semites also; they took her for a whore.

What the women on the ship had found thrilling were their wedding plans. "How romantic," they said, and pressed Louisa for more and more details, which she did her best to supply. Phillip's brother's wife had written asking if their four-year-old daughter could come along to the justice of the peace and be the flower girl. When Louisa tried to imagine her wedding, the other members of the party, including herself, remained shadowy, but she saw the little girl very clearly, with a satin bow in hair the same ash-blond shade as Phillip's, and a white dress embroidered with pink roses.

"Look at you," Otto said in the hotel lobby that evening, holding her away from him so he could take her in. "You're so glamorous."

"Wasn't she always glamorous?" Phillip asked sourly.

"But of course," Otto said with a wink. "Even as a runny-nosed infant. But now she's like a film star, don't you think?" He was smaller than Louisa remembered, disconcertingly Peter Lorre-ish, in a Central European–looking suit with very wide shoulders.

They walked to a smoky bar on Fifty-seventh Street that Phillip had read about, where a tired-looking black man was playing show tunes on a tinkly piano. "So you're a journalist," Otto said, after a pause, when they were seated.

"In a manner of speaking." Phillip snapped his fingers aggressively at the waiter, demanding Scotch. Louisa told Otto about the conference in Chicago; Otto adopted a serious expression and asked respectful questions, as all the passengers on the ship had failed to do. But Phillip's answers were brief and surly; he jiggled his leg impatiently in time to the music. As soon as Otto turned his attention to Louisa, though, teasing her about things that had happened long ago, Phillip set down his glass.

"What's happening with the immigration quota for Jews? Is the Congress doing anything about it?"

"Not that I know of," Otto said politely, transferring his smile from Louisa to Phillip.

"Oh, come now. You must have some rough idea."

"I'm afraid not."

"Well, how many applications are outstanding? Approximately."

Otto's smile had turned wary. He gave a self-mocking little shrug, his ill-fitting jacket rising slightly from his shoulders. It struck Louisa that he was playing a part, an exaggerated version of himself, for Phillip's benefit. "Rolf is the one you'd have to ask. He works for all the committees, he knows everything."

"What sort of committees? What do they do?"

"Whatever is necessary. Find sponsors, jobs, lodgings, raise money, write letters to Congress. All of it."

"I'd like to talk to this chap Rolf," Phillip said, in a clipped, commanding voice, like the ship's captain's. "Could you arrange that for me?"

"He wasn't terribly friendly when I spoke to him," Louisa put in.

"He said you were very charming," Otto told her.

"Well, he certainly didn't seem charmed."

"I'm not sure he meant it as a compliment. He tends to be suspicious of charm."

"Perhaps I could interview some refugees," Phillip said. "Do you think he'd help with that?"

"I don't see why not."

"Splendid. Try to set up a meeting, then." He got to his feet. "Come and dance," he said to Louisa, though on the ship he had never wanted to dance with her.

Reluctantly, with an apologetic smile at Otto, she followed him onto the tiny dance floor, where three couples were moving uncertainly to the pianist's rhythms. The music became slower and slower, until she and Phillip were simply standing there, clutching each other. A man in a black shirt appeared from the back and started shouting at the pianist, who stared at him with a look of intense dislike. "Play faster, goddamnit," the man said, and the pianist stopped altogether, banging the piano shut.

"Well done," Phillip said, nodding with satisfaction, and went back to the table and ordered another Scotch. "What's wrong with you two?" he asked, smiling at them for the first time that evening. "You were supposed to have so much to say to each other."

At eight the next morning, Otto phoned to report that Rolf would be glad to meet with them if they could come downtown during his lunch hour. Otto himself could not make it—it was too far from the dry cleaner's he worked at uptown, where his crazy old boss made his real money taking bets on the horses—but Rolf had given him the address of a coffee shop next to his office. Louisa wrote it down. Phillip, wakened by the phone, groaned and rolled over. They had taken a taxi back the night before, Phillip having drunk four more Scotches after Otto left, and the taxi driver had asked her, in a strong Yiddish accent, why she didn't find a man who would look after her, instead of the other way around: "Believe me, it's the secret to happiness for every woman. I'm an old man, I know what I'm talking about."

Rolf stood when she and Phillip entered—that was how she recognized him. His brown hair was already receding, and there were dark circles under his eyes, visible even behind his glasses. Louisa introduced the two men; Rolf shook hands with them both. "Please sit down," he said, gesturing to the booth from which he had emerged. They sat facing him. "Would you like to see the menu?" He handed it to Louisa. "I can recommend the Reuben sandwich." They both said that was what they would have. Then they were silent. Rolf folded his hands on the table. The waitress brought coffee and took their orders. When she had gone, Phillip pushed his cup aside and, as though remembering that Rolf distrusted charm, said brusquely, "So tell me: when do you think the war will start?"

Rolf did not even blink. "I don't know. Soon. But the Americans will refuse to fight, and who can blame them? It's not their mess."

"Well, the English may not fight either," Phillip said. "The government is handing out gas masks, and they're building more airplanes, but people seem to think it's to stop a war, not fight one. We're about to run a piece from a fellow who was in Newcastle a fortnight ago. The shipwrights' union is on double shifts, but nobody tells them why. 'Hitler wouldn't dare fight us,' they told him. It's what they all believe."

"What about Churchill?" Rolf asked.

"He's still seen as a warmonger. Anyone who says war is inevitable they call a warmonger."

Rolf removed his glasses and rubbed the bridge of his nose. "Otto said you wanted to know about the refugee committees."

"That's right. I thought I might do a piece on them while I was here."

"What sort of information are you looking for?"

Phillip took out the handsome little notebook he had bought for the trip and began with the questions he'd asked Otto the night before. In fact, Congress had recently lowered the quotas for German Jews, Rolf told him, without any sign of emotion; he gave the figures for 1934, 1935, 1936, and 1937; he explained the most recent criteria for admission, and described how the committee set about finding sponsors. Louisa remembered her father, back in the old days, when men from the veterans' organization would come, and they would talk about getting fresh milk to ex-soldiers in the TB clinic. Sometimes there would be other matters under discussion, nothing to do with the veterans; once, half asleep on the sofa, she had heard them make arrangements for somebody's kitchen maid, who was pregnant with the coalman's child. There had been something very comforting about it, the sense that all would be put right, the grown-ups were looking after things.

"I think I should meet with some of the refugees themselves," Phillip said. "Get their personal stories. Can you arrange that for me?"

"If you like. You mean to write about them?"

"People ought to know what's going on."

"Nobody wants to hear such stories. Yesterday I met with a woman whose nose had been broken so badly she could pull the cotton wool up through the top as well as down through her nostrils. She showed me." He looked over at Louisa. "I'm sorry. Your parents are still there, aren't they?"

She nodded. "But Phillip says he'll apply to get them out after we're married." She turned to Phillip, waiting for him to confirm this, but he was just biting into his sandwich.

"Mine are still there also. My father still thinks it will blow over, the Nazis will come to their senses."

"It's strange, my mother was the only one who predicted what would happen. And everyone thought she was crazy."

"Get them out as soon as you can," he told her. "But don't let's talk about it now. Tell me what you've been doing this morning."

They had gone to the Frick, she said, she had loved the Vermeers, and Sir Thomas More . . . "But the John Singer Sargents were wonderful too. I'd never seen one before." Rolf shook his head apologetically; he didn't know them, he said, he had never been there. It turned out he hadn't been to Tiffany's either, or Saks Fifth Avenue, or the jazz clubs on Fifty-seventh Street (but she wished she hadn't mentioned them).

"Tell me where you go, then," she said, laughing. "Go on, tell me."

He had been to the Metropolitan Museum, he said stiffly, several times, and the American Indian Museum, and of course to the Empire State Building; he had walked the whole length of Central Park.

"Do you never do anything frivolous?" she cried, and he turned pink. Phillip was making faces at her, signaling that she should stop, but a peculiar happiness had seized her; the pleasure of teasing him had gone to her head. "Never anything at all?"

"Sometimes I ride the Staten Island Ferry."

"You like being on the water?"

"Yes. And also . . ." He stopped.

"What?"

"I like to see the Statue of Liberty." At first she thought he was joking; she started to laugh again, and then, seeing that he was serious, tried to turn it into a cough. His eyes were so innocent of guile behind his glasses, she felt a sudden falling in her stomach, as though she might start to cry. She and Phillip, of course, had stood on the deck to see the statue as the ship pulled into the harbor. Phillip had quoted, in a mocking voice, the poem the Americans were so proud of, and told her of the signs that used to say NO IRISH NEED APPLY; some of them, he said, who had come to escape the famine, had starved to death in New York instead.

Now the cough got stuck in her throat, she was choking, and had to reach for a glass of water.

"Are you all right?" Rolf asked, alarmed, and she made ineffectual little hand movements, in between splutters, to show she was fine, while Phillip, taking out his notebook, asked Rolf to give him some names and numbers for the refugees.

"He's an odd duck," Phillip said, with a little snort, when they had parted.

"Do you think so?"

"What do you mean? You were the one who laughed at him back there. You were damn rude, actually." She sensed him scowling at her, and looked across the street, at the crowds hurrying along; the hot-dog vendor on the corner, in a dirty apron, was bawling out indistinguishable words. A woman hurried past in a red, belted suit, her face emptied of expression. She imagined Rolf on his way to work that morning; he would not really see those people; he would carry an idea of them in his head.

"Come along," Phillip said. "I need to get back to the hotel and phone some of the people on his list. We don't have much time left here."

But the only person he managed to reach was the pediatrician who had treated Louisa when she was small, a man she hadn't seen in fifteen years. He used to recite nonsense rhymes while he listened to her heart, and sometimes, when he was finished, perform magic tricks for her, the joke being that they never worked. He'd put a pfennig behind her ear, inviting her to remove it and see what it had changed into, which was always just a pfennig; promising to produce a rabbit from his doctor's bag, he brought out his hand with a flourish and peered in dismay at the stethoscope that appeared instead. "The clever devil," he'd say, "he got away again," and sigh loudly. It was his own enjoyment of this foolishness that made her giggle.

Phillip had offered to go to the rooming house where he was staying with his wife and daughter, but the doctor refused. He would prefer to come to their hotel, he said. So they waited for him in the lobby, where the chairs were covered in the same red-and-green plaid as the bedspread in their room upstairs. Louisa, keeping an eye on the revolving door, felt a childish excitement at the thought of seeing Dr. Joseftal again. A man in a loud blue suit entered—"What is it about Americans?" Phillip said. "They all look so newly hatched somehow"—and then two women in feathered hats and clanking gold bracelets. They did not look so newly hatched, it seemed to her, but she refrained from saying this. She was humming to herself, a tune the black pianist had played the night before, and thinking with pleasure of the length of embroidered ribbon she had bought at Saks that morning, when a gaunt shabby man came through the door, blinking, and looked around with the furtive air of a criminal. The desk clerk, his attention alerted to the presence of someone so clearly out of place, narrowed his eyes and watched his progress across the floor, to where Phillip and Louisa sat.

She jumped up, holding out both hands, babbling about how lovely it was to see him, and he parted his lips in a facsimile of a smile, showing two broken teeth. Phillip stood and thanked him for coming.

"Would you like some coffee?" Louisa asked. "Or some tea? I could ask them to bring it."

"No, thank you," he said, seating himself, very upright, in the plaid chair opposite. He pulled the too-short sleeves of his jacket down over his wrists. "It's very kind of you, but no."

"I was just remembering you and the rabbit," she said, in the same bright social voice. When he looked puzzled, she repeated the words in German.

"Do you speak German?" he asked Phillip, and Phillip said no, unfortunately not.

"Then we shall converse in English."

They sat looking at each other.

"What precisely is the information you are seeking from me?"

"I'd hoped you'd be willing to tell me about your experiences in Germany. Your impressions of what is happening there."

"So you said on the phone. You are a newspaperman, I believe."

"Of a sort. A journalist, anyway."

"You are a Communist?" he asked, pronouncing it in the German way. "In my experience, it is only the *Communisten* who are interested in these stories."

"Surely not. Would you tell me what happened to you?"

"It is not so very interesting. Two years ago I moved to München—you would say Munich—because I thought things would be better there. It was not so Nazi a city as Nuremberg. And for a while things were tolerable. I built up a practice. I could not see any Aryan patients, but the authorities did not interfere with me much. Then a little girl was hit by a car outside my house, which was also my office; her mother rang my bell, she was hysterical. I told her I could not treat the child, I was forbidden, but she pleaded with me, she wept and clung to my hands, until I brought the child upstairs to my consulting room. In fact she was not so badly wounded, it is only that head wounds bleed very much, but the mother thanked me over and over; she kissed my hands. I made her promise not to tell anyone what I had done, but she was a foolish woman, or maybe some of the neighbors had witnessed it. At any rate, the next day the Gestapo came and took me away." He stopped, he crossed his legs; he was wearing the same sort of high, round-toed shoes, laced through hooks, that Louisa's father had always worn. Dr. Joseftal's were cracked but highly polished.

"Yes? And then?" Phillip asked, looking up from his notebook; he had been writing while the doctor talked.

"And then they did what the Gestapo does," he said harshly. He breathed through his nose for a moment. "In Germany nobody would ask such a question. It is enough to say they came."

"So they tortured you."

The doctor made a face. "I would not use that word. To me it suggests something more . . . systematic. They shouted, they took out their *Gummiknueppeln*—their police sticks; they got to work. They were very thorough." His attention became fixed on the women in the feathered hats, who had seated themselves at a table close by; they had removed their gloves and were being served coffee, with a plate of brightly iced cakes between them.

"How long did they detain you?"

"Just three days. But I was right to move to München, the police there are still imperfect Nazis. Sophie—my wife—took my war medals to a station and they filed a paper requesting my release."

"Where did the Gestapo take you? Dachau?" Phillip asked, and he grimaced.

"Such interrogations do not take place in the *Lager*, they occur in the prisons. Look here, there is no interest in this sort of story. You are wasting your time." He turned to Louisa. "So you are getting married," he said.

"Yes. When we get to California."

He nodded once; he did not congratulate Phillip, or wish her luck. "And are you keeping well? How is your health?"

She was fine, she said, just fine.

"I remember you used to have many colds when winter came."

"Not for years. Not since I got to England."

"Ah. You are someone for whom the English climate has been a curative. A medical curiosity."

She laughed for longer than the joke warranted. "Will you be able to practice medicine here?"

"I'm afraid that is not possible. But your friend Rolf Furchgott hopes to obtain some work for me, proofreading for a medical journal that is published in German as well as English. I prefer it to being a butler. There are many of us, you know, many doctors, and lawyers too, who attended a school in München that taught the arts of butlery. For Jews trying to get visas. I had a friend who went to England on such a visa, he was quite comic on the subject."

She asked after his wife and daughter. He coughed behind his hand. "They are working already. It is easier for women, it seems, to get employment here, in domestic service. My daughter has found a job cleaning in a cafeteria. When her English has improved she will hope to find something better. My Sophie has been hired by an elderly woman who requires someone to cook and clean. It is not so bad, she says, with just one person in the household. She is only very worried about our son, he is in Czechoslovakia, he went there in '34, but now we think he must leave. Rolf Furchgott is trying to help with the visa, but it is more difficult than we had thought." For a moment his fingers clawed at the arms of the chair. Then, collecting himself, he stood up. "I must really be going," he said, and as Phillip began to rise, "Please do not trouble yourself." He turned back to Louisa. "Remember me to your parents, yes? In happier times your father and I served on a committee together, to help the veterans. I am sorry I had no chance to say good-bye to him."

"Not exactly a charmer, is he?" Phillip said when he was gone. "Christ. I hope they're not all going to be so bloody stiff-necked."

"You can't expect him to be like Emil," she protested, referring to a denizen of the café. "He's not a bohemian."

"Thank you. I think I might have deduced that for myself. That doesn't explain why he treated me like the enemy."

She wanted to tell him how Dr. Joseftal had sat on her bed, patting her hand; she remembered his telling her mother, when she warned Louisa not to waste the doctor's time, that he had all the time in the world. "I should have given him something to take to his daughter."

"Like what?"

"I don't know. Something. I bought that ribbon this morning, remember? I could have given that to her."

"Yes, well, you could have, but you didn't. I don't suppose ribbons are what the poor cow needs, anyway. Let's go upstairs, I want to make some calls. I think this piece could turn into something quite useful, despite the good doctor's recalcitrance."

But he could not get hold of anyone. "Let's go to the park," she suggested, but he waved this aside; she sensed that he was feeling aggrieved again. For a minute he went and stood by the window, staring at the crowds on the street; then he fetched a glass from the bathroom and dug the bottle of Scotch out of his suitcase.

"I wish you wouldn't," she said timidly.

"Why? Are you afraid I'll climb onto my horse and start a pogrom?"

"That isn't funny."

"She is not amused," he muttered, splashing some Scotch into the glass. He took a gulp. "You seem to care a lot more for all these people than you do for me."

"Of course I don't. It was only that he seemed so terribly sad. Sad and gallant. You don't know what he was like before."

"Right. And Otto is like a brother to you, and you seemed awfully fond of Rolf too."

"I wasn't," she said weakly. "He was just odd, like you said." She could not explain the painful tenderness she had felt for them, her sense of knowing them as she would never know anyone else. She could not tell him how alien he seemed in comparison.

He came over, still holding the glass, and started nuzzling her neck. "I'm the one you're supposed to love. So show me, damn it. Show me you love me." His tongue moved across her skin, leaving a sticky trail. She shut her eyes, willing herself to feel the heat in her stomach, so that everything could come right between them again. But rage was mounting in her; she had to fight back the impulse to put her hands on his chest and shove him away.

Now he was unbuttoning her dress, a soft green silk thing she had bought for the trip. She kept waiting for him to notice that she was not responding, but though she kept her arms rigid by her sides, his hands went on moving greedily, onto her breasts. A faint odor of mildew wafted up from the carpet.

She remembered, with a rush of shame, that Dr. Joseftal had not even wished her well for her marriage; he had not said he was pleased for her. He would go back and say to his wife, Louisa Straus is here with a man who is not her husband, and they would exchange troubled glances, both of them thinking of their own daughter.

Phillip had unhooked her bra now, he was brushing his hands in circular movements over her nipples.

"Stop," she said, clutching at his hands. "Please stop."

He drew away from her, blinking, his face puffy. Then he sat abruptly on one of the plaid beds. "Christ," he said; he reached for the bottle on the night table but pushed it away.

Stealthily, she ran her tongue around her mouth; she snaked her hands around her back and hooked her bra back into place. "Don't be angry at me. Please. I'm sorry."

"Are you? I doubt it. I don't think you're at all sorry." Rising from the bed, he went and rummaged through the jumble of objects she had left on the dresser, picking up first one thing and then another. He fingered the keys to his house in London and put them in his pocket. "I'm going out for a bit. I'll see you later." She heard him open the closet and shut it again, and then the sound of the room door closing, not a slam but an oiled click.

Five minutes later, panic had set in: she was crouching in front of the dresser, rifling through the drawers for his passport. If it wasn't there, if he had taken it with him, it would mean he was never coming back. She heard the elevator stop on their floor and stood without breathing, squeezing her eyes shut, but the footsteps went in the other direction. Then she remembered him putting their passports in the tiny safe next to the bed, and knelt beside it, twirling the knob frantically. But there was no way she could open it.

Since they had been in New York, she had forgotten that everything depended on his loving her, she had no right to refuse him. If he walked in now, she would run to him, holding out her arms. "I don't know what came over me," she'd say. "How could I have been so ridiculous?" But already it seemed too late for that.

In a burst of energy, she hurried into the bathroom, determined to go find him. She would start in the bar they had been to last night. But by the time she had powdered her face and smeared rouge into her cheeks, her resolve had faded. Instead she returned to the room and took off her shoes, setting them beside the bed, breathing in the carpet smell as she did so. She seemed to know the shape of the next few hours as though she had lived through them a thousand times.

She arranged the pillows against the headboard and lay back gingerly, so as not to muss her dress. It was how she had arranged herself as a child, when her mother had locked her into her room and she'd had vengeful fantasies of dying. She used to fold her arms across her chest, imagining her mother's sobs on discovering her lifeless body. Then she would picture her father, weeping into his mustache, until her own tears started.

What would happen to her father if Phillip did not marry her? Sooner or later, they would come for him, as they had come for Dr. Joseftal. "They took out their *Gummiknueppeln*

. . . they were very thorough." The ringing of the phone next to her ear was like a reprieve; flooded with gratitude, she snatched the receiver from its cradle before he could change his mind and sobbed out hello. But it wasn't Phillip on the other end; it was Rolf.

CHAPTER FIVE

$\mathcal{H}$e knew from her voice that something was wrong. He was not as obtuse about these things as people imagined, it was just that he always froze at such moments; he could feel the blood vessels in his brain constricting, so that the right words, of comfort and sympathy, never got through. It happened all the time when he was talking to the refugees.

Instead he asked her how she was enjoying her stay in New York.

She adored it, she said, in a bright English intonation, everything was so fast, wasn't it, such excitement, wherever you looked there was always something going on.

He cleared his throat. "I wondered if I might speak to Phillip."

"Oh, what a pity. He's just gone out. Could I have him phone you back?"

Yes, of course, he said, and then she told him maybe it would be better if she took a message. Phillip had gone to meet someone, she wasn't quite sure when he'd be back.

"One of the refugees?"

No, she said, it was a journalist colleague. "But we saw Dr. Joseftal this afternoon."

"And how did you find him?"

"Not well at all."

"No. But he's one of the lucky ones. They let him go."

"They only kept him for three days, he said. But he was completely different. What did they do to him? How could that happen in just three days?" Now her voice had changed; she sounded like the Louisa he used to know. Quite often, turning passionate about something as trivial as how they would line up their tin soldiers, she had sounded on the verge of tears.

"It wouldn't be just the three days that altered him," he said cautiously, reluctant to say too much. Obviously she had no real idea of what was happening in Germany. Perhaps her parents were shielding her as much as possible, telling her things weren't really so bad. Maybe that was the best approach when dealing with susceptible young ladies. He had said too much already, over lunch.

He cleared his throat. "Well, I won't keep you."

"But didn't you have a message for Phillip?"

He had almost forgotten: he had phoned to give Phillip another name, of someone who would talk to him as much as he wanted, who could not stop talking about what had been done to him, so that the other refugees, including Rolf, tried to avoid him whenever possible. His hysteria was exhausting, and he didn't bathe often enough, either. But if it was stories Phillip wanted, Gruenbaum would be happy to provide them. It might even help him to find a really interested listener for a change. He gave Louisa Gruenbaum's number, which she took down. Then she asked him if he knew Dr. Joseftal's address.

Not offhand, he said. But he could get it for her.

"I want to send his wife and daughter something. But I didn't think of it until after he left."

What did she have in mind, he asked her.

"I bought some really lovely ribbon this morning, I thought I could send them that." And then, when he was silent, "Not just ordinary ribbon. It's very thick, it's got blue-and-green peacocks embroidered on it. And I bought a green bead necklace at Best's, sort of like jade, though of course it isn't."

He had thought she was going to say a warm cardigan, or a woolen hat; having seen Dr. Joseftal, with his broken teeth, she couldn't seriously believe that the situation called for embroidered ribbon. Then she said, "I thought I could write her a little note, you know, just telling her how kind the doctor had been to me when I was a child, and wishing them luck." And suddenly he saw that Mrs. Joseftal might, after all, be glad to receive such a note. For all he knew, a ribbon with peacocks on it would likewise make her glad, and the green beads would be just the thing to cheer her daughter.

Dr. Joseftal was coming to see him the next evening, he said. He would get the address from him then.

"Or I could just deliver the things to you tomorrow, and you could give them to him."

It seemed a waste of her time in New York, but he gave her the address of his office. The following morning, shortly after ten, the receptionist told him, in a voice of muffled excitement, that a young lady wanted to see him.

Arnie, the boss's son, had walked into his office a few minutes earlier. Arnie had a habit of dropping in on Rolf after he had been to see his father, whom he visited at odd intervals when he needed money: he directed avant-garde plays, some of them written by himself, at small theaters in the Village; he and his friends launched magazines with bold green or orange covers that tended to run for only a few issues. He seemed to regard Rolf as his private joke. "How's our golden boy?" he would ask, and tell Rolf how highly the old man spoke of him, as though such praise from his father was itself slightly comic. When the receptionist showed Louisa in, he pantomimed amazement, raising his eyebrows in his theatrical way, and then gave Rolf a knowing look.

She was looking quite theatrical herself, in red lipstick and a gray hat with a feather, though her face was drawn. Rolf introduced them.

"Do you work here too?" she asked Arnie, and he laughed.

"God, no. My father owns the place. I just come by occasionally to make sure he's not exploiting the workers too much." He ran his hand through his hair. "Anyway, I don't need to work. Rolf works hard enough for two."

Louisa looked uncertainly at Rolf, as though for a signal. "Louisa is visiting from England," he said stiffly.

"You're visiting Rolf?" Arnie asked in a tone of frank disbelief, looking her up and down.

"She's here with her fiancé," Rolf said, before she could answer.

"Ah," the man said. "Your fiancé. So what brings you to Union Square this morning?"

She looked at Rolf once more, as though seeking protection; it occurred to him that whatever the cause of her distress the night before, it had not gone away. Again, Rolf jumped in. "She's just come to drop something off," he said, feeling the heat rise to his face. Arnie, meanwhile, was clearly enjoying himself.

"Here it is," Louisa said, taking a little package, wrapped in pink tissue paper, from her bag. She placed it on the desk. "I put the note inside, that we talked about. You won't forget to give it to him, will you?"

He shook his head. "I won't forget."

"All right, then." There was a pause. "I'll say good-bye now. I'm sorry to have disturbed you."

"You're not disturbing anything," Arnie told her. "We were just engaging in our usual idle chatter. Where in England do you live?"

"In London," Rolf said. Arnie looked amused.

"Great. I love London. I try to get over at least twice a year. Great theater there."

"Are you an actor?" Louisa asked.

"A playwright." He gave a little bow. "At your service. And a poet. Sometimes. So is this your first visit to New York?" She nodded. "How do you like it?"

She liked it very much, she said politely, without enthusiasm. Then she brightened. "I saw the most extraordinary things as I was coming here. A whole set of living room furniture out on the pavement. And then two taxis that almost crashed into each other, and both drivers leapt out of their cabs and shouted, and then got back in and drove off. In unison. Like something you'd see in a film."

Arnie chuckled, a deep rich sound. "That's New York for you. Pure theater. A movie a minute."

"Yes, I see what you mean," she said, but coolly. It seemed to Rolf she did not care much for Arnie, which pleased him.

"I was just leaving," Arnie said. "I could give you a lift uptown if you wanted."

"That's very kind of you. But I think I'll go to Chinatown next."

Another laugh, louder this time. "Okay. I can take a hint." He winked at Rolf. "Behave yourself."

"Did I seem very rude?" Louisa asked when he'd gone.

"I wouldn't worry about it. Would you like to sit down for a moment? Before you go to Chinatown?"

"I mustn't keep you."

"That's all right. I'm sorry I don't have a better chair to offer you."

"Oh, but this is fine," she said, and sat in the one upright chair opposite his desk, folding her gloved hands over her bag, like someone there for a job interview. There was a pause.

"What's Dr. Joseftal coming to see you about?" she asked, just as he was about to speak.

"We're trying to get a visa for his son, to get him out of Czechoslovakia. Before the Germans decide to march in. But he left Germany when he was eighteen, he's got no skills to speak of, he's been working as a clerk in a hops firm. That makes it more difficult."

"So what will you do?"

"I've been talking to a hops merchant in New York who may agree to sponsor him. It's ridiculous, but that's how it works."

"And you do this for lots of people?"

"I don't, the committees do."

"Otto says you work harder for the refugees than anyone."

"That's Otto being loyal. What he tells me is that I bark at them like a German magistrate, they go away feeling worse than ever."

"Oh, dear," she said, smiling. "That's very naughty of him."

"No, he's right. When he's there he always knows how to put them at ease. He even has them laughing at his stories. They never laugh with me."

"But that's just charm you're talking about. Anyone can learn it."

"I would say exactly the opposite. It can't be learned, you're either born with it or not. Like trying to play the piano when you're tone-deaf."

"You're sure? Have you tried a drink or two?"

He shook his head. "It's no good, it doesn't work."

"Never mind. There are more important things than charm. Anyway, Americans aren't supposed to be charming, are they? They're supposed to be terribly honest and simple and direct."

"Now you are sounding like the others. They love to talk about how simple Americans are, by which they mean stupid. Uncivilized. Not like the Germans, that most civilized of people."

"Don't get huffy. I was only trying to cheer you up."

"In fact Americans are very civilized, in the truest sense. They are only not sophisticated like Europeans. There's a difference."

"What about Arnie?" she asked demurely, and he had to laugh.

"All right, I concede the point. Arnie is definitely a sophisticate. And not necessarily a civilized one."

"I suppose there have to be some exceptions. What was the name of that cowboy you told me about once?"

"I don't remember," he said stiffly, although he did.

"You were going to come to America because of him. And now you're here."

"Yes, now I'm here." He remembered something else: how he had knocked Otto down the day he'd told her about Old Shatterhand, because she had smiled at Otto and not at him. He could have said that to her now, making a joke of it, but like so much else, it seemed too freighted to be safe.

After she had left—he had shaken her hand, and wished her a pleasant journey—he returned, with relief, to the memo in front of him. Arnie's father had asked him to assess the likely risks of buying the lumberyard in Oregon from which the company purchased its wood for making pencils. The owner was interested in finding a buyer. It would reduce their costs considerably, but the geography would make it difficult, and they would have to find an outlet for whatever they could not use themselves; that would mean selling to their competitors, who might be reluctant to buy from them.

We must consider the following, he wrote, colon. *Number 1 . . . Number 2 . . . Number 3.* But it was not as exhilarating, somehow, as such exercises usually were. A sense of dissatisfaction nagged at him. He did not permit himself to break for lunch, but wrote on doggedly, covering page after page of lined yellow paper with his angular script.

"*Wie lieb,*" Dr. Joseftal murmured that evening, when Rolf handed over the little pink package. "*Wie lieb von ihr.*" He seemed overcome.

Then he collected himself. "This will I am sure please my wife very much. You will thank Miss Straus for me? But my wife will want to write to her herself. Will she be here a few days longer?"

Rolf explained that Louisa would be leaving in two days, Phillip was expected in Chicago. Dr. Joseftal shook his head. "I do not feel sure about this man she will marry. What was your impression of him?"

"He was extremely well informed about the plight of the refugees."

The doctor made a face. "That's not enough to make a man a good husband."

"I suppose not. But I don't really know much else about him."

"I know even less. But from his face I suspect he drinks."

That was the report Otto gave too when he came in late that night, as Rolf was making order out of the folders spread on his desk. Otto threw off his coat and sprawled on the couch, watching him in silence, as was his habit. The desk, the most massive piece of furniture in the apartment, occupied the alcove between the kitchen and the living room, where a dining table might have been. Otto usually waited until the papers were cleared away, and then reported on what he'd been doing—the movie he'd seen, the people he'd eaten dinner with; he seemed to expand his acquaintance daily. Sometimes he did not come home at all, until he returned in the morning to shave and go to work.

Now, supine on the couch, he groaned a little. "I'm drunk . . . that man drinks too much, you know."

"Phillip?"

"Of course Phillip. At first I thought he'd decided to like me after all, he was much friendlier than the other night. But I suspect it was only to punish Louisa."

"Punish her for what?"

"I don't know. But he barely spoke to her. He was very amusing with me, very lively, telling stories about all the mad people who wrote for his magazine. And drinking, and urging me to drink. There's a kind of vengefulness in him. It makes me worried for her."

Rolf aligned the folders meticulously with the edge of the desk. At the best of times, he was uncomfortable speculating about such matters. "Do you think they love each other?" he asked, trying to sound casual. All thoughts of Louisa had become disturbing.

Otto gave a sigh that ended in a hiccup. "Who knows? I think she's desperate for things to work out. But she's not very happy, that's plain." He let out a groan. "I must go to bed, I'll feel like death in the morning."

Rolf, waiting for him to finish in the bathroom, read a report on potential sponsors in Philadelphia and made a note to himself about checking the production figures for the lumberyard. It was only when he was in the bathroom himself, brushing his teeth, that his thoughts returned to Louisa. As he replaced the cap on the toothpaste, it occurred to him that if things were really going wrong with Phillip, she might decide not to go out west with him after all, but stay in New York for a while instead. He felt a rush of blood through his body at the thought.

But she left on schedule. Three postcards arrived for Otto from Chicago ("Give my best to Rolf," she wrote, under the signature). They had toured the stockyards, she wrote; Phillip was thinking of writing an article about conditions there. The second card had a Gauguin on the front. "This is the most beautiful painting I've ever seen," she wrote; "I've been to visit it in the Art Institute twice now. Phillip has gone to a meeting of the packinghouse workers. He says they've been swindled by the bosses." Then there was a card with a picture of Lake Michigan, covered in ice: "We're leaving here next week, to take the train out west. They say they're having snowstorms in the Rockies—imagine me in the Rockies! I don't even have the proper shoes." That was the last mail to arrive. The next time they heard from her, it was seven in the morning. When Rolf answered the phone she said, in a high thin voice, "May I speak to Otto, please?" He went and got Otto and then returned to his bedroom, where he had been getting dressed. A moment later, Otto knocked on the door. It seemed she had gotten off the train in Butte, Montana, and waited in the station until a decent hour to call them. She couldn't talk long, she had said, there were two men outside the phone booth staring at her, and besides she had used all her change. But it was over with Phillip, she was coming back. She was very sorry, but could she possibly stay with them for a while, just until she could earn her fare back to England?

CHAPTER SIX

Rolf was having trouble sleeping, something that hadn't happened since the hunger days of his childhood, when he'd lain awake with visions of stars swirling in his head, the vast blue-black skies over Montana. Since he had arrived in New York, even the most worrisome problems had not kept him from dropping off promptly after his scheduled half hour of English reading.

Now there were no swirls and no skies, only a certain disturbance in the atmosphere that kept him wakeful. On the surface, everything had been done to preserve his routine. Otto, who had vacated his bedroom for Louisa and now slept on the living room couch, never prepared for bed until Rolf had finished with his work in the alcove and gone to his room. When he spent the evening in what had become Louisa's room, they kept their voices considerably low, so that Rolf could hear only a faint murmur through the wall.

Nevertheless, everything was different. Sometimes, as he was preparing his evening sandwich in the kitchen, Otto came in—Louisa remained closeted in the bedroom like an invalid—to make tea or coffee, or fetch a hunk of cheese to carry back with him, and would impart to Rolf, indignantly, some further detail of Phillip's iniquitous behavior on the trip. He seemed to be piecing the story together bit by bit;

at first Louisa had been too ashamed to tell him much, but gradually he was dragging it out of her.

In Chicago Phillip had accused her of flirting with everyone from the conference delegates to the Polish slaughterers at the stockyards; he had been drunk almost every night, and would keep her up till all hours, shouting at her, demanding confessions and apologies. "It was terrible for her, frightening," Otto said. On the very morning they were boarding the train to go out west, she awoke in their boardinghouse to find Phillip sitting beside her, in a chair he had pulled up next to the bed. He had not been to sleep all night, he told her, a note of triumph in his voice; he'd stayed up watching her in the light from the streetlamp, wondering how it would feel to put his hands around her throat and squeeze. It might do wonders for his state of mind, he said; one of these days he might not be able to resist the temptation. "Can you imagine how she felt?"

Rolf did not care to imagine it. He confined himself to noncommittal shrugs, to cut these explosions short. There was something almost unseemly, he felt, about Otto's wrath; it seemed out of proportion to what Louisa had suffered. Rolf could have told him a hundred, a thousand more tragic stories gleaned from the refugees. And unlike Louisa, the refugees had not brought their troubles on themselves.

But he was prudent; he kept that thought to himself.

"He said monstrous things to her on that train ride west." Otto was piling Ritz crackers on a plate. "Things no human being should say to another."

Rolf cut him off. "Don't tell me. I don't want to hear."

"No, you're right," Otto said glumly. "But she asked me to phone his brother in California for her. To make sure he arrived safely."

Rolf thought it over. "She's right," he said. "The man is ill."

"I want you to do it instead."

"Why?"

"Because I couldn't bring myself to speak to him. What if the brother puts him on the phone?"

Rolf wondered if Louisa knew of this request; he almost hoped it had been her idea, but he couldn't very well ask her. Since she'd been there, she had spoken to him only about the butter she'd used but would replace, or whether he wanted anything from the shops when she went to Dyckman Street. She seemed embarrassed in his presence; she had said to Otto that Rolf must think her a fool.

"Give me the number," he said. A woman answered the phone, and Rolf identified himself as a friend of Louisa Straus's. "She wanted to know if Phillip arrived all right, she's concerned about him."

"I should think she would be concerned, after what she did," the woman said. "I suppose she didn't have the courage to phone herself. You tell her he's fine, thank you very much, we're all fine, and we don't need her poking her nose into our business."

"She said he was fine," Rolf reported to Otto, who sighed and went off to the bedroom with the plate of crackers. They were going to have cockroaches in the apartment if those two kept eating in the bedroom.

Finally Otto went out alone one evening, to join some friends at the poor excuse for a café on Dyckman Street. Rolf heard him asking Louisa, from the doorway of the bedroom, if she was sure she wouldn't change her mind and join him; there was a murmur from inside the room, and then Otto left. After that Rolf might have been alone in the apartment for all the noise she made, but he was always conscious of her on the other side of the wall. Sometimes his concentration was disturbed by a sudden, startling image of himself getting up and walking into the bedroom. He forced his thoughts back grimly to the papers in front of him: the figures provided by the owner of the lumberyard had some suspicious gaps.

Though he had not paid much attention when Otto spoke of her over the years, he seemed to remember there had been another Englishman before Phillip. As he frowned down at a quarterly report with the operational expenses all lumped together, he wondered if he should get in touch with Hilde. She had been a cellist with the Stuttgart orchestra until the Nazis came to power, but in New York she worked as a secretary to a musicians' union. They had gone to concerts together on the weekends; once she had even taken him to the ballet, a strangely unsettling experience; he had found himself close to tears at the end, while Hilde, gathering up coats and scarves from under their seats, commented briskly on the deficiencies of the orchestra. Everything about her was admirable: she never wasted words or time, or made unreasonable demands, she was as competent in her way as he was. And yet he had felt, from the beginning, a secret disappointment, the sense of some lack that could not be made good. He had examined his conscience and asked himself if it was wrong to sleep with her, feeling as he did. Nonetheless he had been wounded when she confessed to the same absence of enthusiasm. "Our problem is we don't love each other," she said, staring at the ceiling; he had gotten out of bed a moment before and was getting dressed. "What shall we do about that?"

He didn't know, he said, before it occurred to him that it would have been better to lie. He went and sat on the bed, touching her shoulder, but she only glanced at him briefly, with such loathing in her face that he was shocked. He would phone her later in the week, he said, but, remembering that look, he never did.

A few nights later, Otto insisted on taking Louisa to the café. Standing in the vestibule as she waited for Otto to fetch his coat, she smiled wanly at Rolf. "I don't suppose you'd like to come too." He would enjoy that very much, he said stiffly, but unfortunately he had work to do. "You wouldn't really like to," she said. "But thank you for saying so."

Ten minutes after they had left, he got up from his desk and headed for the bathroom; the door of what had become Louisa's room was half open, with the light on inside. Going to switch it off, he stood in the doorway for a moment, halted by the sight of the objects scattered over the bare surfaces Otto had left for her. A library book was open on the bedside table, a woman riding sidesaddle on its red cover; next to it were a pink glass jar and a crumpled handkerchief. The top of the dresser was crowded with a profusion of tangled beads and half-squeezed tubes and smeared brushes surrounding an oval mirror on a swivel stand. There were three stockings—he wondered at the odd number—draped over the radiator and a bright green blouse flung over the single chair. Hilde's room had never looked like that; it was as tidy as his own, with her cello case propped in the corner.

Seated at his desk again, he picked up his Number 2 pencil and began making notes in the margins of the memo he was reviewing: *What internal resources do we need to manage this business? Who will manage the relationships with our competitors?* He leaned back and found himself moving the pencil along the back of his fingers; as he looked down at his hand, it occurred to him for the first time that it was not a very handsome one.

She might remember that she had left the light burning; he had better turn it on again. Retracing his steps, he entered the room just far enough to reach the switch, and then, blind with shame, took three paces forward and opened the closet.

Two of Otto's suits, one blue, one brown—he was wearing the third—hung in the exact middle of the rod, as though placed there with deliberate courtesy. There was an inch of space on either side, and then a green Chinese-looking thing that fell all the way to the floor; it made him think of kept women, of diplomats and long staircases. The rest was a confusion of pale and dark: something tweed, with a velvet collar, a gray shiny something, a dangling pink sleeve crammed between two blacknesses. A gray hat with a multicolored feather sat on the shelf, a fluffy black thing curled round and round it in an untidy heap. Looking down, he saw a pair of black high-heeled sandals lying on their sides, facing each other in curious intimacy, and had a sudden, shocking urge to stroke them, as though they might still bear the imprint of her feet.

Back in the hall, with the door restored to the exact position in which she had left it, he made for the kitchen and gulped down a full glass of water, standing by the sink. Still standing, he ate the liverwurst sandwich he had bought for his supper, discarded the wrapping in the garbage pail, washed his hands thoroughly, and returned to the desk. *How flexible are their cutting facilities? Can they be adapted to other uses if our competitors refuse to buy from us?* he wrote on the top of the memo's front page. *I don't think we have given this sufficient thought.* But he had lost momentum; he no longer felt able to tackle the issues he had raised. *CONCERNS,* he wrote, in capital letters, on a sheet of lined yellow paper. *Number 1:* Then he stood up. He did not want to be sitting there when they returned. He went to his room and sat on the chair in the corner, as he did every night, for a short session of reading. He was halfway through Woodrow Wilson's autobiography. Usually he only managed a few pages a night, but he got through the whole chapter describing the negotiations at Versailles before remembering that he hadn't brushed his teeth. He was safely back in his bedroom when he heard the front door; he changed quickly into his pajamas and switched off the light.

The next evening, when he got home from work, she was sitting with Otto in the living room, talking in her old, animated way: it seemed she had gotten a job, a fact she found inexplicably amusing. She even mentioned Phillip: thank God, she said, he'd gotten her working papers for America. Lord & Taylor had hired her for the pre-Christmas season, putting her at the glove counter on the main floor. She had been instructed to wear nothing but navy blue or black, she was telling Otto breathlessly, and to behave in a ladylike way at all times; she was also expected to catch the eyes of customers as they were passing, to encourage them to stop at her counter. It was this she found particularly comical.

After her third day of selling gloves she forgot to whisper as she was regaling Otto with stories in the kitchen, where she was making an omelet for their supper. It seemed her supervisor had complimented her on her English accent; a Texan had bought a dozen pairs of gloves for the ladies back home and offered to buy her a pair also. A woman in a fur coat had told her a long story about a ruby ring belonging to her mother-in-law, who had failed to leave it to her as promised, which just proved, she said, how duplicitous women could be. "You seem like a very sweet person," she'd said to Louisa, "that's why I'm telling you this. To spare you a lot of heartache later on."

All this she recounted delightedly, changing her voice to play the different parts. Rolf, who was working at his desk, pretending not to listen, felt obscurely wounded, the more so as she was succeeding so well at making them all seem ridiculous.

Louisa glanced over just as he raised his head. "Oh, I'm sorry. We're disturbing you, aren't we? I'll be quiet now."

"You shouldn't talk about them like that," he said, before he could stop himself. "They were nothing but kind to you."

"Oh, God," Otto said, and then, to Louisa, "He thinks you've insulted his precious Americans."

But her face had softened. "Forgive me. I didn't mean to offend you."

"These are the people who have taken us in. All of us. We owe them some gratitude."

Now she was contrite, she said it had been very wrong of her, but he imagined the two of them discussing him in private: "The problem with Rolf," Otto might say, "is that he has no sense of humor." And maybe it was true, maybe it had always been true. Certainly there were fewer and fewer things he found comical lately. On his desk, at that very moment, was an account of a Jewish boy in Fürth who had been trapped in a schoolyard by some of his former classmates and castrated with a knife. An elderly woman in Wuppertal, the widow of a professor of logic, had been beaten senseless in the street. "What is alarming," he had just written to the junior senator from New York, "is that these are no longer extraordinary events. Such things have become commonplace in Germany."

And then one day, forwarded to him from the committee, was an inquiry from Louisa herself. Should she, she asked, try to stay in America, would it be easier to get her parents into America than England? How would the committee advise her to proceed? He went and knocked on her bedroom door; she was lying there reading one of those endless fat novels she took from the library, with a girl in a wimple on its cover. She swung her legs over the side of the bed as he entered, and sat looking at him.

"May I speak to you for a minute?" he asked, holding out the letter. She nodded.

"Why didn't you ask me about this yourself?"

"I don't know . . . I didn't want to burden you with it."

"It wouldn't have been a burden. I would have been glad to tell you anything I could."

"It's just that I don't know what to do." She looked around the room; she got up and removed a black slip from the back of the chair. "Please sit down."

"I'm going to have to ask you some questions," he said when he was seated. "Is that all right?"

"Of course. Anything."

He cleared his throat. "How much money do your parents have, do you know?"

She shook her head, watching his face intently.

"Can you find out for me? Can you find out what they would be allowed to take out of Germany?"

"Is that how it works?"

"For people of their age, it's important. It helps a great deal. But there are other things too. Have they got any relatives here besides yourself and Otto? Anyone who is an American citizen?"

Again, she shook her head. "Does that mean it's hopeless?"

"Not hopeless, no. But it would make it easier if they did. You're sure there is nobody, no long-lost cousins who emigrated years ago, people they might have lost touch with, that I could write to? Or old friends, business acquaintances, anyone?"

"I don't think so."

"Would you ask them, just to make sure?"

"Of course. But wouldn't they have told me if there'd been someone? They would have mentioned it when I was coming to America."

"Not necessarily. They might not have had an address."

"Then what good would it do?"

"I might be able to find them."

"But you might not . . . I should have married Phillip. I should never have got off that train."

"That's nonsense. You couldn't marry him just for them."

"It isn't," she said wildly. "It isn't nonsense, I only had

to do that one thing, and they would have been safe." She fumbled for a tissue on the night table and blew her nose. "I think about it all the time. I had no right to run away, people like me aren't allowed to make choices. Don't you see that?"

"No," he said sternly. "I don't see it."

"You wouldn't," she said, with a flash of bitterness. She shut her eyes. "I'm sorry, I shouldn't have said that. You've been very kind."

"It's all right."

"I just meant you have these . . . these notions, you always had them, of how things are supposed to be, and you won't see it doesn't work that way. You think everyone's like you."

"I hope that's not true."

"I'm not saying it's a bad thing, it's good in a way, it's just . . . never mind."

"It doesn't matter," he said, rising to his feet. "Get me that information as quickly as you can, I'll see what I can do."

Even before the answers arrived from Germany—once they had paid their exit taxes, there would be very little money left; Franz had only one remote acquaintance in America, a fellow lawyer he had had some legal dealings with in Munich before the war and corresponded with until 1914—Rolf got to work. The thought of Jeannette entering domestic service, as other refugee women had done, was too unlikely to consider; even if she would take such a job, she would quarrel with everyone in the household inside of a week. So special financing would be required. He accepted a long-standing invitation for dinner at the Park Avenue home of a couple he knew from the committee, to request their help: would they be prepared to find a suitable sponsor for an elderly lawyer and his wife? "I am very fond of them both," he said awkwardly, by way of explanation, and because he had never made such a personal appeal they promised him, as they sat in their green-and-gold living room after dinner, to treat the matter as urgent. They themselves could not do it, they already had their quota of commitments, but they would find someone who could.

"What about your parents?" the wife asked him, with a certain avidity, never having presumed to inquire even that far before, and he told her, which was true, that he had all the affidavits ready. He had saved enough money to serve as their sponsors himself; he was only waiting for them to declare themselves ready to come.

He began preparing similar affidavits for Louisa's parents; he requested, and received, copies of their birth certificates, the results of their medical examinations; all the papers were waiting for the moment when a sponsor was found. When the couple on Park Avenue reported that their first approach had been refused—the man in question felt it was the young who must be gotten out—it only increased his determination. He began writing letters to everyone on his list of sponsors, rising to new heights of eloquence, describing Franz's charitable work for the veterans and the unwed mothers back in Germany. If there was anyone who had earned the right to be assisted, he declared, it was this man.

He imagined himself bringing the sponsor's letter home, placing it before her, then leaving the room. But when the papers came from Germany, he only thanked her and put them in his briefcase; he did not want her to know the strings he was pulling, the favors he was calling in. Ever since that night in her room, she had been unnaturally humble with him: she was always offering to share her supper, she asked him polite questions about his work, though he was sure it bored her. Already, it was clear, she felt under an obligation. He would not take advantage of it—that would be blackmail, more dishonorable than what Phillip had done. Best to stay out of her way altogether.

He began leaving for the office earlier in the mornings, and taking the committee's files downtown with him, so that he could work on them in the evenings, when everyone else had left. The cleaning woman no longer looked startled when she poked her head into his office and found him there. On weekends he had the whole place to himself; he got more work done than ever. It was, he saw, the ideal arrangement; he should have adopted it months ago.

Throughout those weeks, he kept thinking he saw Louisa on the street—a woman in a gray hat crossing Fourteenth Street, a woman in a blue suit emerging from the subway, even a red-haired mannequin he caught sight of in a shop window on his way to work. When he turned around a fat man in a checked waistcoat was unbuttoning its dress. Meanwhile, he avoided encountering the real Louisa as much as possible, and hardly spoke when they did meet, resisting all her attempts to draw him out.

Early one Thursday morning, as he emerged from the bathroom after shaving, she was waiting for him in the hall in her Chinese dressing gown, clutching a towel and a pink drawstring bag.

"May I speak to you for a minute?"

"What is it?" He was uncomfortably conscious of standing there in his bare feet, with his shirt unbuttoned; he sucked in his stomach.

"I just want you to know I'm saving as much of my salary as possible. As soon as I find out what's happening with my parents, I'll either get an apartment here or use the money for my passage back."

"Don't worry about it."

"But I do worry. I realize what a nuisance it is, having me here."

"It's not a nuisance."

"Of course it is. Don't pretend." Her lip trembled. "You're never friendly to me any more."

He cleared his throat while he tried to think how to answer, and then wondered if she'd mimic him to Otto later, if she'd clear her throat in exactly that way. "Have you talked about this to Otto?"

"A little."

"And what does he say?"

"He says you're just preoccupied, that's all, I shouldn't take it personally. He says it has nothing to do with me."

"That's not true," he said, suddenly angry, the blood pounding in his ears.

"Yes, I know. That's why I'm telling you this."

"I didn't mean that. I meant . . . Never mind. Forgive me. I should let you get ready."

"But I want to hear what you meant."

"No, you don't."

"I do. Really." Her face, clean of makeup, had a naked look; her expression was so sad and puzzled it was almost more than he could bear.

"You're not a nuisance," he said thickly, and then he took a step toward her. Somehow he had his arms around her, pink bag and all, and was kissing her. He had never known how heavy a weight he'd been carrying all his life until he felt the shock of her body against his own.

CHAPTER SEVEN

*O*tto, as was only fitting, served as their witness. Finally his luck too was changing; he had been offered a job in Baltimore, teaching German at a private school. They set the wedding date for his last day in New York. He not only bought Louisa a whole sheaf of roses but managed to borrow a fine German camera for the occasion, so he could take their picture on the steps of city hall. It was one of those glittering fall days in New York when the wind was up and the air seemed to give off sparks; trees and scarves and flags all fluttered rhythmically. In one of Otto's snapshots, you can see not only the newlyweds but a young girl in a shiny coat, also with a bouquet, peering anxiously down the steps to the street, as though afraid that her intended might not show up.

Louisa, of course, looks very glamorous, in her cape with the velvet collar, her brown hat pulled down slightly over her face. There are flowers pinned to its brim, and she cradles the roses like a baby. But it is the groom, in his bulky overcoat and trilby, who seems almost deranged with happiness, his eyes gleaming crazily, his mouth cracked open in a smile of painful joy. The truth is, it does not suit him, this radiance; stripped of his dignity, he looks ordinary, even homely, his mouth too thin, his cheeks already going jowly. So perhaps it was for the best that his ecstasy would be so short-lived; soon enough he could resume his becoming gravity.

First, though, there was the trip to Havana, that incongruous fleshpot, where he was being sent on business by his firm, the first such trip ever. It allowed them the luxury of a honeymoon, like other couples. Louisa wore her wedding outfit on the flight, though she left the flowers behind. There was her old pigskin suitcase; there was a dressing case with her new initials on it, Rolf's wedding gift to her, a pledge of all the trips they would take together some day. She did not mind that her husband worked ten hours a day on their honeymoon; she could hardly imagine him not working. In the mornings, she accompanied other married ladies, whose husbands were also there on business, on guided tours of the city arranged by the hotel. They drove past marble villas with filigree iron gates, to disembark at churches studded with glass rubies, with bright blue heavens painted on their ceilings. When the other women spoke of "my husband," she did so too. She gave handfuls of pesos to the skinny children who surged around her on her way from the tour bus to the church; they grabbed the coins and ran away quickly, as though she might change her mind. In the afternoons, she swam in the hotel pool; she sat on the balcony and read the novels she had brought with her; she painted her toenails and let her hair dry in the sun.

She did not even mind that they were expected to entertain the clients, so that their evenings too were often not their own. They ate dinner in restaurants with heavy, mustachioed men, the customers of the pencil company, who seemed delighted with the situation: to the honeymoon couple, they said, winking raffishly, and raised their glasses high. They had orchids delivered to the table, they flirted with her and pinched her cheek. They told her about their mothers, crossing themselves; they ordered special, peppery dishes for her, and roared with laughter when she gasped and sputtered. They were almost brutally jovial, with an edge of cruelty, she thought—Rolf protested at the idea—but she wasn't frightened. Nothing could frighten her just then.

And then, when the gentlemen had dropped them off at their hotel, kissing her hand, they went upstairs to their room and shut the door. Sometimes, while he was shaving at the sink—for he did not want to scratch her—she would take a bath and, stepping naked out of the tub, do a mock-Spanish dance behind him, until he caught sight of her in the mirror and turned around, laughing. She always felt a thrill when she made him laugh, though really it wasn't so hard to do, even if he seemed taken by surprise each time. Otherwise she might have felt too humble, a cheap silly person compared to him. She would like to work with him on the refugee committees when they got back, she said; she wanted to do something to help. It hurt her feelings when he did not seem pleased, when he only said she might find it very boring. "I'm not expecting to be entertained," she said.

He worried that after a while he too might bore her. He told her that in bed; he told her many things in bed. She remembered supposing, before she went to bed with Julian, that two people could say anything to each other then. Only it had never happened. She had not learned until now how talking could feed desire, make it urgent again.

Nobody had any right, living in those times, to be happy. She knew that, and yet she was. She had never anticipated loving him like that, she had only expected to feel grateful, relieved, full of good intentions. To find herself joyful when she caught sight of him in the lobby, to get such pleasure from touching his face, so that she had to shut her eyes: it seemed remarkable to her, more than she deserved. The smell of bougainvillea and hibiscus came in through the balcony windows as they lay in bed. She marveled at that, and at the balminess of the night air: it was the first week in November. In New York, they read in the paper, there had already been some light snow.

They took a taxi from the airport to the apartment on Bogardus Place, another unwonted luxury. Among the bills crammed into their mailbox was an airmail envelope containing a letter from Franz and a photograph of the two sets of parents, who had celebrated the marriage together in Nuremberg. There they were, on the horsehair sofa in Jeannette's drawing room, in front of the portrait of Jeannette's brother, raising their glasses in a toast to their children.

The women's heavy silk dresses are cut square at the neck, to let them display the double strings of pearls their own fathers gave them when they got married. On the table beside them are a plate of iced petits fours and a large open box of chocolates, their crinkled papers mostly empty. The glasses they hold aloft are of leaded Bavarian crystal; so is the chandelier above their heads. From the way they are smiling at the camera—even Louisa's mother has mustered a smile—one might almost think that their snug and prosperous lives had gone on uninterrupted since the departure of their children five years before. Of course the chocolates and the cakes had to be purchased at certain hours, the times set aside for Jews to do their shopping; Mrs. Müller and Ilse had long since departed, Aryans no longer being permitted to work in Jewish households; the chandelier itself had been taxed with a special tax. Still, the women are only slightly thinner than before; the men exude *Gemütlichkeit*; there is no trace of the special armbands with the yellow stars that have to be worn on the street.

But earlier on the day that Rolf and Louisa returned, the horsehair sofa had been ripped open with a butcher's knife, to see if there was gold hidden in the cushions; the chandelier had been smashed with an ax, the pearls snatched from the jewel case in Jeannette's bedroom. The remains of the box of chocolates had been hurled from the sideboard and trampled into the carpet, along with the shards of crystal. The two proud fathers, with Otto's father Emil, who had taken the photograph, were dragged from their houses with shouts and curses, and kicked down the steps. Both Sigmund's eyes were blackened; Emil lost three of his teeth. They were shoved into the back of a van that, when it had its full complement of Jews, rattled through the darkness toward Dachau. It was what the American papers would call the Night of Broken Glass.

Because all three men had been awarded the Iron Cross in the war, their names appeared on the list issued by the Reichs-bureau a month later, allowing for the release of decorated front fighters from the Bavarian camps. But by the time the seals had been properly affixed and the orders arrived in the office of the Kommandant, Emil was dead, having collapsed during the morning roll call a week earlier. The young SS guard—he could not have been more than twenty; he had just been promoted to captain—shouted at him to get to his feet. When he failed to do so, the boy kicked him in the head and dragged him over to the flogging blocks; there he began whipping him, but halfheartedly, because he had stopped moving. The SS guard threw the whip aside and stalked off. Later two of the prisoners were ordered to bury him in the pit set aside for that purpose.

So it was only Sigmund and Franz, Rolf's and Louisa's fathers, who returned to Nuremberg, driven home by the Red Cross, because it was clear that Sigmund was in a terminal state. Somehow Franz managed to carry the dying man up the steps of his house—he weighed under a hundred pounds, Franz himself had hardly more flesh on him by then—and then to his bedroom, where he lowered him, in his stinking, shit-smeared camp uniform, onto the remains of the mauve eiderdown that had been part of Rolf's mother's dowry, and which the SS had likewise slashed in their hunt for diamonds. For an hour Franz sat in a chair opposite while Trudl bathed the scabs on Sigmund's face and spooned broth into his shriveled mouth. Each time the liquid came up again, pure greeny-gold, shiny with the putrefying fluids of his stomach lining, until she put the bowl aside and stroked his face, murmuring the same words she used to say to him when he'd had a bad dream. Then Franz left to go tell Jeannette he was safe.

She wept hysterically when he walked in. She had been out of her mind, she said, wringing her hands. She had hardly slept, she had hardly eaten since they'd taken him away. But she did not think to offer him food. He sank down on the sofa, and though its stuffing was spilling out and its carved back was full of gashes, it agitated her to see it soiled by his filthy rags. He had better take a bath, she said, her tears having dried.

The next morning he put on his yellow star and walked to Sigmund's again—all Jewish telephones had been removed by order of the authorities some months before—where Trudl told him that Sigmund had died during the night. He stayed with her until her sister could come and then went to the post office, where he filled out a form requesting permission to send a telegram notifying Rolf of Sigmund's death. After examining his papers, and Sigmund's papers, and grudgingly stamping the telegraph document in all the required places, the woman behind the counter made him lay the money down before her, unwilling to take it directly from his Jewish hand; she counted it twice to make sure he was not trying to cheat her. As he walked outside, a marching band was passing by, preceded by two men bearing the SA flag. On both sides of the street, people stopped and raised their arms. A bent old woman shifted a string bag full of vegetables from her right arm to her left, so that she could give the Hitler salute, and stepped to the curb, shouting *Perish Judah!* Franz stepped back into the post office vestibule until the marchers had passed.

Back at the house again, he headed for Louisa's old bedroom. He had gotten into the habit of going there when he wanted to be alone; he would sit, incongruously, on the tufted chair in front of her vanity table, moved by the sight of her powder puff, with a mauve bow on the back, and of the silver heart on its tarnished chain that she had draped over the mirror years before, and by the thought that she at least was safe. In the camp too he had thought of her, insofar as he could think at all. He had not really believed that he would get out alive, but after a while that hardly mattered; the important thing was that she had escaped.

Nothing in her room had been touched since the night the SS came. Among the clothes and lipsticks and books and smashed trinkets strewn over the flowered carpet was a pale green chiffon dress that quivered slightly at his entrance and then subsided again. He picked it up and went to lay it on the bed, whose mattress, like so much else, gaped open. The wardrobe had been smashed, and tilted dangerously forward. He righted it with an effort and then, one by one, picked up the drawers from the dressing table, which had been yanked out and flung onto the floor. They would not slide in all the way, but still he put the broken pots of rouge and face cream carefully inside them.

Stooping to retrieve a bundle of letters curling inside a rubber band, he noticed, jammed up against one leg of the dresser, the little cameo brooch that his mother, shortly before she died, had wrapped up for him to give to Louisa on her tenth birthday. Unlike all the rest, it seemed unharmed. The girlish profile was as smooth and unblemished as before, the pin on the back still sat securely in its clasp. He fumbled a small piece of tissue paper out of the drawer he'd just replaced and, folding it around the pin, placed it in his jacket pocket.

It was still there, still in its flimsy wrapping, when he and Jeannette boarded the SS *Manhattan* in Hamburg three months later. In December 1938, their visas had arrived from the U.S. Consulate, the affidavits Rolf had obtained being deemed sufficient. At the end of January, in 1939, Franz had been summoned to an interview at the Office of Reichs Emigration above the police station, where the Herr Präfekt, a gloomy man who smelled of schnapps, examined his papers suspiciously, holding them up to the light and peering at the stamps on the visas through a magnifying glass. But finally, as though sick of the whole business, he had produced two exit permits from his desk, slammed the drawer shut, and handed them over with a grimace.

They were allowed to take two trunks with their possessions. In addition to warm clothing, a German–English dictionary twenty years out of date, two leather-bound volumes of Goethe, and several large envelopes full of photographs, Jeannette had packed the vast lace-edged tablecloth, embroidered with lilies and peacocks, that had been the pride of her trousseau, a set of gold-handled fish forks, and the portrait of her brother.

As the ship pulled away from the dock, a small boy in a fur hat came running up to Franz and pummeled him on the leg. "Now I'm in America," he shouted, in German. "I'm going to be an American."

"Good for you," Franz said, but already the boy had whirled away from him, racing up and down the deck. On the shore too, men were running, pointing excitedly at a vast crane lowering a railroad carriage onto a flatbed truck. A gust of wind rippled through the red and black banners lining the pier, making their swastikas dance. Meanwhile the seagulls were circling the ship, closer and closer. As it pulled away, Franz heard a woman sobbing behind him, but having no comfort to offer he went on staring ahead—at the banners, the gulls, the railway car—willing his heart to turn to stone.

PART II

CHAPTER ONE

The army rejected him not, as he had feared, because he was German, although the examining sergeant seemed suspicious about that, but on the grounds of his myopia and the punctured eardrum he had suffered in a football game twenty-two years before. They did not even let him finish the physical, but told him to get dressed halfway through, when he was still holding his arms stiffly by his naked sides and trying to stand straight. It was almost a relief when the navy turned him down, since he had been seasick all the way to New York on the boat. The air corps was out of the question for someone with his eyesight. In desperation, he tried the merchant marine, but even they refused him.

By early 1942 Otto and the others had all enlisted or been drafted, and had scattered to training camps around the country. Alex Starin was working in army intelligence in Washington; even the hysterical Gruenbaum, who had managed to train as a taxi driver in the intervening years, had been taken by the navy, despite his mental imbalance. Drunks on the street accosted Rolf to ask why he wasn't in uniform; at Rexall's on Fourteenth Street, where he sometimes went for his lunch, the waitresses, hearing his accent, gave him dirty looks and slapped down his sandwich without speaking. He did not try to defend himself. However much blood he gave, however many war bonds he bought, however many chocolate bars and copies of *True Detective* he shipped to GIs overseas (the American Legion provided lists of those without families to send them parcels), he would still remain safe, while every other man his age was in danger. For the first time in his life he felt morally compromised.

Even his mother seemed ashamed for him, perhaps remembering his father's Iron Cross for bravery, though it had not saved Sigmund at Dachau. Her sister's boy, Hans, having escaped to England with his parents and sister just in time, had been released from internment as an enemy alien and was serving with the British Army in the Middle East. But Trudl, though she spoke of him proudly, seemed to brood about that also. The English had made him anglicize his name—he was no longer Hans Metzger but John Mercer—but she still worried what would happen if he were captured by the Germans.

Three times a week, on his way home from work, Rolf went to visit his mother in her tiny apartment around the corner from his and Louisa's. These visits always followed an identical pattern: she served him cake and coffee at the little round table in front of the window, on the same blue-and-white Meissen and with the same swift decisive movements he remembered from childhood. She sat with him as he ate and drank, asking how his work was going and telling him any war news she had heard on the radio that day, her voice particularly brisk when reporting battles in the Middle East. Then, after exactly fifteen minutes, she would stand. "I mustn't keep you any longer. Your wife will be expecting you." If he suggested that she come back with him for supper, she always shook her head. Not today. Today she was feeling a little tired. Some other time.

Louisa was allowed to pay longer visits, during which they sat at the little table playing Chinese checkers. Louisa was with her on the day the telegram arrived from her sister, announcing that Hans was missing in action; it was Louisa who phoned Rolf at his office and told him. When he got there that evening, the two women were bent over the star-shaped board. His mother let him in in silence and listened in silence as he told her she must not despair; Hans might have been taken prisoner, and the Germans would know him only as John Mercer. Yes, she said, with a flash of scorn, Louisa had mentioned that already. "If he is a prisoner, they will realize soon enough that he is Jewish. They will see that he is circumcised." Now if he wouldn't mind she would return to their game.

Two weeks later, a letter came for Trudl from her sister; Hans had been confirmed dead. "At least he died with honor," Trudl said to Rolf that night. "At least there is that. He died as a soldier. Not as a prisoner in the *Lager*." And Rolf, whose clearest memory of his cousin was of Hans telling him that his missing cat was probably hanging in a butcher's shop, felt that she was reproaching him.

On the morning the Allies took Cologne, Louisa went to Trudl's apartment and, getting no answer to the bell, used her key to let herself in. She called her mother-in-law's name several times before opening the door to the bathroom, where she found Trudl, her hair neatly covered by a hairnet, lying in the tub, wearing her wedding ring and the pearls her father had given her when she was married, the skin of her narrow body shriveled and puckered from the bathwater in which she had drowned.

"I didn't want you to see her like that," Louisa said, when Rolf asked that evening why she hadn't called him right away. Instead she had managed somehow to lift Trudl up, carry her to the bed, dry her off, and cover her with her robe and a blanket. After she phoned Rolf and told him to come, she had also phoned the doctor, even the funeral parlor. When he got there, she was waiting for him in the doorway and led him by the hand into the apartment; she made him sit down on the couch. "She was so unhappy," she said. "At least now she won't be unhappy any more." But he could not accept this as consolation. His mother had never spoken of being unhappy. Only later, when he could not sleep, did he wonder if Louisa had meant something else. Maybe Trudl had drowned herself deliberately. Maybe she had left a note, and Louisa had hidden it. When he asked Louisa, the next morning, he thought she hesitated for a moment before she said no.

"What did you talk about with her? You can't just have played checkers all the time."

"Once," Louisa said, smiling at the memory, "she told me about the first time she met your father. About how she was strolling with her sister in the park, and he rode up beside them on a chestnut horse and doffed his hat to her." Rolf tried to remember if his mother had ever told him that story; he thought not. She had never been demonstrative with him; he and she had been alike that way. His father had been the emotional one. Even as a child, he understood that Sigmund, and the effort to keep him calm, required too much of her attention for there to be much left over; he himself had better not trouble her too much. Now he wished he had found more for her to do in New York; he should have encouraged her to find some outlet for her energies, her organizational skills.

He had bought her German books sometimes, from the stalls on Broadway, near his office, but she never gave any sign of having read them. Louisa brought her American ones from the library, but she never spoke of those either. He saw that as the war had dragged on, and especially after the telegram about Hans, she had spoken less and less, as though speech itself were an effort for her.

At the funeral, in the unfamiliar synagogue on Dyckman Street, the young rabbi, who had never met Trudl, tried to compare her to the children of Israel. Like them, he said, she had been forced to leave her homeland and wander in the desert before arriving in the promised land. Then, as though realizing that the analogy would not hold, he hurried the eulogy to its end.

A dozen of the refugees who had known his mother were in attendance, seated on the opposite side of the sanctuary. After the service several of them came up to him to offer their condolences. A small lean woman with bright blue eyes, whom he could not place for a moment, approached him. She had spoken to his mother only the previous week, she told him.

"Our apartment is very near here. Will you come back and have some coffee and cake? Then we can speak truthfully of your mother." He must have looked startled, because she clucked her tongue. "I do not mean I am going to tell you ugly secrets. I meant to remember her. After a funeral one should remember the dead." At this she nodded swiftly, with a birdlike motion of her chin. He had remembered by then who she was: Sophie Joseftal, the doctor's wife. He had seen her once or twice at his in-laws' place over the years. And so he and Louisa, with Louisa's parents, went back to the one-room apartment on Inwood Avenue where she and the doctor lived, with its neat rose-colored couch that served as their bed at night, the furniture unadorned except for photographs of their two children. Their son, whom Rolf had helped get out of Czechoslovakia, was in his U.S. Army uniform. On the wall was a single painting, of a dark, gingerbready-looking house in the Black Forest.

"That was my family's summer home," Sophie said. "Your mother visited us there one year, when we were at school together. She sketched all the scenes in the vicinity, and painted them too, she was very artistic." He had never known that, Rolf said. "Oh, yes, even my father, who knew something about art, thought she was quite talented. We used to tease her that she would be famous one day. But her father would not permit her to attend art school; that was something young ladies didn't do then. And then she was married, and the war came, and Sigmund became very moody. Perhaps she had no more time for such things."

"Did you see much of her here in New York?" Rolf asked. His mother had never mentioned Sophie to him.

"No . . . I invited her many times, for lunch and supper and to come with me to the park, but she rarely agreed to come. So I did not press her any more. But I continued to phone her, every week."

Meanwhile Jeannette, twisting her hands in her lap, was telling Dr. Joseftal how she had never really cared for her English governess, or developed any love for the language; she had always preferred French, she said fretfully, though Emmy Loeb, her best friend at school—who lived on Indian Road now—used to make fun of her accent. She blamed

Emmy (whose husband had been killed on *Kristallnacht*, whose two sons, hiding in France, had been denounced and deported) for the fact that she had given up her French studies after the second year. But perhaps it was for the best; what good would French have done her here in America, where nobody spoke anything but English? "I have a cousin who emigrated to the Dominican Republic. I am sure that Spanish is a much more *gemütlich* language than English. But it would be too late for me to learn it now."

Sophie, overhearing this, said briskly that she must show more gratitude to her new country, she must not be so discontented. "You spoke of Emily Loeb," she said. "We must think of what she has to endure, and not make so much of our small troubles." Jeannette became agitated; she half rose in her chair, as though propelled upward by her indignation at being addressed this way. The doctor, who up till then had been almost silent, told her gently, "Don't be offended. My Sophie is a great one for enjoining us to gratitude. And of course she is right. I myself need these reminders, I have a tendency to melancholy. We should not read the newspapers too much, I think."

"One must naturally keep up with the war news," Sophie said. "But there is no necessity to read some of the other stories they carry."

"Like what?" Louisa asked.

Sophie looked at her husband, who sat with his head bowed, still smiling faintly, as though to remove himself from the discussion. "These sad stories about animals that die in the zoo. About old women found dead in their apartments."

"I didn't think they carried such stories in the *New York Times*," Rolf said.

"Yes, they do. On the inside pages. They upset Gustav very much."

"I am afraid I am not the soldier my Sophie is," Gustav said, smiling at Jeannette. "But she is right, we must try to be grateful, to America especially. You would not find the Dominican Republic more congenial than New York, I am sure of that."

Three weeks after Trudl's funeral, reports began appearing about the *Lager* the Allies had liberated in their march through Europe. The women read the accounts, in German, in the Washington Heights paper, the men in the *New York Times*. But they were afraid to say too much. Did you see the pictures in the *Aufbau*, one woman might ask another, and the other would nod; they would both fall silent for a moment, before telling how the butcher on Dyckman Street had failed, once again, to trim the fat off the stewing meat.

Even husbands and wives could not talk of those things; when they turned off the light, they lay silent, their backs to each other, and did not shut their eyes. The thoughts they had then might be of trivial things, petty squabbles they had had with neighbors, fallings-out with second and third cousins in Stuttgart or Frankfurt that had caused them to cut off contact years before the trouble began—people they had loved once, and now saw that they loved still, whose fate they did not know. They wondered if friends they had lost touch with when they came to America had perished, or if the visas they had been waiting for, to Singapore or South Africa or Argentina, had come through. And some of them thought with shame of scornful remarks they used to make about the *Ostjuden*, the immigrants from Poland whose rusty black jackets, long beards, and guttural Yiddish had embarrassed them so when they still thought of themselves as good Germans.

In search of their relatives, they went to the offices of the Joint Distribution Committee to look at the lists of the dead, which grew longer every week—another thousand names, another hundred thousand. But still they did not speak of these things to each other; they grieved in the dark, remembering the photographs in the newspapers, the mounds of skeletons, and hoped crazily that maybe Rosa or Gottfried or Friedrich had survived after all.

Shortly after Germany's surrender, when the whole world reeked of death, the word circulated among the refugee women that Louisa was pregnant—a piece of news that might have seemed just ordinarily cheerful a few months before but now took on almost a holy resonance. In the midst of the horror, the nightmares, the thoughts of what the dead had suffered before their end, here was a new life beginning, an American child would be born from the ashes. It was enough to make them hum the tunes they used to sing to their own children as they went about their chores, enough to make them stop and smile at the children in the playground at Isham Park.

Many of those women had never cared for Louisa: they remembered their first, terrible weeks in the city, when they had looked to her for succor and been disappointed. She had shown up, breathless and late, in their near-empty apartments, with useless gifts of lace doilies or French soap, when what they needed was to be shown where to find brown bread and lightbulbs. They had also needed an audience for the stories they'd brought with them, and she had not provided it; instead she had told them her own stories, amusing little anecdotes about America they could not quite grasp. They suspected that they bored her; they suspected she preferred her new, American friends, the Park Avenue matrons who worked on the committees with Rolf and invited her to their grand apartments for cocktails. No doubt her frivolous stories, her breathless laughter, went over much better in their drawing rooms; no doubt those rich women were relieved to have found one émigré, at least, who was not grim and reproachful, who did not insist on telling them things they would rather not hear.

But now the refugees drew around her, ready to forgive her everything, even the way she spoke about her baby. For she was no more serious than ever. She joked that the child seemed very bad-tempered, and threatened to knock it out with brandy if it didn't stop its kicking at night. Whereas they began knitting tiny sweaters—they dug out their embroidery silks too, their fingers, stiffened with arthritis, remembering how to make baby bonnets, how to stitch little flowers and leaf patterns—Louisa had given up on her own knitting after a single attempt. It would be cruel, she said, holding up a tiny red scarf, still on its needles, that was curling into a tube, to inflict such a gruesome object on a helpless child, even one with a vile temper.

It was just a manner she had, Sophie told them, when the others shook their heads and rolled their eyes—something she must have picked up in England, where everybody talked that way. She wasn't really unfeeling. Look at how much milk she was drinking. Look at how happy she was. But later the women would say she had been *too* happy; that there'd been something feverish about it, as though she'd had a premonition all along.

When the dizziness started, three months before her due date, and the headaches got so bad she was sick to her stomach, they all remembered, for her sake, the cousin of a cousin or a sister-in-law's sister who had had the most frightening symptoms, and everything had been fine in the end. As she began to look less blooming, as her vision became blurred and her walk unsteady, they told each other she needed to rest more, to eat more meat; she had been a child during the famine; no wonder she wasn't very strong. One or the other of them, organized by Sophie, brought food to the apartment at lunchtime, schnitzel or sauerbraten, with a slice of plum cake from the bakery on Dyckman Street. Afterward they tucked her up on the living room sofa with a crocheted comforter.

But sometimes she could not keep down the food they brought; sometimes she dropped her knife or bumped into a chair on her way to the table. Then she might press her clenched fists against her temples, rocking back and forth, and ask them to leave the veal dumplings or the liver and onions in the kitchen; she would heat them up later. Whichever of the women had come that day would flutter around her, anxious and frightened, telling her with diminishing conviction about a friend or a neighbor back in Nuremberg who'd been nauseated and dizzy for nine months before miraculously giving birth to a healthy child. When they arrived home they would phone Sophie to report.

Jeannette too had taken to phoning Sophie, always at the most inconvenient times, when Sophie was breading veal cutlets or expecting a call from her son Kurt, now enrolled in Ohio State on the GI Bill. Everyone was lying, Jeannette said, all the women, and Louisa's fool doctor too. Anybody with half a brain could see that something was wrong.

She, Jeannette, had tried to speak to Rolf, but Louisa was pretending for him, as everybody else was pretending for Louisa. She should have taken to her bed and stayed there throughout her pregnancy; Jeannette had told her as much, but of course she had not listened to her. The stupid American doctor saw no reason why she shouldn't be climbing mountains. Now look what was happening. Already it might be too late.

"You mustn't worry her," Sophie said. "The last thing she needs now is more worry."

But she herself, Jeannette said, was out of her mind with worry; she could not digest her food properly; the constant acid in her stomach was ruining her health.

"Then you are the one who must see a doctor," Sophie told her sharply. "I've been going to a very pleasant young man, right here in Inwood. I'll give you his number."

"It's all very well for you," Jeannette said, sniffing. "You're not her mother."

"We cannot be telling our children what to do any longer. If she needs another doctor, Rolf will see to it."

But in the end it was Louisa who saw to it. On a gusty fall morning, after Rolf had left for work, she put on the brown felt hat that she had worn for her wedding, walked unsteadily to the corner of Broadway, and hailed a cab. At the hospital on 168th Street, she tottered down the strip of carpet in her high heels, like a drunken model on a runway, and leaned, trembling, against the reception counter. A plump blond nurse carrying a roll of rubber tubing stopped on her way past and asked if she was all right. She was fine, Louisa said: now that the time had come to say out loud what she had been thinking for five weeks and three days, that something was wrong with her baby, she had changed her mind. But when the nurse touched her arm she started to cry.

"Hey," the woman said, shifting the tubing to her left hand. "Hey hey hey. I'm Bonnie. Why don't we take you into the back there and talk for a sec." She steered Louisa, blinded now by tears, through some swinging doors and into a cubicle with a white metal table, where she set the tubing down and gently removed the brown hat. After that Louisa became wholly submissive, allowing Bonnie to take her coat and help her up onto the table. When she was down to her underwear, Bonnie tied a gray hospital gown around her and went to fetch a doctor, who spoke hardly a word, but worked his fingers over her scalp the way the girl at the hairdresser did when she was giving her a shampoo and then shone a light into first one eye and then the other. Bonnie tucked Louisa's hair behind her ear for her before leaving the room. The doctor pinched the skin on her temples and pressed his thumbs, hard, into the back of her neck.

When he too went away, Louisa sat there for a long time, waiting anxiously for Bonnie to return. Instead, two men in rumpled green uniforms arrived, rolling a gurney between them and telling her to hop on and lie down; they had orders to bring her downstairs. In the elevator they had a disagreement about someone named Lena: one of them thought she was just being friendly to Josie's husband, the other that she was after him. "Come off it," the taller one said. He looked as though he needed a shave. "The guy's sixty if he's a day."

"Yeah, well, when Lena's hitting the sauce she don't care how old they are."

Down in the basement, they wheeled her down the corridor and inside a musty beige room almost filled by a huge machine with steel arms swiveling out in all directions. Each arm had a different-shaped attachment at its end. A man who'd been sitting at a desk in the corner got up and swiveled a stubby, cone-shaped one toward Louisa until it was pointing at the right side of her head. A light flashed. "What are you doing?" she asked.

"Just relax. This won't take a minute." He pointed the cone at the other side of her head, then at her forehead; again, there was the flash of light. Then he went and opened the door, and the same two men came and wheeled her out into the hall. Without a word, they aligned the gurney carefully with the wall before stepping into the elevator, leaving her there. She began to cry, weak helpless tears, her bare legs cold against the table.

Several times, she heard the elevator descend and then stop; finally the doors opened and a nurse stepped out—older than Bonnie, skinny, with a starched cap. "Now now," she said, in a neutral voice, handing Louisa a pink pill and a tiny cup of water, and propping up her head so she could swallow. "You mustn't cry, you know. It's bad for the baby." Louisa lay back, both hands on her stomach, and whispered to her child that it was all right, they would be all right, everything would be fine. Then she remembered Phillip, back in London, saying those words to her one wet afternoon: she had not heard from her father for two weeks, the *Manchester Guardian* had run an article that day about the proscription of Jews from the streetcars and parks in Germany. "I promise," he had said, kissing her eyelids, "I promise you'll be fine," and as he unzipped her dress, "It'll all be all right. You'll see. We'll get them out. We'll be very happy. Everything will be just fine." But it had not been all right in Chicago, and she knew, even before the doctor came back, that it was not all right now.

CHAPTER TWO

*I*t was Rolf they consulted, not the patient. Rolf was summoned to a room with tall windows, on the top floor, the dizzying heights of the neurology department. Two bony doctors, professorial types in hairy jackets, met him at the elevator and escorted him there. They had already arranged for him to go, the very next day, to a doctor on Park Avenue, a Dr. Channing, who was a leading expert in the field.

After he left them he came and sat by Louisa's bedside, drawing up the pink visitor's chair and speaking in a measured voice, very low, to keep the women in the other two beds from overhearing. Louisa listened in silence, her mouth trembling slightly, as though with the effort of concentrating on his words, which weren't his at all: meningioma, basal ganglia, occipital lobe.

"It's all right," she said then, sounding cross, "you can talk in a normal voice. Really." She looked around at the other beds. "It won't matter if they hear, they won't understand what you're saying either."

When he had finished, she asked if they could save the baby.

"What do you mean?"

"If I die."

"You're not going to die," he told her, too quickly.

"What did they say about the baby?"

"They said it would be fine. Absolutely fine."

"No they didn't," she said, in a voice so tender he could hardly bear it. "You're making it up."

"They said the heartbeat was normal."

"And what else?"

"They said it seemed perfectly healthy."

"You're lying to me. I can tell because you lie so badly."

"I'm not. They don't think the tumor will affect it."

"But they're not sure."

"I suppose not."

She asked him to feel the baby. He got up from the chair and sat on the edge of her bed, while she guided his hand onto her stomach. Immediately, the baby kicked. "It feels fine," he said. "It feels exactly the same."

In fact he could not remember how it had felt before.

"Are you a lucky man, Mr. Furchgott?" Dr. Channing asked him the next morning. "Because I'm afraid it's ultimately a matter of luck." He was a tall, plump, beautiful man with snow-white hair and the radiant pink skin of an infant. There were hunting prints and maps of the ancient world on his office walls, and a large brass letter opener lying on his handsome desk, which he tapped on the blotter as he answered Rolf's questions.

Only when Rolf asked about the baby did Dr. Channing look slightly annoyed. If the tumor had been discovered earlier, he said, he would have recommended a termination. As things stood, it was hard to say, really, what damage might have been caused. The oxygen supply to the fetus could have been interfered with.

And what would that mean? Rolf asked.

"I can't say with any certainty. We don't encounter this situation very often, as you can imagine. But brain damage can't entirely be ruled out."

What did he mean, it couldn't be ruled out? Was he saying the baby was brain-damaged?

"Good heavens." Dr. Channing tapped the letter opener against his gleaming white cuff. "Nothing of the sort. The child might be perfectly normal. I only meant the possibility can't be ruled out." It was then that he asked whether Rolf was a lucky man.

Louisa, it seemed, had her own luck, in that the tumor was benign. They could leave the whole matter alone, if Rolf chose; the mass in the brain might remain the same size indefinitely. "On the other hand," Dr. Channing said, shifting the letter opener into his own other hand, as though to illustrate this formulation, "it might not." He produced a multicolored diagram of the brain, a surprisingly humble object, like an illustration for a school textbook, with what looked like sweat marks on it, from the drawer of his elegant desk. Taking up the letter opener again, he used it as a pointer. If the tumor spread to the right—a coil of grayish blue—there was a risk of blindness, whereas here on the left—a bilious yellow-green—was the center that affected speech. Then there was the purple area directly in front of where the mass was now. He tapped twice.

What happens if the tumor goes there? Rolf asked.

Dr. Channing set down the letter opener and cracked his rosy knuckles. "It all depends. Sometimes there are personality changes. Only sometimes. But we don't want it to reach the basal ganglia, that would be a very bad business. Pressure on the basal ganglia is always a very bad business. A terminal situation."

Again: what were the chances?

"I'm afraid there aren't any reliable statistics." He looked a little less cheerful now. "I will say, though, that it's improbable—it's not, let's say, extremely likely—that the tumor will remain at its present size indefinitely."

"I see."

"Well, then," Dr. Channing said, brightening. "Perhaps we'd better start thinking about treatment." There was a team at Dana Farber, up in Boston, that had been using radioactive substances to shrink such tumors. "Unfortunately, they haven't had the results they hoped for. It may be some time before we can pinpoint the cancerous cells."

"So you wouldn't recommend it for my wife."

"I wouldn't personally, no."

They sat in silence for a moment. Dr. Channing resorted to the letter opener again, passing it deftly along his knuckles. "There's a Dr. Seidelbaum who's been doing some interesting work," he said, as though he had just remembered. Dr. Seidelbaum, it seemed, had been performing a procedure of his own devising on cranial tumors. "I'm not personally acquainted with his methods, but he's extremely well regarded." He could make a referral if Rolf wanted; he could even phone right then and there. Though he believed, he said, raising an eyebrow, that Dr. Seidelbaum charged rather hefty fees.

Out on Seventy-ninth Street, cars seemed to be veering toward the curb; the wind had been high for days, and candy wrappers and paper cups blew merrily in the gutter; Rolf had to cram his hat down onto his head. Dr. Channing would send the X-rays to Dr. Seidelbaum, who'd agreed to see Rolf in his office the following day. Nobody, it seemed, thought it necessary to see Louisa in person. "Oh, no, sir, I don't think that would be a good idea," Dr. Seidelbaum's secretary said, a little shocked, when Rolf asked if he should bring her along.

On a bench outside the park, a red-haired boy was angling a sugar cone piled with strawberry ice cream toward the mouth of a girl who kept giggling and ducking away. The yellow cabs heading downtown obscured them from Rolf's sight for a moment and then revealed them again, the girl holding up her hands in protest, the boy trying to zigzag the cone past them. Rolf stood staring from the other side of Fifth Avenue, his vision blurring and clearing, blurring and clearing, light coming at him in waves. Just as the girl surrendered, as she was licking the pink ice cream from her chin, she looked up and caught his eye. Immediately he swerved away, hurrying to Eightieth Street and crossing against the light. As he entered the park, a patch of red and yellow flowers, fiercely bright in the sun, made him dizzy for a moment; the vivid green of the grass brought on a nausea he could only just contain.

Louisa was being discharged; she lay on the bed in her street clothes, her shoes neatly aligned on the floor, her hat on the bedside table. The nurse had to come and take her pulse before they could leave, she said. He told her about Dr. Seidelbaum's promising procedure, stressing his high success rate. (He made no mention of blindness, impaired speech, personality changes.) But she only nodded tiredly in response; her eyes were fixed on the painting on the wall opposite—a cheerful beach scene with striped umbrellas and blond children—and her expression was one of strained politeness; he could not even tell if she was listening.

Then she turned and looked at him. "Poor Rolf," she said. "Poor Rolf." She held out her hand, and he took it. "Let's talk about something else. About other people's problems. What was in the paper today?"

He had carried the *Times* with him onto a half-empty subway that morning, having left for the office at six to get his work done before he went to see Dr. Channing. For once he could have opened the paper out fully in front of him, instead of reading it column by folded column. But he could not summon up the interest. Seated across from him had been a squat bronze-skinned woman with a face like an Inca carving, stony with exhaustion; a crumpled shopping bag full of rags and worn-out brushes swayed at her feet. For just an instant he seemed to see into her—he felt the weight she carried inside her, he saw the dark room where she lived alone—and it made him afraid.

He might have told Louisa about her, or the couple outside the park, but he could not explain the blinding vividness of them. Instead he tried to remember the previous day's news. The UN was under attack for failing to resolve the Iranian crisis; the Russians had vetoed the U.S. plan of action. Many members of Congress felt that America should resign. There were speeches about it in the House every day.

"Go on," she said. She was looking at the painting again, her lips were slightly parted.

A truck strike was threatened at the city's sugar refineries. Retail prices had gone up by 13 percent in the past year. Meat-price controls had been removed. Thousands of Jewish war veterans had marched on Washington to demand the resettlement of homeless European Jews in Palestine. President Truman had agreed to meet with them.

"Go on."

The Civilian Production Administration was considering canceling the regulations regarding women's clothing. Skirts might be longer again by early 1947, and sleeves wider. He'd thought she might smile at that, but her expression did not alter.

The clocks had just gone back—already, at four, it was dusk outside. On the street below, a young woman in a plaid skirt was wheeling a baby stroller; a skinny boy hardly old enough to be a father slouched protectively by her side, hands in his pockets. As they waited for the light to change, a grizzled man in a peacoat came barreling around the corner and almost slammed into them. The boy seized him by the arm, but the other shrugged him off and hurried on his way.

Again, nausea rose in him. The growth in Louisa's brain made a certain kind of sense: it had definite meaning, required definite action; there were causes and effects to think of— even, despite Dr. Channing, the laws of probability to consider. When he listened to the doctors, his heartbeat, like the baby's, was normal. But looking at a velvet coat on a child, an ice cream cone, a middle-aged cleaning lady, had become unsafe.

"We have forgotten there are sorrows in the world that have nothing to do with the Nazis," Sophie had said the night before. Jeannette had told her the news. The child would need to be looked after, Sophie said briskly, while Louisa was in the hospital. If she could help in any way, he had of course only to ask.

Thank you, he said stiffly. Always before he had been the one to offer help. How was Gustav? he asked her.

"You are wondering why he doesn't talk to you himself. As a medical man."

No, no, he said, though the thought had crossed his mind.

"He wanted to, but I advised against it. I was afraid he might become quite emotional, it would only upset you. But he asks you to send Louisa his love."

Of course, he told her. And how were her children?

"I am trying to explain why I will not invite you for dinner while Louisa is in the hospital. I am not sure it would be relaxation for you."

"I understand."

"Then we won't speak of it again."

He'd been relieved that he did not have to go there. He did not want to sit in that small room, with the sound of Gustav's breathing, the smell of veal and cauliflower and damp wool, and the fog of sadness that even Sophie, so brisk and sensible, could not dispel. It was the silence, the thin air, of his office he wanted, with the door shut into the corridor. It was being alone with a yellow legal pad and a sharpened pencil and the figures Mr. Starin had asked him, once again, to review: the question had been reopened of buying the lumberyard in Oregon from which they purchased their supplies of wood. In 1938 they had missed their chance; someone else had moved more quickly, but now that buyer was himself putting it on the market—for health reasons, he said; he was recovering slowly from a heart attack. Mr. Starin wondered if that was the true and only reason.

Rolf had sat with the numbers, breaking them down every way he could think of, for half a day before Louisa took herself to the hospital. Now, as the church bell wobbled across the way and they waited for the nurse to come, his thoughts returned to them. It was clear that the business was not flourishing, but there were opportunities to be seized.

New efficiencies would be needed, they would have to achieve economies of scale, but the potential was there. The crucial figures—production for the last three quarters, margin percentages for the different lumber types—made a clearing in his mind, glowing faintly, with a pleasing luminosity. The image of a misshapen, oxygen-deprived creature growing in Louisa's belly sank back again, into the swamp from which it had come.

CHAPTER THREE

"My good Sophie. My good Sophie. You cannot take this on yourself. You will wear yourself out."

"You talk as if I were planning to look after the child myself. I am only going to make a few arrangements."

"Even so. It is terrible, what happened. *Schrecklich*. But this is not your responsibility."

"Whose responsibility should it be then? Jeannette's?"

He gave her a wounded look. "She is no better?"

"Who, Jeannette?"

"You know who I mean."

"No."

"*Schrecklich*," he said again, under his breath. Sophie stood up and began clearing the table. "Think of how fast it happens," Gustav said. "A person's destiny decided just like that, in an instant. A life destroyed so fast. And why? For what reason?" He shook his head. "If we knew when we were born what lay in store for us, none of us would have the courage to see it through." But Sophie, scraping the gristle from his plate into the bin under the sink, could not be thinking about destiny just then, or the courage required for existence.

It was seven weeks since the birth. Everyone had been mindful of the danger; the obstetrician had sent Rolf a letter enumerating the risks—herniation, excessive intracranial pressure, pituitary malfunction—although he hadn't specified what the results of these might be. In the event, although Louisa's contractions had come in irregular, violent patterns over a period of forty-three hours, and she lost far too much blood, both mother and baby came through all right. Franz had been with Rolf in the waiting room—the obstetrician had long since turned the case over to a resident and gone home to rest—when a plump, boyish-looking man in sweat-stained surgical whites had come through the swinging doors, a broad grin on his face, and told Rolf in a Southern accent, "You got yourself a baby daughter. All her fingers and toes, and she can scream like anything. So don't worry, okay?" Reporting back to Sophie the following day, Franz said that this was the moment when he began to believe in America.

The hospital kept them there for a week, while Louisa was recovering. Everyone had been optimistic then, everyone had predicted that things would be right as rain, as one of the nurses put it: Louisa even tried the expression on Jeannette, who came and sat by her bed, twisting her hands in her lap, as Louisa waited for them to bring her the baby. Dr. Seidelbaum was monitoring things from his own hospital, farther downtown; he phoned Rolf to congratulate him on the birth and tell him about an article on his new procedure in the *Journal of Neurosurgery*. His father had emigrated from Stuttgart in 1909, he told Rolf; Rolf should call him Leo.

Louisa herself was hectic with gaiety, laughing at everything. In the month that she was back in the apartment, before heading downtown to Dr. Seidelbaum's hospital, Rolf would wake in the night and lie there listening, half expecting to hear her sobbing in the dark, but it was only Emma who cried—Louisa said the moment she looked at her she knew she was an Emma—and then Rolf would get up and warm her bottle. Louisa slept more heavily in those weeks than Rolf had ever known her to, he had to shake her sometimes to bring her back to consciousness. There was always a moment when he was afraid he could not rouse her, but then there she was, radiant with happiness.

On the morning of the day she had to check into Mount Sinai, Louisa lifted Emma high into the air and lowered her to her face, kissing her with loud smacks, while Emma squealed with delight. The babysitter, an Irish girl from the neighborhood whose chief training had been as the eldest of twelve children, wished her luck. "I really really hope it'll all go okay today. I'm going to say a prayer for you." Louisa smiled a vague secret smile, as though amused at this burst of fervor. It was hard for Rolf to know any more what she was thinking.

Rolf carried her suitcase, packed with three nightgowns and several paperback books as well as her toothbrush and makeup. Franz was waiting in a taxi downstairs. Complex negotiations, mostly out of Louisa's earshot, had been conducted about who should accompany them to the hospital; Sophie had persuaded Jeannette that the two of them would be needed to keep an eye on the babysitter, who had never been alone with Emma for more than a few hours before. Otto had written to Rolf and offered to come. He had been discharged from the navy at last and was living in California, about to get married to an émigré teacher he had met shortly before shipping out for the Pacific, who had been writing to him throughout the war. He mustn't come, Rolf had told him, not yet, anyway; he mustn't leave his fiancée so soon after they'd been reunited. But the night before, Louisa had phoned him—to congratulate him, she said—and talked to him for what seemed like a long time. Rolf didn't know what they'd said to each other.

The cab driver, who had just returned from visiting his daughter in Minnesota, told them New York was no fit place for human beings to live. When Louisa said she loved New York, he turned around to look at her and said it was funny, she didn't look like a crazy person. Then he swung onto Broadway and speeded up. There was a large dray horse pulling a flatbed cart on the other side of the road, something they all agreed they had never seen there before. Wouldn't it be lovely if we could get Emma a pony, Louisa said dreamily. Franz took her hand and squeezed it.

The waiting room in the maternity ward uptown had not yet been rescued from wartime austerity; its mismatched chairs, in various grimy checks and tweeds, had looked like discards from various basements. The one in Dr. Seidelbaum's hospital was airy and opulent, flooded with light. There were Persian carpets in deep reds and blues, curved chintz sofas, matching drapes held back with woven red ropes. It was like wandering into a model living room at B. Altman's, lacking only certain personal touches—knickknacks, photographs, domestic clutter—to bring it to life. Rolf and Franz sat opposite each other on the two sofas, each of them composing his features for the other's sake. The operation was scheduled for eleven; it had been explained to them in advance that they would not be permitted to see Louisa until afterward. At 10:45 Dr. Seidelbaum bounded in, dressed in his street clothes, and greeted Rolf exuberantly. Rolf introduced him to Franz, and instead of shaking Franz's hand he held both of his own up to him. "See? Completely steady. No shakes." He explained to Franz, as he had to Rolf, that his father had emigrated from Stuttgart in 1909; Franz did his best to seem enthusiastic. He had never been to Stuttgart. He had been to Heidelberg, to Frankfurt, to Hamburg, to Berlin, but never to Stuttgart. Dr. Seidelbaum asked him if he knew they used a saw, an actual saw, to cut through the skullbones. Franz said he didn't. The doctor squeezed Rolf's shoulder before turning to go. "Relax," he said. "It'll all be over soon."

Rolf had brought a book with him, a heavy, navy blue volume that he opened on his lap as soon as the doctor had left. Every few minutes he turned a page. Franz took a copy of *Life* from the coffee table and spent the next hour looking at photographs, unable to comprehend the captions. He would never know in what country someone had photographed an emaciated dog lying on whitewashed steps, or where the men were fighting in the streets, or whom the monks were praying for. He paused at an advertisement for Alka-Seltzer, and a smaller one for false teeth, two smiling fair-haired people with their arms entwined. Meanwhile the rhythmic ticking of the grandfather clock in the corner, with its handsome gold face, seemed to be growing louder.

When Dr. Seidelbaum returned the sun was streaming in through the picture window; Franz could not see his face properly. The man sat down next to Rolf, putting his head in his very clean hands. Immediately, in some part of his mind, Franz thought, he's an actor, this one. "Is she dead?" Rolf asked.

The surgeon looked up. No, no, he said, it was nothing like that. "We've succeeded in removing the tumor. She's absolutely out of danger." Then he returned his head to his hands. "I can't tell you how sorry I am."

"What is it?" Rolf asked sharply. "Tell me."

Dr. Seidelbaum let out a long breath. He did not excuse himself, he said, he alone was responsible. But the tumor had extended farther into the ganglia than he'd thought. He had had to cut into the gray matter. In ridding her of it certain nerves had been severed in her brain.

"Which nerves?"

He wasn't sure yet. An optic nerve, certainly, but apart from that, he wouldn't care to speculate. They would have to wait until she woke. The morbidity might be considerable.

Then he said, "You don't have to pay me," but Rolf said he had sent the check the day before. After that nobody spoke for a long minute. Franz listened to the clock. When it seemed that Rolf was not going to break the silence, he asked if he could go to her. As a child she'd been prey to nightmares; if he heard her cry out he had always tried to get to her first, before Jeannette or the grumpy nursemaid could scold her for waking them; he would turn on the light and sit on her bed, holding her tight. It was mice she used to dream of then, or Russian soldiers. He did not want her waking now to an empty room, to blindness or deafness or whatever this bouncy young man had inflicted on her.

Dr. Seidelbaum said he would take them to her; she might be coming to already. It was Franz, again, who asked the questions. What was *morbidity*? "Damage," said Dr. Seidelbaum. What had the doctor meant by *considerable*? "We can only speculate until we know what to expect." At the very least, Dr. Seidelbaum said, her ambulatory functions would be impaired. It was a question of degree. "And at the very most?" Franz asked. But the doctor did not answer that one. Instead he led them down the corridor, ushered them into an elevator, steered them down another hall, and pushed open a door. Louisa was lying on a gurney in a brightly lit, salmon pink room, a sheet pulled up to her neck, her head swathed in a neat little cap of bandages—like the green turban she sometimes wore, with a small gold pin on it, only this was white. There were dark hollows under her eyes, her face looked much thinner than the day before, as though the operation had drained the flesh from her bones. Dr. Seidelbaum felt her wrist and pulled up her right eyelid. "I'll be back in a minute," he said.

The two men approached the bed together. It seemed to Franz that Louisa was struggling to wake; she gave a little moan, her eyelids fluttered; then she went to sleep again. Meanwhile Rolf hung back, looking over Franz's shoulder. Franz could feel his fear, he wanted to say something to him, but he could not take his eyes off Louisa. A minute later she opened her eyes and gave him a lopsided smile, seeming to recognize him. It appeared that the doctor had been wrong after all. But when Franz reached down to take her hand, which was lying on the sheet, it was stiff and lifeless in his own. He squeezed it harder, and then harder, waiting to feel some pressure in return, but she only went on looking at him, smiling that same half-smile. He tried to lift her hand to his face, in order to kiss it, and discovered that it would not bend.

CHAPTER FOUR

*A*fterward, of course, when the doctor had returned and the necessary experts had been summoned, the real assessment could begin. Within twenty-four hours, they had ascertained the precise extent of motor function impairment: weakness in the left leg, paralysis of the left arm (it was unfortunate that Louisa had been left-handed, a propensity Jeannette had tried to rid her of throughout her childhood). The damage to her sight was quickly identified: blindness in the left eye, the right only minimally affected. It was the left side of her mouth that drooped too, causing a certain slurring in her speech. The balance problems were trickier to quantify—a whole battery of tests was required. And it would never be fully determined how much the other changes, the unmistakable decrease in charm, the vagueness and timidity, were due to cortical deficits, and which might have been avoided had other circumstances been different.

Dr. Seidelbaum, on the grounds that none of this was his area of expertise, turned the case over to the neurologists and the physiotherapists, who, in consultation with each other, decided that the patient should be sent home as soon as possible, rather in the spirit, as one of them explained to Rolf, of throwing a child into water to teach her how to swim. Meanwhile more permanent arrangements had to be made for the care of the real child, the infant Emma, whom Katy from the neighborhood had no intention of looking after permanently. Babysitting was strictly her part-time vocation; she was taking classes in cosmetology, she explained to Rolf, who had to ask her what that meant. Two of her sisters were roped in. But Deirdre was surly, Maureen washed Emma's face with a dirty flannel, and she got an eye infection. It was this situation that Sophie, in consultation with Franz, had determined to amend.

The last time Sophie had gone to Bogardus Place, Maureen was squatting on the living room floor, changing Emma's diaper. The baby was smeared with what looked like milk and carelessly applied powder, which was also distributed at random on the living room carpet, some in the shape of footprints where it had been trodden on. The air smelled bad; Emma was grizzling and writhing, flailing her arms about. Louisa, her useless arm folded crookedly against her chest, kept trying to rise from her armchair across the room and falling back again. Bristles of red hair were poking through on her shaven scalp, standing straight up.

Sophie waited until Maureen had finished and took the child from her, wrapping her more snugly in her none-too-clean blanket, so that she could not wriggle too much. Then she laid her carefully in Louisa's lap, propping her against Louisa's good arm and hovering nearby in case she started to fall. For a minute, mother and baby gazed at each other, both perfectly still, Louisa's face alight with joy. So she feels it, what we have all felt, Sophie thought. That at least isn't dead in her. Then the baby lifted up her arms to be held, and started to cry. Sophie took her away. The girl knocked over the tin of powder, which she'd left on the floor, and headed for the bathroom, trailing the dirty diaper behind her.

Rolf would get ill, Franz said; Rolf could not go on getting up with the baby all night and going off to work in the morning. Somehow the money must be found to pay a proper housekeeper. But even when this decision had been made, when Rolf himself had agreed, no likely candidate presented herself. Rolf had put an ad in the Sunday *Times*, without result. Gustav had tried the *Aufbau*. Jeannette, clearly unable to take on the job herself, wrung her hands and cried that there were too many situations vacant since the war, everyone was crying out for workers. Nobody wanted to look after a baby in a crowded little apartment uptown. Nursemaids were for those who lived downtown, on Sutton Place.

Sophie brought the problem to Mrs. Timpson in 5B. For several years they had been exchanging news of their soldier sons in the elevator, and Mrs. Timpson once told Sophie that her husband was the only gentleman left in the building: Gustav, it seemed, always took off his hat when he saw her. She had to put the ad in the *Daily News*, Mrs. Timpson said, the kind of person she was looking for would never read the *Times*. "You're looking for a widow, and women only read the *Times* if their husbands get it." Sophie took the subway to Herald Square and filled out a form; the harried-looking young woman in the classified department crossed out all the articles and charged her $3.20.

Nothing happened on the first day, but at 8:30 the following morning, just after Gustav had left for work, the phone rang. "I'm calling about your ad in the paper," a voice said. "This is Mrs. Sprague. Who am I speaking to?" But she laughed when Sophie said her name. "Well now, I could never pronounce that." Her voice was girlish, but she told Sophie she was fifty-nine, with three grown children. "I got plenty of energy for my age, though, don't worry." She was from Maine; her husband, a lobster fisherman, had died the year before. She was staying on East Seventy-first Street with a family she knew from back in Bucks Harbor: "They always came for the summers, and I used to help the Mrs. with the kiddies. Oh, they were lovely, real little lambs, the pair of them, but they've grown now, they're too big for their old Aunt May to be much use to them, so the Watsons are just putting me up while I look around for a position. Now you tell me about your baby."

It wasn't her baby, Sophie said stiffly. She had not thought this through properly; she had not planned how to tell Louisa's story to a stranger. "Look here," she said. "I think it would be better if we met in person. Then I can tell you what's what." (*What's what* was an expression she had heard Mrs. Timpson use.) And so, three hours later, they met at the Old Vienna Café on Dyckman Street, where Sophie managed to explain the situation.

"Oh, that poor woman," Mrs. Sprague said, sighing. "My heart goes out to her. To all of them." She was a large, handsome, oddly childlike woman in a shaggy brown fur coat with bald patches. Sophie was not convinced of her sincerity—she seemed to listen without really listening; a moment after speaking of her heart, she tucked with evident gusto into the cream cake that the waitress had brought her—but told herself she was being unfair. After all, why should Mrs. Sprague feel for Louisa, whom she had never met? She wished Mrs. Timpson had been there to pronounce judgment.

Anyway, as Mrs. Sprague said, the important thing was the child. That was why she had come uptown, so that Sophie could take her to meet the baby, and let the baby meet her. "Because we've got to jell, her and me," Mrs. Sprague had said on the phone. "It's just like any two people, baby or no. There's got to be chemistry. Though I've rarely met a baby I couldn't take to. And they take to me pretty good too. You'll see."

It was plain when they got to the apartment—Sophie had phoned Louisa and told her to expect them—that that much at least was true. A girl called Hazel, a friend of Katy's, was walking Emma up and down, back and forth, in the living room, with the baby's head resting on her shoulder. "It's the only way to keep her from crying," Hazel said, sounding very fed up, and even with the constant movement, Emma was sniffling. But when Mrs. Sprague went and put her face close to the child's, pursing her mouth as though for a kiss, Emma stopped her fussing and looked expectant; when Mrs. Sprague clapped her hands, Emma gurgled happily; pretty soon she was reaching out her arms, demanding that Mrs. Sprague take her, as though this was the person she'd been waiting for all along. Meanwhile Louisa sat watching from her green chair, with a look of dazed exhaustion.

"There you go," Mrs. Sprague said happily, a rich coo in her voice. "Yes, I know. I know you want to see what this old woman is all about. You take a good whiff of your old Aunt May. And I'll do the same." She buried her nose in Emma's neck, until the baby squealed with delight. She made loud smacking noises. "Don't you smell delicious. Don't you smell like the most beautiful little girl in the world."

"And this is Mrs. Furchgott," Sophie said.

"Pleased to meet you," Mrs. Sprague said, taking her eyes off Emma only very briefly. She dove again into Emma's neck; Emma gave a loud laugh, and clutched at her hair. "Aren't you a naughty thing," Mrs. Sprague said, laughing.

"Isn't she a naughty one," she repeated to no one in particular. "Bright as a button, I can see that. The naughty ones are always the best." And to Emma again, "Isn't that true, my darling?" Now she turned her attention to Hazel. "How's about you straighten things up a little while I'm tending to her?" She gestured with her free hand toward the mess of plates and bottles and tissues on the coffee table. "Go on, I've got the baby now, you might as well use the time to get the place tidied up."

The same idea had occurred to Sophie; she could not have said why hearing it from Mrs. Sprague made her uneasy, except for the fear on Louisa's face. Sophie went over and asked in a semiwhisper, "What do you think?"

"Rolf will be pleased," Louisa said slowly, still without taking her eyes from Mrs. Sprague. "He hates finding everything in a mess when he gets home, he's always telling me I must get them to clean up." Suddenly she reached up with her good hand and gripped Sophie's with startling force. "I don't think so, Sophie, I don't think I want her here. Please. Please make her go away."

CHAPTER FIVE

$\mathcal{I}$n that morning's dream, they were demanding proof of his identity—his passport, his *Landkarte*, a letter signed by the consul general. He searched through his briefcase, while they stood at the barrier, blocking his way. Others, meanwhile, whom they had waved on, were streaming past him toward the exit. He had a panicked memory of setting down the papers on a ledge somewhere, even as he hunted through his case for the dozenth time. The officers detaining him, stolid red-faced men in badly fitting suits, kept shouting that he was wasting their time. He stood frozen, anguish spreading through his chest, until finally he woke up.

He did not think of Louisa right away. For some reason he remembered the story of the boy who had been dragged into a corner of the schoolyard by some of his classmates and castrated with their Hitlerjugend knives. Later, he'd heard, the boy had been taken away on *Kristallnacht*. Maybe it was best that way, the boy's brother had told Rolf, in the very room where he was lying now. Who knows what his life would have been?

He turned on the light, to see what time it was: 5:42. At any minute, Emma would start crying, and he would go into the room she shared with Mrs. Sprague—what used to be his room, back in the days when he and Otto had lived there—and rescue her from her crib. He was sleeping on the living room couch these days, so that Louisa, who had such difficulty sleeping now, could rest undisturbed. At least that was the explanation he had given, on the day he moved out.

He rose to fetch the bottle from the icebox, where Mrs. Sprague had left it the night before, and filled a saucepan with water, to heat it. This was his favorite part of the day: Emma was at her most cheerful in the mornings, patting her bottle happily with one hand in time to the arias he sang her in his tuneless voice. If he stopped for even a minute, she would let the bottle slip from her mouth and look at him in distress until he started again. Then she'd give a little gurgle of bliss, puff out her cheeks, and go back to sucking.

Already he had bought her, though he knew it was too soon, a huge furry teddy bear with a chocolate brown back and a ginger face. He found himself looking at dolls in the windows of toyshops with a covetousness he had never felt for any material object: there was a glossy blond one on Fourteenth Street, in a smocked yellow dress, with bright china-blue eyes, sitting beside a little table where a miniature pink-and-white tea set was laid out, with a tiny pitcher and sugar bowl. He wanted the tea set too.

That morning Emma woke while he was shaving, and by the time the sounds penetrated to the bathroom and he had rinsed his face and gone to her room, Mrs. Sprague was just lifting her out of her crib. As soon as he entered, though, Emma began wriggling toward him, swimming out of Mrs. Sprague's grip with her arms held out to him. He lifted her over his head, feeling a flash of pure joy as she squealed with delight, though a moment later the panic from his dream was with him again, as if her tiny body were a great weight smothering him. But still he went on raising and lowering her, gently, as Mrs. Sprague had shown him. With Mrs. Sprague making clucking noises behind them, he carried her into the living room, sitting with her on the green chair while with the other hand he groped in the box that held her toys, to find the red-and-white rattle, with hearts on it, that Louisa had bought before she was born. Meanwhile she clung to him anxiously, imprisoning his other arm, and when he tried to free it she wailed in protest.

"Look here," he said, with a mock frown, "do you want me to stay here with you all day? Do you want me to be fired from my job? And then who will pay for your milk, little Emma?" He rubbed his face in her hair. "Who will keep you in arrowroot biscuits?" Immediately she smiled and gurgled, she was happy again, until he made the next attempt to rise, and she howled louder than before.

"All right," he said, "two more minutes," settling back down again. Beaming, she raised a hand to his face, knocking his glasses sideways. Everyone said that she looked like Louisa. "Thank God," he always answered, but he didn't really see it. It was in her baby smiles, her sudden swoons into happiness, that Louisa, the old Louisa, came back to him.

Sometimes, these days, he had to help her to dress and undress. On her first night back from the hospital, after the operation, he could not get her bad arm into her nightgown, the shoulder opening wasn't large enough. He went to get one of his shirts for her to wear instead, and when he came back she was slumped on the bed, her stomach still distended from the birth, sagging over the top of her pants. Seeing him watching her, she tried to cover her body with her good arm. Before, she used to walk around naked, in only her high-heeled slippers, hunting for a bobby pin or a pencil to write something down with. She had been just as easy in her body when she was pregnant, pushing her stomach at him and pretending to dance. Now she would never dance for him; she would never wear her black satin shoes or the green silk blouse, with the dozen tiny buttons in a diagonal line across the front, that she had bought to wear after the baby was born.

Mrs. Sprague came in to summon them to the breakfast table, where Emma finally consented to leave his arms for her high chair, and sat patting her bottle and kicking out her feet. He made faces at her while he drank his coffee and ate the bacon and eggs that Mrs. Sprague insisted he needed, being a man with a hard day's work in front of him.

"And what will you girls be doing today?" he asked, swallowing a rubbery mouthful of bacon.

"Well, let me see. I think we'll go shopping, won't we, my little one, we'll go and buy something nice for your daddy's supper."

"And then aren't her grandparents coming this afternoon, to take her to the park?"

Mrs. Sprague looked annoyed. "They mustn't take her out for so long, they really mustn't. They're overtiring her. Besides, the weather has been so changeable lately, she could catch a cold. The other day they brought her back with her hat half off her, and when I said something her grandmother said the fresh air was good for her. So I said maybe that was how they thought in Europe, but in America we keep our babies bundled up, and do you know, Rolf, I read somewhere that we have the healthiest babies in the world. Why don't they just take Mrs. Furchgott? She needs to get out more, she ought to be practicing her walking. The little one can stay home with me."

He had heard all this before, just as he had heard from Franz of the difficulties involved in getting Emma away from her. "She is immune to my charms," Franz had said. "I believe she suspects I am a spy."

"Try to be patient with them," Rolf said now, to Mrs. Sprague. "They mean well. And she is their grandchild, after all."

"Oh, he's all right in his way. It's her that gets my goat."

"Yes, I know. Everyone feels the same. But we must be pleasant to her for his sake, otherwise we only make his life more difficult." As he said it he remembered the look of pleading on Franz's face the last time he had taken Louisa there, as though Franz knew, when Rolf took Louisa's arm as she stumbled, the effort it cost him to touch her.

And then there she was, standing in the doorway, in her gray housedress with the zipper, staring at Mrs. Sprague, who seemed not to have noticed her. Mrs. Sprague had taken Emma on her lap now, she was tipping the bottle up so the child could get the last drops of milk. Usually he did not see Louisa in the mornings; she stayed in her room—asleep? hiding?—until after he had left. He met her eyes for a moment and looked quickly away.

Mrs. Sprague too looked up for a moment, before returning her attention to Emma. "Of course I'll be nice to your granddaddy, won't I, darling," she said, "but I've got to make sure he doesn't give my little girl a cold. You know your Aunt May will always do what's best for you, she's always going to look after her precious lamb. You know she loves you best in the whole wide world."

CHAPTER SIX

*H*e counted on having the office to himself when he got there in the mornings; he liked the silence in the hallways, the sense of undisturbed dust, which reminded him of his schooldays. Until the others arrived at nine, he could think undisturbed, far-seeing and satisfying thoughts about the future of the business, new avenues they ought to explore. He had begun asking for suggestions from the men on the factory floor, who understood the manufacturing processes better than anyone, and how they could be made more efficient, how the products could be improved. One of the foremen had come up with a very promising idea for coating the lead in the pencils to make them write more smoothly; together they were planning its implementation. He'd been costing it out and drafting a memo to Mr. Starin, to persuade him to fund it.

But that morning, as he stepped out of the elevator, he heard the clacking of a typewriter. Connie Maggiore, Mr. Starin's new secretary, was seated at her desk in the corridor, her red nails striking out a sharp rhythm on the keys.

"Hi there," she said, when she saw him. "I bet you're surprised to find me here."

He blinked at her, removing his hat as he did so.

"I had to get these reports done for the sales force before their meeting, so I got up at the crack of dawn and came on in. I've been working since 7:45. I bet even you never get here that early."

"Sometimes I do."

"Come on," she said, tossing her head. "At least let me think I'm the only virtuous one around this joint."

He wished he could think of some breezy joke to make in return, but he never could; he could never manage the banter that came to Americans so naturally. He gave her an apologetic smile. "Don't let me disturb you."

"You're not disturbing me, Mr. Furchgott."

"Please," he said. "Call me Rolf."

"Okay, Rolf. And you call me Connie. That's short for Constanzia. Can I get you some coffee?"

"No, no. I didn't mean to interrupt your work."

"You're not interrupting. Would you know how to spell *subsequent*? When I was taking dictation I put it down *s-u-b-s-i-q-u-e-n-t*, but now that looks funny to me, and some joker has walked off with my dictionary."

"I believe it has two *e*'s," he said, clearing his throat. "But don't take my word for it. My English is far from perfect."

"There's nothing wrong with your English I can see," she said. "Hey, you're blushing." He stammered a denial and was about to walk into his office when he remembered that he had to talk to Mr. Starin about money, something he had been putting off for weeks. Already the bank loan to cover the expenses of Louisa's surgery was running out; he would need to borrow more to pay Mrs. Sprague's wages.

"Can you tell me if Mr. Starin is free any time this morning?" he asked her, and she got out the leather-bound book in which his appointments were kept.

"Nine o'clock looks good," she said. "Before he meets with the sales reps. Should I tell him you want to see him?"

"Yes, if you would." She looked at him expectantly, but he could not think of a plausible reason. So once again he smiled apologetically before retreating to his office.

At nine exactly—by that time the other secretaries, including the one he shared with the general manager, were hanging up their coats and settling down at their desks, calling out greetings to each other—he came back and asked her if Mr. Starin was expecting him.

"Sure," she said, typing away. "I told him it was something mysterious, you wouldn't say what." Then, looking up and seeing his face, she took her hands off the keyboard. "You don't think I really said that, do you? I'm just kidding. Me and my big mouth."

"It's all right."

"You look like you're going up against the firing squad or something. He's not that bad."

He was spared having to reply by Mr. Starin calling out to him to come in.

They said good morning, Mr. Starin pointed to the red leather chair opposite his desk, where Rolf always sat when they were conferring, and by the time Rolf was seated it seemed as though the silence had already gone on too long. Mr. Starin looked even more dyspeptic than usual; he folded his hands on the blotter and waited with an air of barely contained wrath for Rolf to speak. But just as Rolf was about to start, he snapped, "I know what you're going to say."

It wasn't so surprising if he'd figured it out. Everyone in the office knew what had happened to Louisa, though nobody ever referred to it directly; they asked him about Emma instead, they cooed over the picture of her that sat on his desk in a leather frame. But some of the women gave him compassionate smiles when he greeted them in the halls; they offered to bring him coffee more than they used to, and asked if he wanted anything when they went out for lunch. Mr. Starin was very good with figures; he must have realized that the situation would entail extra expense.

"I'm sorry about this," Rolf said, and the other man made an impatient noise.

"So where are you going?"

"What?"

"What kind of job have you found yourself?"

It took a minute before Rolf understood.

"I haven't found any job. I'm not looking for another job."

Mr. Starin frowned. He popped something into his mouth and swallowed. "You're not here to tell me you're quitting?"

"Not at all," Rolf said. "Nothing like that."

"Hardworking young man like you," Mr. Starin said, "all this postwar expansion, there must be plenty of jobs out there now. The big companies are looking for people."

"I like the job I have," Rolf said firmly, and took a deep breath, but the man cut him off before he could begin.

"So what are you here for?"

"Well, sir"—he never called him that. "I wondered if you'd be willing to lend me some money."

Mr. Starin grinned suddenly; he swiveled from side to side in his chair. Rolf could not remember him ever looking so cheerful.

"What do you need it for?"

It seemed harder than ever to mention Louisa with the man smiling like that. Somehow he managed to stumble through it: the bank loan, the monthly repayments, Mrs. Sprague. "The bank won't allow me to borrow any more. If you can lend me this money, you could deduct a certain amount from my salary every week. I'd expect to pay interest, of course, whatever you thought was fair. You could have papers drawn up, and I'd sign them."

"How much?"

"I was going to ask for two thousand dollars."

Mr. Starin stopped swiveling and gave Rolf a speculative look. Then he turned and looked out the window, then back to Rolf again.

"How much would you pay back every week?"

"Say, fifteen dollars?"

"With interest, that could take three years to pay back. What if you leave before three years?"

"I wouldn't do that. Anyway, I don't want to leave."

"You might. Somebody might offer you a better job."

"I wouldn't leave owing you money."

"Okay, okay, don't get huffy." Mr. Starin was silent for a moment, puffing out his cheeks and sucking them in again. Then he placed his hands squarely on the blotter and leaned toward Rolf. "How's about this? You don't have to sign anything. I give you the money, and you give me your word you stay with the company until it's paid off. Or five years, because you might pay it off quicker than you think. Mr. Price is about to retire in two years; you could wind up general manager. And then you'll get a raise, and you could pay it off quicker. But you still have to stay five years. What do you say?"

"You gave me my first job in this country. I'm not going to quit on you. But you can still have papers drawn up."

The man brushed this aside. "I have a hunch it's better not to deal like that with someone like you. Then you've got to keep your word, I'll have trusted you. That's right, isn't it?" He didn't wait for Rolf to answer. "I'll call my bank manager; you should have the money in a few days. That good enough for you?"

"Of course. I can't thank you enough."

"Don't worry about it. You're going to make me a lot more than two thousand dollars." He became expansive, leaning back in his chair, talking about his problems with the lumber suppliers; they were raising their prices, they were delaying shipments; they had too many customers right now to care about him. "So I think we should go ahead with buying that yard in Oregon. Guaranteed supply. I think he'd give me a good price. But I need to find out what it would take to run the business. Maybe you could go out there. Check things out. What do you say?"

"Of course," Rolf said. "If you think I could do it."

"I know you could do it. The question is just whether you can get away, what with the situation at home right now." It was the first time he had ever referred to it.

"How long do you think I'd need to spend?" Rolf asked him.

"Say, two weeks."

He hesitated. He would have to talk to Mrs. Sprague, and Franz; someone would have to look after Emma on Mrs. Sprague's day off.

"You could go twice if you wanted," Starin said. "A week at a time."

"That would be better, I think."

"The problem is, you're too good for this place. I've been waiting for you to quit ever since the war. You could go work for General Electric, one of the big boys; they love guys like you, smart straitlaced gung-ho types that take work home every night. They'd jump at the chance."

"Perhaps not with my accent. Have you thought that might be a problem in Oregon? A man with a German accent asking questions?"

"I'll tell the guy why you had to leave. But you ought to change your name one of these days. Call yourself Ralph First or something like that."

"I'll think about it."

"No, you won't." Mr. Starin laughed again; he was positively jovial. "Let me know when you can go to Oregon. The sooner the better. Here"—he opened his top drawer— "here's the file, with all the projections from October. You'd better refresh your memory."

"Well, you're looking more cheerful," Miss Maggiore said when he stepped out into the corridor again. "Did you get a raise or something?"

"No, no," he said, "nothing like that." He was walking down the corridor to his office when she called out to him. "Hey. You were right."

He turned around. "About what?"

"It has two *e*'s. I got my dictionary back."

"I'm glad," he said absently. His thoughts were on backward integration, pricing models, the difficulties of selling wood to their competitors. But somewhere at the back of his mind was an image of the plane flying west, over the Rocky Mountains. He would visit the redwood forests, the Pacific

Ocean; he would be surrounded by the light-filled vistas he had dreamed of as a child.

Maybe, after all, America was not lost to him for good, though for the past few months he had been thrust back into the Old World, or that was how it felt, with all its weight of helpless suffering. And this time there were no visas out, no papers to submit that could restore Louisa to what she had been. What was happening to them could have no part in an American life.

CHAPTER SEVEN

I love this one like she was my own baby," Mrs. Sprague announced, which Sophie wasn't sure was in good taste. She wasn't sure, either, that Emma's face was any cleaner than it had been when Katy was in charge, but the child was obviously happy, almost aggressively so, banging lustily with a serving spoon on the little tray of her high chair. Meanwhile Mrs. Sprague was putting away the fruits of their recent excursion to Dyckman Street: brightly colored packets and tins, Wonder Bread in shiny red-white-and-blue wrapping, pressed turkey, and other things that Sophie had never seen before.

As she moved around, chatting animatedly, she paused frequently to make little noises at Emma, who became agitated and held up her hands. "How's Aunt May going to get her work done with you on her shoulder, you little devil?" Mrs. Sprague cried, but she picked her up nonetheless. When Sophie offered to take her from her to free up her hands she surrendered her reluctantly, laughing in admiration as the baby grabbed a lock of Sophie's hair and pulled at it. "She's such a smart little thing, isn't she," she said proudly, and then took her back uninvited, Emma squirming toward her in her excitement.

"Yes, you want your Aunt May, don't you," she said with satisfaction. She shook some frosted cookies from a packet onto a plate. Since Sophie's last visit, the kitchen table had acquired an oilcloth covered with red and orange squares; a sampler hung on the wall that said, in shaky cross-stitches, *Hope springs eternal.*

"Where is Louisa?" Sophie asked her; it was Louisa she had spoken to on the phone earlier, to ask about coming.

"Oh, she's in her room," Mrs. Sprague said. "I thought she needed a little rest. She's got herself a typewriter now, she says she's going to learn to type, although what she wants to do that for I really couldn't say." Then, when Sophie was silent, she asked her in a not entirely friendly voice how she liked America.

"I like it very much," Sophie said levelly. "It is a wonderful country."

"Because I guess you had to get out of your own country, didn't you," Mrs. Sprague said. "Mr. Furchgott was telling me about it. Oh, the wicked things that man Hitler did, I've read about them in the papers. You can't believe there are such wicked people in the world, can you?"

No, Sophie said, it was hard to believe. They sat in silence for a moment. The baby's cotton shirt had worked its way up her chest, leaving her little stomach exposed; suddenly Sophie remembered her children's small bodies, how she had kissed their stomachs and their pudgy legs while they squealed with joy.

Well, she for one couldn't understand taking against people that way, Mrs. Sprague said. "Look at Mr. Furchgott, nobody could be more of a gentleman. It's a real pleasure to work for him, I can tell you." She sat down, bouncing Emma on her knee, and reached for a cookie: one of her grandsons always loved that kind, she said, and so Sophie asked about her grandchildren, and Mrs. Sprague explained about her three sons, and the girls they had married back home, and the mischief her grandchildren got up to. Several of her stories, which set her laughing, were about her laconic neighbors back in Maine: where she came from, she said, nobody used two words when one would do. Yet she herself seemed the most loquacious of women; it was hardly necessary to contribute anything beyond an occasional murmur.

Finally Sophie managed to excuse herself and went to knock on Louisa's door. "Who is it?" Louisa asked, in a wary voice, and then told her to come in. She was sitting at a small desk in the corner. In front of her was the typewriter Mrs. Sprague had mentioned, a heavy old Remington with a sheet of paper in it; another sheet, covered with typing, lay beside it.

"How are you coming along, Louisa?" It seemed more tactful than asking, "How are you?"—it couched the question in terms of progress, of moving into the future. Things were bad and then, however slowly, they got better; they came along.

But Louisa brushed the question away with her good hand, as though it weren't worth discussing. She seemed different from when Sophie had last seen her, not huddled and slow but with an air of nervous defiance that Sophie found disquieting. "I'm finding new ways to amuse myself. One-handed typing. Not that I was ever much good at the two-handed kind. Do you know how to type, Sophie?" No, Sophie said, she didn't. "It's quite satisfying in its way. You ought to try it."

"What is it you type?"

"Just this and that," Louisa said craftily. "It strengthens my hand. Have you been discussing me with Mrs. Sprague?"

"You know I would not do that."

"She thinks it's silly, my learning to type. She thinks I should just lie there."

"She seems very fond of the child."

"Yes, I know. I know all her virtues. How is Gustav?"

"Very well, thank you," Sophie said. "He sends you much love." She tried to think of something to add, some cheerful detail, but Gustav was getting less cheerful all the time.

"Please give him mine."

"You must not let this woman bully you. Shall we go out together, and tell her we will bathe Emma? I would like that very much, and you would enjoy it too."

It was Sophie who spoke to Mrs. Sprague, while Louisa smiled and waved at Emma. "It would give me great pleasure," Sophie said, conscious that she was asking permission of the other woman, that she felt the need to charm her. "I haven't done it in such a long time, since my own children were small." Mrs. Sprague was gracious in her assent; she even filled a little basin for the purpose, which they placed in the bathtub. Emma wriggled and splashed and clapped her hands, sending water all over the bathroom, while Louisa blew kisses at her from behind Sophie's shoulder, her mouth quivering in nervous excitement. Afterward they sat with her between them on the sofa, and Louisa, looking flushed and happy, stroked the baby's wet hair back from her forehead. But when Mrs. Sprague came in, proffering more cookies, she excused herself, returning to her room.

"You have seen her?" Gustav asked, when he came home from the office, looking gray with exhaustion. Sophie nodded once and turned away, opening the door of the oven to peer at the calf's heart within. She was expecting a call from their son Kurt, who was studying for his law degree in Ohio now; she wanted Gustav to be steady in his mind when he spoke to him. There had been some shameful scenes lately, with Gustav sobbing over the *Kindertotenlieder* on the radio, or an item in the paper about a panda grieving for its mate in the Bronx Zoo. She was glad their children were far away—Kurt in Ohio, Gabrielle in Pennsylvania, where she was teaching German and Latin in a private school. She would not want them to see their father like that.

The first time it had happened—a mother of two had thrown herself in front of a subway train when her husband deserted her—she spoke to him sharply: "Look here, you must get yourself under control." But more recently, if she found him with tears running down his face, she simply looked away, or left the room to fetch a clean handkerchief.

"And how did you find her?" he asked now.

"Not too bad. We bathed the baby together, I think that was enjoyable for her."

He sat at the little dining table in the alcove, from where he could watch her. He had not even removed his suit jacket. "She always seemed so eager to seize life. I wonder if she knew," he said then.

"Knew what? What are you talking about?"

"Maybe she sensed she did not have much time." It was what some of the women had said too, at the time they learned of Louisa's tumor.

"That's nonsense. It was her character, that's all. And she'd had it easier than others, don't forget. She left so early for England, she didn't see the worst things."

"You sound as though you are blaming her for that."

Just then the phone rang: it was Kurt, punctual as always. He thanked her for the food parcels she had sent, while teasing her for believing that he could not possibly be eating properly in Ohio. Kurt was like her: nothing he had seen—either back in Europe or while he was serving in the Pacific—would destroy his nerves, she was certain of that. It was Gabrielle, the quiet one, she worried about.

Then Gustav spoke to him, taking on the mantle of the father again, standing very straight by the little table where the phone was kept. "You must show me some of this one day, I would like to see it," he said. "I would like to see what these laws are, in America."

But when he replaced the receiver and sat down again, he returned to the subject of Louisa. "You never really liked her."

"I didn't dislike her," she said.

"But you disapproved of her."

"I never spoke against her. It was the other women who complained. She could have helped them with so many things, the shops, the subway, the English words they needed, but she preferred her American friends. She only ever visited when Rolf did, on the weekends, never during the week."

"I seem to remember she gave you presents when we first came. And something for Gabrielle."

"Ribbons," Sophie said. "She sent me French ribbon with embroidery. And a string of green beads."

"And that was wrong of her?"

"Of course not. It was her nature. But not very helpful. We had no winter coats, or pots for cooking. I would not have brought someone beads in that situation."

He patted her hand. "No, you would have cooked a good stew and brought warm clothing. That is *your* nature." But she was not sure it was a compliment.

"She is learning to type."

"Louisa?"

"Yes, with her right hand."

"The poor child," he said in German, and she knew he didn't mean Emma.

The typing was a foolish idea, such as only a thoroughly impractical person would come up with—in that way, at least, Louisa had not changed. But perhaps there was something gallant about it too; she wished now that she had said so to Louisa. She hoped that Rolf would say it, and doubted that he would.

When her children were young, and like all children wailed, "It isn't fair," she used to tell them, "Never expect that life will be fair," believing it the most important lesson she could teach them, the root of her own philosophy, on which she had prided herself for as long as she could remember. Even later, in the worst of times, she had refused to complain. Instead she had done what was needed: standing in line, sending telegrams, bribing officials to get their exit stamps. Once in America she had told herself to be grateful for all the terrible things that hadn't happened, or not yet: for their children's safety, for the friends who had managed to get out, for any kindness she received or heard of. She had learned how to darn socks, how to clean a toilet, telling herself, and believing it, that she was lucky to be performing such chores. When she heard of the death of her beloved cousin in the back of a mobile gas van, she had gotten on her hands and knees, like someone praying, and scrubbed the floor.

But now, with the war over for almost two years, something in her had started rebelling; she herself wanted to howl, like a child, that it wasn't fair. That must be why this business with Louisa had affected her so badly: it seemed one loss too many; it seemed unnecessary for Louisa to be sacrificed like that, in what felt like an afterthought, a careless postscript to the general destruction. And all she could do was to pay another visit, which she would do very soon, bearing presents approximately as useful as French ribbons and beads made of glass.

CHAPTER EIGHT

They were in the living room together, Mrs. Sprague having gone into the kitchen to prepare dinner. Emma was in her playpen, and Louisa was waving and smiling at her. In between blown kisses, she told Rolf that Otto was coming to visit—to be introduced to Emma, he'd said. But Rolf wondered if she had summoned him.

"Will he want to stay here?" Rolf asked, for something to say, and Louisa said no, no, he had a friend in New Jersey, someone he'd met in the army, who was putting him up. She wrinkled her nose at Emma.

"Well, you'll be pleased to see him."

Only then did she look at him. "I thought you might be pleased too."

Of course, he said. Of course. It had been too long.

But he wasn't pleased; he imagined that Otto was coming to judge him. When they were children, he had sometimes had the feeling that Louisa and Otto did not really like him as they liked each other; they had allowed him to dominate in most things, but almost as though they were sorry for him— sorry that it should matter so much to him. If he grew very adamant, insisting that something be done in a particular way and no other, he would catch them giving each other secret smiles.

Otto would not flinch at the sight of Louisa; he would only be full of sorrow, and love her more than ever. But then it was easy for Otto. He would not have to see her naked body, or feel the old hunger stymied, remembering her as she had been. Otto would go home and make love to his wife, full of judgment against his old friend for his hardness of heart.

The next morning Rolf got to the office early again, to work on his proposal, but for the second time Miss Maggiore was there before him.

"Well, would you look what the cat dragged in," she said when she saw him. "I was thinking on the train this morning, I bet even Rolf won't be there this early. Won't he be surprised to see me sitting there when he walks in."

He couldn't tell if she was making fun of him or not. Surely she had not really thought that on the train, but he felt himself flushing as he wished her a good morning and backed into his office.

Half an hour later he was well launched on his proposal, laying out alternative strategies for reorganizing operations, when she appeared in the doorway. "What are you working on there?" She approached his desk and looked down at the yellow pad.

"Just a proposal for the business," he said guardedly.

She tossed her head. "Never mind, you don't have to tell me." But then she advanced another step. "There are lots of things around here that someone should be proposing about, if you ask me. I've worked in four places now, and the other three all had the same system for certain things, and it worked great. I don't know who came up with the systems here. Like the way you file things. Why should you do it by date all the time? It means you can't find anything unless you know the date it was written. It's crazy."

"You should mention that to Mr. Starin," he told her.

Again, she tossed her head, her stiffly lacquered, waved black hair hardly moving as she did so. It was a curiously girlish gesture, especially since she was not, after all, as young as he had first thought; seeing her up close like this, he realized she must be in her mid-thirties. "It's too early for me to be telling them how to run things. Wait till I've been here a little longer." She laughed, and he did too, half wishing she would leave him in peace and half charmed by her brassy innocence.

Then Miss Adams, the earnest young secretary he shared with the other junior manager, popped her head in the door and seemed put out to find Miss Maggiore there. "I wondered who was in here."

"We were just having a chat, weren't we, Rolf?" Miss Maggiore said, and sauntered out.

"Can I get you some coffee?" Miss Adams asked, looking wounded.

"No, no, I'm fine. And how is your mother doing?"

She brightened. "Much better, thank you. The doctor says she'll be back to herself in no time."

"Good, good."

"I'll bring those letters for you to sign."

Mrs. Sprague phoned shortly after eleven. He should buy some camphor, she said, to rub on Emma's chest, and maybe some lavender oil to mix with it. "The poor little thing is sniffling, and I don't want to take her out shopping again when she's poorly. I think it was that wind yesterday. They kept her out in the park too long, her grandparents."

"I'm sure she'll be fine."

"Well, it makes more work for me, that's all I can say. She wouldn't go down for her morning nap, she clung to me so, it was sad to see."

Mrs. Sprague never complained of Emma causing her work unless it was somehow connected to Louisa and her parents; they had had this conversation before. He did his best to soothe her, thanking her for all the care and trouble she took, and at lunchtime he went to the nearest drugstore to buy the things she'd asked for.

Miss Maggiore was at the front counter when he went in, paying for a bottle of nail polish. "Hello, there," she said. "How's your secret proposal coming along?"

"Pretty well, thank you." And then, because that didn't seem sufficient, he told her he was there to buy some camphor for his baby daughter, that she had the sniffles.

"Aw," she said reverently. "What's her name?"

"Emma."

"That's a beautiful name. And I bet you're a real proud father, right?"

"Well . . ."

"Is she your first?"

"Yes, she is." He stiffened slightly, wary of being asked about Louisa. Or she might make one of her jokes about his wife phoning him at the office to send him out for baby medicines. Instead she said, "I bet you don't mind that she's a girl, either. In my neighborhood, all the men are crazy for sons. They've got to have boys, boys, boys, the more the better. You can get awful fed up with it, believe you me."

"Where do you live?" he asked, handing a dollar to the man behind the counter. He was conscious of her watching him as he pocketed the change. She must be lonely, he decided; she had just started in the job, and probably had no friends yet among the other secretaries.

"In Brooklyn," she said, falling into step beside him as he turned to go. "East New York." He nodded, trying to look as though this meant something to him. He knew about Brooklyn Heights, and about Williamsburg, where the *Ostjuden* lived, but East New York was out of his ken.

"Have you heard of it?"

He shook his head, feeling caught out.

"I knew you wouldn't of. It's not the kind of place someone like you would know about." They walked along in silence for a moment, Rolf wondering what sort of person she imagined him to be. Then she burst out, "Not that most people *really* know about it, they just think they do. They think everybody who lives there must be some kind of gangster." He turned to look at her, bewildered.

"It's an Italian neighborhood, see. If you're Italian in this city, everyone thinks you go around rubbing people out for the mob. My father, God rest his soul, would never hurt a fly. He went to Mass twice a week, and if the roof was leaking over at St. Sebastian's, or the rectory needed a new stove or anything like that, it was always him they came to. He got all my brothers to help the nuns too. And he was a fourth-degree knight in the Knights of Columbus. Not many people get that high, you know."

"What did he do?" he asked, with genuine curiosity.

"He was a contractor," she said proudly. "With thirteen people working for him. How about yours?"

"He had a toy company," he said. It had been a long time since anyone asked him what his father had done for a living.

"Is he still around?"

He shook his head. They had arrived at their building; he stepped aside to let her go through the revolving door before him. "Gosh," she said, as they walked through the lobby. "Just imagine how they'll all talk in the office if they see us come in together."

"Surely not," he said, a little shocked at the idea, and she told him she was only teasing.

"It's hard not to tease you, you're so serious all the time."

"I'm sorry. I don't mean to be."

"You look like you're carrying the world on your shoulders." She screwed up her eyes and pursed her mouth into a frown of pure gloom, effecting such a startling transformation that he laughed out loud.

"I think that's the first time I've ever heard you laugh. You should try it more often, it'll do you good."

"You're probably right."

"Of course I'm right."

When they got to their floor, she gave him a little wave and headed for the ladies' room; later that afternoon, when he went into Mr. Starin's office, armed with his legal pad, to present his projections for the lumberyard revenues, she was sitting at her desk, painting her nails, and gave him another little wave, this time with fingers spread carefully apart, as he passed her.

CHAPTER NINE

On the Sunday before Rolf left for Oregon, Sophie and Gustav paid a visit to Bogardus Place, bearing a cake chosen by Gustav from the German bakery on Dyckman Street. It must be soft enough, he had said, so that Louisa, as the hostess, could cut it without difficulty. Sophie stood by while he peered into the glass case containing the pastries and questioned the women behind the counter before settling on an elaborate chocolate confection with whipped cream roses.

This fussing over cakes seemed like part of a pattern, another symptom of the softening of his brain. *Meine arme Sophie*, he called her these days, my poor Sophie, sighing; he made her sit in the living room after dinner, when she wanted to be tidying the kitchen, so he could bring her a cup of tea. She looked so tired, he would say anxiously, though she was not the slightest bit tired.

Sometimes she woke in the night to find him gone from their bed; he would be sitting on the chair in the dark, staring out at the streetlights of Seaman Avenue. She was afraid he might be thinking of his time in prison, or of his younger sister, who had died, along with her two children, at Treblinka. But if she asked him, it was always something innocuous—a milking song, in Bavarian dialect, that his old nurse used to sing to him, or the painting of the Schwarzwald that had hung in his parents' living room. It was almost worse that he should talk of such banal things with so much sentiment.

The night before, when she'd gone to find him, he'd been thinking about a maid his mother had hired right before she gave up her own household and moved in with them; he had just remembered, he said, that they had found a place for her with Jeannette. "Ilse was her name. She had just moved to Nuremberg from the country."

"You can ask Louisa," Sophie said briskly. "Perhaps she will remember."

He nodded. "Yes, I will ask her." But he still made no move to come back to bed.

As it turned out, Louisa remembered Ilse very well; she laughed delightedly when Gustav spoke of her, the first time since they had arrived that she showed a flash of her old animation. Before that, she had hung back, looking from one of them to the other; when, trying to stand to take the cake into the kitchen, she fell back down onto the couch, she gave Rolf a cringing, apologetic look before starting over. Everyone was very polite, very concerned to show goodwill. Rolf and Gustav spoke at some length about the political situation, the recent election, in which the Republicans had gained a large majority in Congress; they discussed whether it was better when one party was dominant, if it meant that more could get done. Rolf explained the purpose of his forthcoming trip to Oregon, and they said he must be sure to see the redwood trees while he was out there; all of them had heard about the redwood trees. Sophie said how much she had always wanted to see them. Louisa took them in to see Emma, who was sleeping peacefully on her stomach. It was the first time Gustav had seen her, and he exclaimed at her thick head of auburn hair, all that was visible of her. Rolf did not come with them. In all the time they had been there, he had not spoken to Louisa once. Sophie wondered what would happen when the child woke up, since there was no sign of Mrs. Sprague.

"Mrs. Sprague is still working for you?" she asked Louisa, who said, with an air of constraint, "Oh, yes, she has just gone out for the day, to see her cousin in New London."

When they returned to the living room, Rolf was emerging from the kitchen bearing a tray with an embroidered cloth, on which were a teapot and cups and saucers and the cake on a stand. They all exclaimed at how delightful the cake was, and then silence fell. Gustav was looking with melting eyes at Louisa, who lifted her fork awkwardly to her mouth, crumbs falling onto her green dress. Sophie was worried that he would say, "*Arme Louisa,*" if someone else did not speak soon.

"Gustav was just talking of a maid his mother had," she said, setting down her cup. "He thought you might remember her, Louisa; it was your mother who gave her a place when Irma came to live with us."

Louisa was chewing solemnly, concentrating hard, her eyes round with effort; she brushed a crumb from her lips and said, "I don't have any memory of that. What was her name?"

"What did you say her name was, Gustav?" Sophie asked, though she remembered perfectly well.

When he told them, Louisa seemed to tilt sideways in her excitement. "Ilse! Ilse! Oh, my God!"

He beamed at her. "So you remember her."

"Remember her? She was the heroine of my childhood. I was a supplicant to her, I used to go to her room with my little presents, cakes and almond pretzels I had stolen from the hoard in the kitchen, or chocolates someone gave me for my birthday, and then, if she was in a very good mood, she'd let me come in. Sometimes she'd just take the food and slam the door on me, but other times I'd sit on her bed while she told me stories. Terrible stories, of her drunken father and the beatings she'd had, how her family almost starved to death one snowy winter, she had no shoes to wear to school, but she'd laugh the whole time, as though it were the best joke in the world. I remember how lovely she smelled, and her pink eiderdown from home, and the pictures on her wall, of the Virgin Mary and an angel, and two little ragged children crossing a stream in their bare feet. They all looked like her to me, even the angel, with her blond hair and rosy cheeks. My God! I'd forgotten about those pictures. Ilse was totally faithless, she didn't love me a bit, but I adored her the way I never did poor old Frau Müller, who would have died for me."

Gustav was smiling at her as though she were still that child. "She stayed with your family for many years?"

"Oh, yes. Of course she had to leave when Aryans were no longer allowed to work in Jewish households, but that was after I was in England. And she came back once to see my father. She had a Nazi husband then, she looked much more severe, Franz said, in a drab green dress and a braid coiled around her head, like a proper Nazi wife. She didn't laugh even once, he said. She stood in the hallway, she wouldn't come in, and told him he must get out, things were going to get very bad for the Jews. And then she sent me her love and went away again."

"So she was not so faithless after all," Gustav said gently.

"No. No, you're right. I wish I knew what had happened to her. They say nobody in Germany can get sugar now, and she loved sweet things. I would send her Hershey bars. But I don't even know her married name."

Then Rolf made a little sign to her to wipe the crumbs from her chin, and she subsided again. Sophie said how much Kurt was enjoying his studies, and Rolf inquired about the classes he was taking. Sophie waited for Gustav to answer this question, but when he didn't—he was looking fixedly at the teapot—she jumped in quickly and said he was studying every kind of American law, and Gabrielle's school was very pleased with her, though it had been a little difficult at first. But the headmistress was a very kind, understanding person.

There was another silence. Gustav raised his head, giving Louisa one of his dangerously tender looks. "And how are your parents, my dear?"

She glanced at Rolf before she answered. "Pretty well," she said uncertainly, and then, her face lighting up in the old way, "Franz is in love with Emma. He's convinced she is smarter than all of us, she is laughing at us the whole time. You'll be the same when you have a grandchild, Gustav."

"Perhaps. I'm not sure this world is any place to bring children into."

Rolf cleared his throat and started to speak, but just then Emma began crying in the other room. "I'll go," he said. Louisa followed him with her eyes as he walked out.

Gustav leaned over and gripped her hand. "It will come right in the end."

"Don't be foolish," Sophie said briskly. "Of course it will come right. And now perhaps Louisa will let me have some more of your lovely cake."

But Louisa ignored this; she looked at Gustav's hand where it lay over her own and said in German, "Don't feel sorry for me, Gustav. If you start feeling sorry for people it never ends. But you could help me by phoning Franz, I'm worried about him."

"Of course," he said.

Just then Rolf returned with Emma, who was grizzling and rubbing her eyes. "I'll go warm up her bottle," he said. Louisa adjusted her posture and patted her lap, but he ignored this, carrying the child with him into the kitchen.

"Did you see what lovely eyes she has got, Gustav?" Sophie asked, and Gustav nodded. When Rolf came back, settling Emma on his knee with her bottle, they rose to take their leave.

Gustav was silent during the walk home. When they got back to their apartment it was dark, and he took up his post by the window, staring out at the street. "What shall we have for supper?" Sophie asked, hanging up her coat; he had not removed his.

"Whatever you wish," he said, without turning around. "Whatever is easiest for you."

She got out the beetroot from luncheon, and some gherkins and cervelat, and sliced up the rest of the bread and made a salad. After they had eaten, with the radio on to mask the silence, he said, "You must talk to him."

She knew very well whom he meant; there was no point in pretending. "And what would I say? If he wanted my opinion he would ask for it. Am I supposed to go to him and say, your mother was my girlhood friend, therefore I will tell you how to live your life?"

"But something must be done. You saw how things are there. She is afraid of him."

"Perhaps she is only afraid of being looked at, of people seeing how she is. She hates to be seen now, just as she loved it before."

"It's more than that. She is afraid of his cruelty."

"He has never been cruel that I know of," Sophie said.

"And I would say he has never been kind. Only just. He does his duty by others, he doesn't love them."

"I am sure he loved her."

"Yes, in his way. When he could be proud of her. But not any more."

"Even if that's true, you said yourself he was just. So he will be just to her also."

"It's not justice that is required of him now."

"He is suffering too, I'm sure. All the more because he knows how he should be."

He made a little noise of disgust. "Yes, he cannot think well of himself at present. It's very important to him, to think well of himself."

"You forget the things he has done for us all. For you, for Kurt, for so many people."

He pushed away his plate and stood up, looming over her. "That has nothing to do with what I am talking about. Nothing at all. Of course you admire him, you always admire those who do their duty. But pity, tenderness, imagination for others, these things mean nothing to you. I think you even distrust them, you cannot understand why others do not control themselves as you do. You and Rolf. You are more German than the Germans, both of you."

He was shouting at her now, the spit was flying from his mouth, onto the table, onto the top of her head. In the thirty-two years of her marriage there had never been a scene like this, he had never shouted at her in this vulgar way; she wondered if the people upstairs, immigrants like themselves, though from Bremen, could hear him, if the old lady next door was listening, but thank God she was deaf.

Blindly, she stood up too, and began clearing the table, rattling the plates as she stacked them. "What are you doing?" he cried.

She drew herself up. "You can see perfectly well what I'm doing."

"That's your answer? To clear the table?"

"Somebody must. There are no longer servants to do it," she said, and then stopped, confused, because it sounded as though she were reproaching him for the lack of servants, which would be vulgar in itself.

As she turned away, toward the kitchen, he blocked her path. "Sit down," he said. He gripped her shoulders. "Listen to me."

"I'm sorry, Gustav. I have listened enough for one day. Please let me take the plates to the sink."

"My God, you're like a stone. I touch you, and you're like a stone."

"You think I should cry, you think that would do any good? I should cry because a panda is mourning in the zoo? You think I would help someone that way?"

"Please. I'm pleading with you. Please. For God's sake."

"And where is to be the end of it? When the dead come back, when the suffering ends, when everything is as it should be in the world?"

He shook his head; he stumbled to the sofa and sat down heavily; then he put his head in his hands and sat there, rocking back and forth. She went into the kitchen with the plates, she put on the water for coffee, taking deep breaths to steady herself, and then the phone rang, making her jump. It was Kurt, who was getting five days off for Thanksgiving, he said; he had decided to take the bus to New York.

CHAPTER TEN

*N*aturally, as was customary, Sophie was going to phone Louisa the next day, to thank her for their lovely visit. What was less usual was her awareness that, it being Monday, Rolf would be at work: she could, if she wished, go beyond the dozen words she normally felt it decent to speak down a telephone and try to talk to Louisa a little bit, to get some sense, perhaps, of whether Gustav was right to think Louisa was afraid.

She hoped it wasn't true—for Louisa's sake, of course (mostly for Louisa's sake, she told herself sternly), but also for her own, so she could stop wondering if Gustav was right to accuse her. She even asked herself if it could possibly be her lack of pity, of imagination, that accounted for the change in him, if people would look at her one day and say, *That woman drove her husband mad.*

Gustav had spoken to Kurt in his usual way the evening before, inquiring after his classes and the route the bus would take to New York as though nothing was wrong. She told herself she was glad—that had been her great fear, she reminded herself, that he would break down in front of one of the children. But it showed he could behave normally when he wanted, which made his loss of control less excusable. Once again, she had awoken to find him missing from the bed, but this time she had not gone to find him; she had lain there rigid until he returned—it was past four—and pretended to be asleep. In fact, she had not slept for the rest of the night, though he had snored away beside her. She wondered what he would have done if she had gone and put her arms around him; she tried to remember if, in all their marriage, she had ever done such a thing, or if she had always waited for him to do it first. She could remember apologizing to him on various occasions, after a quarrel, when harsh things had been said on either side: she had not been so unyielding as all that. But whether she had ever put her arms around him, whether she had ever turned to him in bed and touched him before he touched her, she could not remember that.

And so, because it was connected with Gustav in her mind, she put off making the call to Louisa, telling herself she would ring in the afternoon. Then Rolf phoned her from the office.

At first she thought he was going to ask her about Gustav, she was afraid he had noticed something strange, but it was Louisa he was phoning about.

"I have a favor to ask of you," he said in his measured voice. "I wondered if you would be kind enough to look in on Louisa while I am out west."

"Of course," she said, the old pride flaring up for an instant—she was the one he had singled out—before she quenched it. "I suppose it will be difficult for her to look after Emma by herself when Mrs. Sprague has her day off."

"That's not a problem. Katy has agreed to come."

"I see," she said, although actually she didn't see. She no longer knew what he was asking of her. "But I will check whether she might need assistance of any kind," she went on, when he was silent.

"I am worried about her moods. She gets very despondent sometimes. Irrational. Mrs. Sprague has told me some alarming things she's said."

"What sorts of things?"

"About Emma," he said after a pause.

"But what sorts of things?"

"She complains that Emma's crying is driving her crazy. And one day when Emma would not go to sleep she said she was going to throw her down the incinerator."

"Every mother feels like that sometimes, I assure you. I cannot believe Louisa was serious." She remembered how reluctant Mrs. Sprague had been to hand Emma over to her the day she visited the apartment. She is trying to get rid of Louisa, she had thought. That's why Louisa was so tense. "Look here," she said, "have you considered that Mrs. Sprague might be jealous of Louisa, she wants the child to herself? She is very possessive of her. And perhaps she would like it better if there was no one there all day to oversee her."

"I think you are doing her an injustice," he said stiffly. "Her main concern is always for Emma."

"I will see for myself," Sophie said, more sharply than she'd intended.

"Yes, of course. If you would only look in once in a while, or telephone her."

"I will do both. And I hope your trip will be very pleasant and successful."

She decided not to tell Gustav about this phone call; she was not going to tell Gustav anything until she had made up her own mind. But she kept thinking of Mrs. Sprague, of the jealous way she had taken Emma back that day, and her enthusiasm for Rolf. Perhaps she thought, why should a man like that be saddled with a crippled wife? Why should we have to have her here, when neither of us wants her around?

You don't know, Sophie told herself. You are making up stories now. Be careful.

Later, when she had done the shopping and the mending and scrubbed the bathroom tiles, she phoned Louisa. First she thanked her, ritually, for a lovely time, and Louisa told her that she had just seen Franz, and Gustav had phoned him that morning, for which she was so grateful. "He's such a kind man, your husband," she said.

"He's very fond of you," Sophie told her.

"As I am of him," Louisa said. "Would you thank him for me? And thank you so much for phoning."

It was well known in their circle that Sophie never talked on the phone more than was necessary, Louisa was only respecting this fact, but now Sophie wanted to detain her.

"You will miss Rolf, I'm sure, when he goes to Oregon."

"Emma will miss him dreadfully. She listens for him to come home at night, she listens for his key, truly. No wonder her grandfather insists she is a genius."

"But you will manage all right with her? You and Mrs. Sprague?"

There was a pause. Then Louisa said drily, "I'm sure Mrs. Sprague thinks she'd manage even better without me."

Sophie was silent. It made her uncomfortable to have Louisa say it outright like that; she wasn't sure, after all, that she wanted to know what was happening on Bogardus Place. "I mustn't keep you," Louisa said then. "I'll say good-bye for now."

"Shall I visit you soon? We could take Emma to the park."

"That's very kind of you, but it isn't necessary. My parents take her to the park with me."

"But I would like to see you," Sophie told her.

"We'll talk soon," Louisa said. Sophie had the strangest feeling that she knew about the conversation with Rolf.

She was conscious, as she busied herself in the kitchen afterward, that her phone was often silent recently. The other women—Rosa, Hilde, and the others—did not call on her for advice as they used to. She had never been one to phone them, waiting instead for them to seek her out, as they had always done, with questions, complaints, tears, wild pronouncements that they could not go on. Then it was her job to prop them up, either by recalling them to their duties or simply suggesting what they might do about their sons' unsuitable girlfriends or their husbands' bad feet.

She had always told them, when they complained of being lonely—for of course, with the housework to do, and without the rich social framework they had lived in all their lives, they got out a great deal less than they had been accustomed to, even in the Nazi years—that she herself was perfectly content with her own company, with a good book to read, or some embroidery and the radio to listen to. Now that they had evidently taken her at her word, she missed their need of her, which it seemed she had needed in her turn. They had taken to playing bridge, she knew, but after she had scoffed at the idea once or twice they had given up urging her to join them. No doubt they were all gathered at one of their apartments, serving up coffee and cake and scolding each other for the way they had played their hands. She wished that one of them would phone her now, needing her advice. She even wished, though it was out of the question, that she could talk to one of them about Gustav.

She told herself not to be ridiculous, not to get morbid; it wasn't her way. And so she decided to go to the greengrocer, though she had already done her shopping for the day, and see if there were any nice pears for Gustav's dessert.

Mrs. Timpson was in the elevator when the doors opened, her shopping cart loaded with library books, and beamed at the sight of her. "Isn't that something, Mrs. Joseftal, I was just thinking of you."

"And why is that?" Sophie asked, smiling back.

"Oh, my son's stationed in Germany now, waiting for his discharge, and there was a letter from him this morning about how terrible things are there. Half the Germans are starving, he says, and there's rubble everywhere from the bombs, a lot of them don't have homes to go to, and the children follow the GIs through the streets, begging for Hershey bars. He sent some photographs too, of buildings like skeletons, with the windows and the roofs gone, and you can see the remains of people's furniture inside, it's a sad sight for sure."

"Yes, I too have seen such photographs, in the papers," Sophie said warily, uncertain how Mrs. Timpson expected her to respond.

"Sure, so have I, but it feels different when you're looking at someone's actual snapshots. But what I was thinking was, how do Mrs. Joseftal and her people feel about this? I remember my husband, when there were all those pictures of London in the Blitz, how he said the English were finally getting what they deserved, but I just couldn't feel like that.

It was the poor who were suffering there, that's what I told him, not the oppressors. And then I wondered, how do you feel when you hear about the Germans starving?"

"I am afraid it is the same thing. Probably the decent ones are starving, the others have found some way to line their pockets."

"I just hope Tom doesn't decide to play white knight. The next letter might tell us he's coming home with a German bride and her three brats from some dead soldier husband. That'd be just like him. Saving the world."

Sophie laughed; she told her how Kurt was coming home for the university's Thanksgiving break. She supposed—in fact it had just occurred to her—she should cook a turkey.

"Oh, you've got to. For his sake. With stuffing and sweet potatoes and the whole works."

"Perhaps you could advise me on how to cook such things?" Sophie asked shyly.

"Mrs. Joseftal, I would adore to advise you. I'll even give you my sister-in-law's famous recipe for cranberry sauce, handed down from her grandmother. She's third generation, and don't we all have to hear about it. And then maybe you can advise me what the hell to do with the German delicacies that came from Tom the other day—maybe he should have given them to the starving Germans instead. But I guess he's trying to turn us into cosmopolitans. There are some hard little sausages in cans, and flat chocolate cakes with paper stuck to them. What I can't figure out is, do we eat the paper or not? Should I boil the sausages, or fry them, or are they already cooked enough, and I should just serve them cold? Do you think you could educate me on those questions?"

"I would adore to," Sophie said.

CHAPTER ELEVEN

O n Thursday—seven days before Thanksgiving, two days after Rolf had left for Oregon—Sophie went to call on Louisa. She had spent an instructive few hours with Mrs. Timpson, who had not only shown her diagrams of how to truss and stuff a turkey, and given her the promised recipe for cranberry sauce with orange peel, but even demonstrated how to make sweet potato casserole with a brown sugar crust. She had also told a story that interested Sophie very much: her youngest brother, formerly a football coach at a school in New Jersey, had decided that kids should not be taught to play football. It only brought out their competitive instincts, he said, which was what made for wars. When Mrs. Timpson asked him what he was going to do with himself in that case he had said he might get a job as a gardener, at least that way he would not be harming anyone. And when she said he ought to go back to college and make something of himself he had shouted at her that that was how the world had gotten into this mess, he refused to think in terms of getting ahead.

"And what do you think caused this exactly?" Sophie asked her.

Mrs. Timpson, who was mashing the sweet potatoes, flicked a piece of tobacco off her lower lip; at first Sophie had been shocked that she would cook and smoke at the same time, but now there seemed something delightful about it, something insouciant and American. "I suppose it must have something to do with what he saw in the Pacific, right? Something about all the cruelty he witnessed, he can't stand any more. He won't even go hunting with his buddies. It's like he's been rubbed raw. What do you think?"

"I think you are right," Sophie said. Then she added, "My husband is like that also."

Mrs. Timpson did not seem scandalized by this revelation, so momentous for Sophie herself. She did not seem curious, even; she just shook her head. "Not that it makes him any nicer to his friends and relations. His wife is getting frantic, she wants him to go to Rutgers on the GI Bill and be a history teacher, he's always reading books on the Civil War, but no, she's just thinking of the money, he says. Now he's apprenticed himself to a gardener for five bucks a week or something."

"This is nonsense, what he says. Just self-indulgence. What good does it do anyone if he wastes his brains also? Maybe he could help someone as a teacher."

"Oh, I know. But when I tell him that, about wasting his brain, he goes lofty on me. Says that's been the fate of most of humankind throughout history, what does it matter if it happens to one more Irishman?" She blew smoke out of her nostrils. "I suppose he's kind of a Communist. But sometimes when he's ranting away, saying I don't care if people are dying in Africa, I think, 'He's right.' I read about it in the papers and then I fry some eggs. So maybe he has a point."

"Yes," Sophie said. "Gustav also." She did not go so far as to tell Mrs. Timpson that Gustav had accused her of having no pity, no tenderness, no imagination, but she was thinking about it as she headed to Louisa's through the cold, with a small bouquet of chrysanthemums she'd bought on the corner.

Mrs. Sprague greeted her at the door, exclaiming over the flowers as though they were meant for her. "Aren't they beautiful! So thoughtful of you. But you shouldn't have, you really shouldn't. Here, just you give me your coat, and I'll go put them in water." She ushered Sophie into the living room, where Louisa sat on the sofa, in her crumpled green dress, waving a rag doll at Emma, who sat on a little pink blanket on the floor, clapping her hands. "You make yourself comfortable, and I'll be back in a jiff with some coffee."

"Hello," Sophie said, bending down over Emma, "hello, little treasure, and how are you today?" Emma lifted her face as though to the sun, scrunched her eyes together with what seemed to be an appraising look, and then laughed up at her. "Her grandfather is right," Sophie said to Louisa, "she is laughing at all of us."

"Is that true?" Louisa asked Emma. "Are you really laughing at all these good people who love you so much? It's very naughty of you." It all seemed perfectly natural, her voice was like any young mother's talking to her baby, but it struck Sophie that Louisa had not yet looked at her.

"Are you keeping your mother company while your daddy's away?" she asked Emma, holding up a rattle in front of her. "And do your grandparents come to visit you, and take you to the park?"

"Not the last few days," Louisa said flatly. "The weather hasn't been good enough."

"But you are keeping well, Louisa?"

"I'm all right." She spoke to Emma again. "You've been in a good mood all day today, haven't you?" Emma reached her arms toward her mother just as Mrs. Sprague bustled in, with Sophie's flowers in a tall blue vase.

"Just look what Mrs. Joseftal brought," she said brightly, and then, setting them on the table, swooped down on Emma. "My little girl wants to be picked up, doesn't she," she crooned. "She wants her old Aunt May to pick her up, I can see that."

Sophie glanced at Louisa, who had slumped back on the couch. "Come," Sophie said briskly, "why don't you put her next to her mother? I will sit on her other side, and we can have a little visit."

"No, she wants to be held now that I've got her," Mrs. Sprague said, "she'll only make a fuss if I set her down again. Her stomach'll get upset and I'll be up half the night with her. I've got enough to see to."

"Perhaps I could hold her," Sophie suggested.

"I don't think she'd take to that, she don't really know you."

Sophie could feel Louisa's eyes on her in warning: she was not to offend Mrs. Sprague, she was not to let this escalate. "It's only that I know you have so much to attend to," she said smoothly, "I would like to help if I could." Grudgingly, Mrs. Sprague transferred Emma to her arms, hovering there for a minute as though waiting for Emma to protest; when she didn't, Mrs. Sprague had no choice but to leave the room and go do all those things Sophie had referred to.

"Here, I will put her in your lap," Sophie said to Louisa.

"You'd better not," Louisa said sullenly. "Mrs. Sprague won't like it."

Sophie jiggled the child in her arms for a minute—she could feel her getting restless—and then said, "You cannot let her bully you like this, Louisa."

"Ssshhhh." She raised an eyebrow in her old, mocking way. "She may be listening. She listens at doorways sometimes."

"But this is ridiculous," Sophie said in German. "You have to take charge. You must make her understand that you are the mistress here."

Louisa reached out her hand to Emma, who grabbed a finger. "We mustn't talk German in front of you, must we? We don't want the first word you speak to be German."

"Did you hear what I said?"

"Yes, I heard you. I've tried it, and it doesn't work."

"Then you must get rid of her, you must find someone of a different character."

"And what character would that be?" Louisa asked, with a flash of anger. She shut her eyes. "Please. Please don't talk about it any more."

Emma began to cry. Sophie jiggled her energetically, but the child did not stop.

"She wants you to rest her head against your shoulder," Louisa said. Sophie obeyed, and immediately the crying subsided.

But Mrs. Sprague had heard. "Is she all right there?" she called, on her way into the room. "I don't mind taking her, I can put her in her high chair in the kitchen and talk to her while I'm cooking."

"It's all right," Sophie said. "Look, she is happy now."

"Make sure her nose isn't pressed against you, she's got to breathe."

Louisa was leaning back, her bad arm folded in front of her. One of the cushions had come dislodged, and was half on the floor; Mrs. Sprague rescued it, tucking it behind Louisa's back. "Thank you," Louisa said, without opening her eyes.

"I was thinking we could have a nice piece of pie round about now," Mrs. Sprague said, a mug of coffee in her hand. "I'm just warming it in the oven." The phone rang; Louisa started up, pushing herself off the couch with an effort, but Mrs. Sprague got there first.

"Furchgott residence," she said, and then, turning her back on them, laughed girlishly. "Yes, yes, it's me, Mr. Furchgott, I like to answer the phone properly, just in case. How are things out there in Oregon? I'm sure you're getting much nicer weather than we are here . . . Yes, gray and cold, not a peep of sun . . . Of course she is, she's fine and dandy, happy as can be, aren't you, my little lamb?" Here she turned around and winked at Emma. "You don't have to worry about her, you know that, I've got everything under control . . . Yes, about four o'clock, and I was just heating up some pie for Mrs. Furchgott and Mrs. Joseftal, she's come to see us. Would you like to speak with her? I mustn't take up all your time." She set down the receiver, took Emma out of Sophie's arms, and stood there crooning to her, just next to the phone; Sophie was sure Rolf could hear.

"Hello, Rolf," she said stiffly. "I hope you are having a successful trip."

"Yes, thank you. Everything seems to be in order. And there?"

"Yes, everything is fine," she said. "We're all fine here. A nice little visit. I caused a little upset by bouncing Emma too hard a moment ago, but Louisa knew exactly what to do. That's always the way with mothers. Shall I put her on?"

"Please," he said. Louisa struggled to her feet, while Mrs. Sprague looked at Sophie with unconcealed dislike.

"Hello, Rolf," Louisa said.

Sophie turned to Mrs. Sprague. "We should let them speak in private." Mrs. Sprague seemed about to protest, but Sophie forestalled her. "Come," she said decisively, and turned and walked down the hall to the kitchen, with Mrs. Sprague, Emma in her arms, following behind.

But Louisa's voice was still audible. "Yes, I did . . . It was all right . . . No, I haven't yet, I haven't had a chance, I'll do it tomorrow . . . Yes, I told him . . . I will . . . I haven't forgotten . . . I was going to do it when the weather cleared up a little."

Aware that both she and Mrs. Sprague were listening, Sophie launched into conversation.

"I have never been to Maine," she said, as Mrs. Sprague settled Emma into her high chair and handed her a rusk. "I understand it's very beautiful."

Mrs. Sprague addressed herself to Emma, who was sucking blissfully. "If it weren't for you, my precious, I'd go back there right now, wouldn't I? There's not many people who would put up with this setup. They don't know what it's like for your old Aunt May, do they, darlin'?"

"I am sure it is not easy for Mrs. Furchgott either," Sophie said, on an intake of breath.

Now Mrs. Sprague turned to look at her. "She ought to be put away, that's the truth of it. Better for her and everyone else."

Just then Louisa called out, "Mrs. Sprague, Rolf would like another word with you if you're free."

"If you'll excuse me, Mrs. Joseftal," she said grandly, getting to her feet. "He must have forgotten something he needed to tell me. Maybe you could keep an eye on this little girl for me."

But Emma, her face smeared with crumbs and spit, began to cry as soon as Mrs. Sprague left the room, drumming her legs frantically against her high chair. Sophie wiped her face with her handkerchief and lifted her out, but Emma would not be consoled. "Don't you worry, it will be waiting for you when you get back," Mrs. Sprague was saying down the phone.

"Now that's what I call a real gentleman," she said triumphantly, reentering the kitchen. "So nice to be appreciated, isn't it, Mrs. Joseftal?" Emma, turned calm again at the sight of her, was restored to her high chair. Mrs. Sprague twisted open a jar of orange baby food and began spooning it into the child's mouth. "Won't we be happy," she crooned, "when, your daddy's back with us . . . won't we just."

Sophie went down the hall to the living room, where Louisa was staring, like Gustav, out at the street. The light was just starting to fade; following Louisa's gaze, Sophie saw a woman in a red coat wheeling a stroller to the entrance of the apartment building, a shopping bag dangling from her arm. She pulled open the door with one hand, propped her shoulder against it, wheeled the stroller up the steps and halfway through the door, then reached back for the shopping bag, which she had set on the top step. Sophie was suddenly conscious of how much of ordinary life required two good hands.

Crossing the room in swift strides, she sat beside Louisa. "Listen," she said in German, "you must gather your strength together, you must get rid of that woman. If you cannot do it for yourself, then for Emma's sake."

"Emma loves her better than anyone in the world. And why shouldn't she? She has the right to her loves."

Sophie could think of no answer to this, except to repeat what she had said already, on a rising note: Louisa had to rouse herself, she had to muster the strength to defeat Mrs. Sprague. And still Louisa stared at her, slumped and beaten. "Listen to me. You have got to fight now, it's the only way. You cannot let yourself go under." But what if Louisa had no fight in her? She touched her hand. "I'll help you, Louisa, I promise. Let me help you."

Just at that moment Mrs. Sprague appeared, humming a little tune. "Wouldn't you know it, I forgot to drink my coffee, and now it'll be cold. Seems like I never have a chance just to enjoy a nice cup of coffee these days."

Sophie stood. "I will come for you on Saturday, Louisa, and we will go to the park. They say it will be fine on Saturday, I heard it on the radio this morning."

CHAPTER TWELVE

*L*ying in a lumpy hotel bed on his first morning in Oregon, awakened by the cries of strange birds he hoped might be eagles, Rolf had remembered his parting from Louisa—a peck on the cheek, a falsely cheery line about enjoying herself while he was gone—and been flooded with remorseful tenderness. It seemed to him, struggling out of sleep, that his love for her was intact inside him, only walled away waiting to be reclaimed. This optimism did not last through his first evening at home.

He arrived on a Sunday. Louisa, seeming not to notice that Emma was shrieking in her playpen—was actually turning blue—greeted him and told him wistfully about going to the park with Sophie the day before, about Emma clapping her hands at the birds. It was Mrs. Sprague, of course, who had to pick Emma up and soothe her.

There was a chicken roasting in the oven, courtesy of Mrs. Sprague. The Sunday papers were waiting for him—Mrs. Sprague went very far in her solicitude. She had put on lipstick for the occasion, and a red necklace. "Get away with you now," she said, thrusting out her hand, when he complimented her. "What do you mean flattering an old woman like me?" It would have been pleasurable to bask in Mrs. Sprague's own pleasure, to sit listening to her account of Emma, to describe for her the redwood trees and the immense circular saw at the lumberyard, descending as though from heaven to slice through the logs of some lesser wood. There had been as much solemn majesty in the one as in the other.

But Louisa, sitting opposite in her zippered housedress, choked on her very first mouthful of chicken, her eyes bulging. Mrs. Sprague jumped up nimbly and handed her a glass of water. "You must be careful, dear. I thought I'd cut that meat up small enough for you, but you let me know if you want it smaller." Each time he looked at Louisa after that, she was chewing doggedly, or wiping the plate with one finger and then furtively licking it, to sneak the food into her mouth. When she finished—Mrs. Sprague was just asking him about the birds out there, wondering if they had the same seagulls as in Maine—she stood up, plate in hand, and started for the sink. "You leave that for me, dear, I'll clear up," Mrs. Sprague said, and after hovering for a minute Louisa disappeared from the room.

A couple of days later Otto arrived—sweet, kind Otto, so unlike Rolf. Rolf was a hero at the office, and to Mrs. Sprague, but even Sophie disapproved of him now, he had heard it in her voice when he spoke to her on the phone that morning. "This woman believes she is the child's mother. I cannot think she is the right person to have there with Louisa." There was nothing wrong with Louisa, she told him, that time would not put right. No doubt Otto was waiting for his chance to say the same.

When Rolf got home from the office, Otto was dancing around the living room like a sprite, Emma in his arms, while Louisa laughed at them from the sofa. "Hello, Rolf, I'm in love with your daughter," Otto said. Rolf told him drily that everyone felt that way and went to hang up his coat.

Then he went into the kitchen to say hello to Mrs. Sprague, who grumbled that Otto was getting the little one overexcited. "I'll be up half the night with her," she said, and he had to repress a sense of gratification that someone at least was not charmed. It was the first time Emma had not clamored for him on his arrival.

When he returned to the living room Louisa was smiling at him, a gay inviting smile, not a plea for forgiveness; she asked him in a wifely voice how things had gone with Mr. Starin that day. Pretty well, he said. Otto was crooning to Emma, but Rolf could tell he was listening. He should have been pleased that Louisa was so vivacious, he should have been pleased with the whole scene—his wife, friend, daughter laughing together—but it felt like a fraud, something manufactured to reproach him. Otto, he sensed, was willing this mirage into being for his benefit, keeping Louisa afloat on his own effervescence. He retrieved Emma from Otto's arms and brought her into the kitchen for her bottle. Mrs. Sprague seemed more than ever like an ally.

It was Otto who cut Louisa's pork chop for her at dinner, deftly, talking all the while. Rolf had always left it to Mrs. Sprague. "Remember the penknife you gave me on my birthday? Remember the pony ride?" Otto said, ignoring Mrs. Sprague altogether. But already Louisa's energy was fading, her expression confused. She didn't remember, she said apologetically, she had no memory of a pony ride at all.

"It doesn't matter," Otto said, "of course it doesn't." He asked Rolf about his trip out west; he asked about the business, and many other questions. He was going to see Franz and Jeannette the next morning; then he had to go downtown to make some purchases; he wondered if he could meet Rolf for lunch. Louisa put down her fork and looked tensely at Rolf, as though much hinged on his answer. Of course, he said. That would be very nice. Mrs. Sprague scraped back her chair and stood.

"Well, I'd better get on with things." His purpose accomplished—that was how Rolf saw it—Otto remembered his manners and insisted on helping her, complimenting her on her cooking. Meanwhile Louisa was still watching Rolf.

He got to the coffee shop seven minutes early the next day, but Otto was there already, in a corner booth. "How was your visit this morning?" Rolf asked him.

"The usual," Otto said lightly, although Rolf knew it would have been different in at least one respect: the talk would have been of Louisa, and then of his own behavior. "Jeannette complained, and Franz wanted to know all about my life, he wanted to see pictures of Margaret, and the apartment, and the cat. But he doesn't look at all well."

"I know." Neither of them said what both were thinking: when Franz's life was shattered, when his brother died at the hands of the Nazis, when he came to America with nothing, cooped up with Jeannette in two dismal rooms, eking out a living by dealing in old stamps, when the news came after the war that his sister and her family had been gassed at Auschwitz, the one thing still left to him had been the certainty of Louisa's happiness.

Otto looked around at the other diners. "Do you think they are enjoying themselves?" He gestured toward the booth opposite, where a young couple were hunched over ice cream sundaes. They looked weary beyond their years, drained of hope; perhaps they had just had a fight, they had come out for ice cream to try to salvage something.

"No," Rolf said reluctantly, as though this admission would compromise him. "Not at this moment."

"When I first came to America I half the time wished Americans would not smile so much and the other half wondered why they didn't smile more, why they weren't smiling all the time."

"Some of them do."

A freckled waitress in a striped apron appeared to pour them coffee and ask what they wanted. Rolf said the BLTs were good there, and they ordered two. They stirred cream into their cups in silence. Otto rearranged, meticulously, the knife and fork the girl had placed on the chipped Formica in front of him. Then he said, "She will never be able to do what's necessary for the child, all the practical things, in these early years especially. But to be there with her, to see her, to touch her . . . they have such wonderful smiles for each other."

"Of course." Rolf glanced at the young couple again. The girl had put down her spoon and was leaning across the table, talking in a low urgent voice, while the man went on callously shoveling ice cream into his mouth. And all the while he could feel Otto's eyes on his face.

"If it were anyone else, I wouldn't be so worried. I'd think, well, he'll take a mistress, that's how it will be managed. But you won't do that. You virtuous ones are more dangerous than the rest of us."

It was intolerable, indecent, that Otto of all people should speak of it. "That's enough," he said, "I won't sit here and listen to this," but his voice, instead of being stern, was hoarse and cracked like a madman's. For a moment they stared at each other, frozen, until Otto reached over and touched his hand.

"Forgive me. It's none of my business. You will do what you have to. But I ask you, please, don't give up on her completely. Not yet."

"I haven't," Rolf said, clenching his teeth.

"I think the idea of it has become possible to you. But the other is also possible. You don't know how much she will recover, not her arm, her walk, but her old self. I still see flickers of it, I feel it alive in her. It hasn't died, she just can't inhabit it in the old way any more. But she might. She might. You don't know. She could still come back to herself."

Rolf took a deep breath, steadying himself. "I don't see that happening, frankly."

"Because you see only the other things, the clumsiness, the veins that show in her forehead. How can you help it? But I tell you, there is grace and grace . . . Why are you looking at me like that?"

"I was thinking you sound like a preacher. Did you find God in the trenches, Otto?"

"There were no trenches where I was. I'll shut up if you want me to."

"You're not saying anything I haven't told myself dozens of times. In my own more pedestrian way. I'm doing the best I can. I'm sorry it's not good enough. As sorry as you are."

"I'm thinking of you as well as her. About what will become of you afterward."

"You think my guilt might kill me?"

"No. But you will carry it with you, it may be too heavy a load to bear. Heavier than she would be."

The waitress arrived with their sandwiches. Rolf sat staring at his, Otto picked up the pickle from his plate and took a careful bite, seeming to signal a return to normalcy—he would speak of something different next—but this time it was Rolf who could not stop. "What if I can't love her the way she is?"

"I don't know," Otto said sadly, the pickle still in his hand. "But you haven't tried yet."

Rolf went on looking at the lettuce curling out of his sandwich; he was not sure he'd be able to eat the thing. He wanted no more of Otto's wisdom, if wisdom it was, not when it meant the zippered dresses, the bristles of hair, the lopsided mouth. Alone with her that morning, with Mrs. Sprague and Emma in the kitchen, he had felt she was about to say something he would not want to hear; he had begun talking about the snow they were expecting, about Emma's checkup next week, about the Congress, the UN. And she had sunk back into herself again, successfully warded off, her eyes full of misery.

What was Otto telling him, if not that he must live like an old man, resign himself to his duty, which it seemed to him he had been doing for most of his life? (He forgot the joy there had been, the Sunday outings with Louisa, the picnic on Bear Mountain, the night she had told him she was pregnant.) He stared at his hands on the table, remembering Miss Maggiore's scarlet nails. She had brought him a yellow rose in a water glass when he got back to the office on Monday. "There you go," she said, without quite looking at him, "the yellow rose of Texas. Except it's Oregon you've been to. But it's the thought that counts, right? It's from all the girls, not just me. But it was my idea."

"It's very sweet of you," he said gravely.

"Oh, I'm awfully sweet. Sweet is just my middle name." She seemed to be watching him with a special alertness. "Well," she said finally, "can't stand here talking all day. Or not talking. There's work to be done, right?"

She was the secret he was keeping from Otto. Nothing had happened between them, apart from those curiously charged encounters, but more and more the thought of her interfered with the workings of his conscience, made him mutinous in the face of reason. And he sensed that she knew this, and was excited by her power; she knew she had awakened in him some avidity that was dangerous. She may even have understood how foreign it was to what he had always believed was his nature. For all her brash innocence, she was shrewder than he was; that too was part of her charm.

But here was Otto, trying to sell him on Louisa as surely as the man who had come to his office that morning had tried to sell him on a new line of graphite. Delight, adventure, all that would be deferred for one more generation, something for Emma, not for him. Certainly that was Franz's view of it. At the thought of Franz he knew he was trapped; in a minute he would pick up his sandwich and start to eat, and when he was dead they could write on his tombstone, *He saw it through.*

CHAPTER THIRTEEN

$\mathcal{A}$s it turned out, it was Louisa who left him, if a woman with a crippled arm and a pronounced instability to her gait can be said to leave anyone. It happened late on Thanksgiving, after their dinner, prepared of course by Mrs. Sprague, with Otto in attendance, and Emma blowing out her cheeks and making rude noises as Otto had taught her, then shrieking with laughter. Otto had brought two bottles of wine; Mrs. Sprague was too good a Baptist to partake, but the others toasted her with it, complimenting her on each dish in turn. Afterward Sophie and Gustav were coming with Kurt, just for a cup of coffee, and to say hello.

When they had eaten their turkey and stuffing and sweet potatoes and pumpkin pie Louisa, with the confidence lent to her by the wine and Otto's presence, had insisted charmingly that they would clean up. Mrs. Sprague had done enough for one day, she should go to the living room and rest. Rolf had put Emma down for her nap; it was just the three of them in the kitchen, with Rolf washing and Otto drying and Louisa wiping the table and high chair and putting things away, maneuvers she managed by a painstaking exertion of effort. She had improved, Rolf saw, she could do more with her right hand than he had supposed.

Even of old she had never really been graceful; she was too physically careless for that. She might turn around too quickly with a full cup of broth in her hand and spill some on the floor; she might set the jar of cinnamon too close to the counter's edge and catch it with her sleeve. But her movements had always seemed so emphatic, so swift and certain, that it didn't matter. He would sit in the kitchen in the evenings and watch her, smiling as much at her lack of method—she was always forgetting things, always having to open the oven door again and add one more thing to the casserole—as at the stories she told him, about something ridiculous that had happened to her that day. Chatting, she called it, a word she had picked up in England; he did not know anyone else who used it. And then she might burn the rice, and have to scrape it off the bottom of the pot.

Now here she was, picking up a wine glass laboriously with her good hand, wrapping the fingers of her other one around the stem, using her free hand to open the cupboard door, then prizing the crippled fingers off the glass to set it down.

"Look at her!" Otto cried, flinging out his arms, the dish towel snapping. "Isn't she wonderful?" Rolf turned around for a moment and then went back to wiping the sink.

"Stop it, Otto," Louisa said, her voice rising.

"But you are, you're wonderful."

"You're embarrassing Rolf."

"Then damn Rolf."

"Oh, no," she said, "you mustn't say that, you can't damn Rolf. Rolf is . . . he's the model citizen. And I, you see, I'm no earthly use to the state. To nation-building."

"Don't be ridiculous," Rolf told her, turning around fully now. "Nobody's ever suggested such a thing."

"No," she said hysterically, "of course not. Nobody would ever say a thing like that. But then nobody talks to me much, nobody talks to me at all. Except Mrs. Sprague, she tells me lots of things. While you were away she told me about a widow lady who lives in a house on Park Terrace West, and rents out rooms to invalids. Such a very nice lady, she said, she just happened to strike up a conversation with her in the supermarket one day. Mrs. Rafferty is her name, she'd love to take me to meet her. Why do you suppose she said all that?"

"I presume because she was trying to make conversation."

"Oh, God," she said. "God. What a coward you are. Even Mrs. Sprague is more honest."

He stalked out without looking at either of them. In the living room, Mrs. Sprague had fallen asleep on the sofa, her head lolling on her flowered apron. For a few minutes he sat opposite her, taking deep breaths, and then the doorbell rang. Sophie and Gustav had arrived with Kurt.

Afterward, Rolf could hardly remember a single thing that had been said. They must have spoken of the usual subjects—the political situation, Kurt's studies, Franz and Jeannette (they had come that morning, Otto was going to see them later). Gustav must have asked him about his trip out west. But only Kurt, a stocky untidy young man with a cowlick, spoke to him with normal kindness; the others all seemed to sit up straighter when he talked, they were stiffly correct, tight-lipped, while bestowing all their warmth and smiles on Louisa. He and Mrs. Sprague were cast out.

She tried to press her pumpkin pie on them, but they refused even that. Sophie had also made a pumpkin pie, Gustav told them proudly, patting her hand, a magnificent concoction; she was becoming a real American now. Rolf had never seen him so cheerful, or Sophie so girlish; only when they addressed themselves to him did the old severity return. Louisa, meanwhile, was part of the general radiance—Louisa, who a few minutes before had been shouting insults in the kitchen, beamed at them, leaned forward excitedly on her chair, told a funny little story about Emma with the old breathlessness. Mrs. Sprague got up and disappeared in the direction of the room she shared with Emma.

A few minutes later, when Sophie, too, rose and said they must be going, Louisa pushed herself off her chair and went over to her. "I'm so glad," she said, clutching Sophie's hand. "I'm so glad for you both." It was the sort of thing people said to a young couple who'd just announced their engagement, but neither Gustav nor Sophie seemed at all embarrassed; their faces were alight.

Then it was just the three of them again. Otto announced to Louisa—he still had not looked at Rolf—that he must be going, Jeannette and Franz were expecting him. Louisa told him to bring them the rest of the pumpkin pie. "Perhaps we should ask Mrs. Sprague about that," Rolf said, with careful mildness.

"Leave a piece for her," Louisa said to Otto. "Cut a piece and put it on a plate." The whole time Otto was in the kitchen, busying himself with the pie, she did not speak, though she stared fixedly at Rolf, forcing him to meet her eyes. Only when Otto had left, promising to come in from New Jersey again on Saturday, did she break the silence. "Please sit down," she said sharply. Just at that moment there was a wail from the bedroom.

"Mrs. Sprague must be asleep," he said, when it did not stop right away. "I'll go get Emma."

"Not now. She'll wake up in a minute. I need to talk to you alone."

Reluctantly, he sat down. "I really can't concentrate while she's crying." But just then the crying stopped; they could hear Mrs. Sprague cooing to her. In a minute, he knew, she would appear in the living room with Emma, on the way to the kitchen to heat up a bottle. He willed her to come soon, to rescue him.

"What are we going to do?" Louisa asked him, her voice low, and then, desperately, "Look at me." But he could not do even that much; he was too full of dread. He was only waiting for Mrs. Sprague to emerge with Emma in her arms; otherwise it could not be averted, something terrible was going to happen.

"Very well," Louisa said, harsh with contempt. There were no more sounds from the bedroom, Emma must have gone back to sleep. "There's nothing we can do, that's what you mean, isn't it?" And still he could not answer.

"Look at me, for God's sake, can't you even look at me?" Finally he raised his eyes; he stared at her, growing more and more frightened, waiting. This was the moment when he had to beg her forgiveness, when he had to swear he would be different. Only he could not do it.

"All right then," she said fiercely, "that's that, isn't it," and shut her eyes. When she opened them again she told him she was leaving. She would go to Mrs. Sprague's friend, she would do whatever she had to, go anywhere. She could not stay there any longer. He knew he should say *Don't go*, he should cry, or cry out, he should stand and put his arms around her, but he could not manage any of those things. All he could do was sit there, with limbs heavy as stone and molten heat deep in his belly; his mind was stripped of words. There was silence for a long minute.

"What are you thinking? Tell me."

"Nothing."

"Don't say that. You must be thinking something."

But he wasn't. With immense effort, he ran his tongue around his mouth.

"Maybe . . ."

"Maybe what?"

"Maybe you can come back after a while."

She laughed shrilly, rocking back and forth, her bad arm folded across her chest. But just when it seemed she might lose her balance and topple over, she straightened up and met his eyes, her face full of such bleakness he had to turn away. The door to the bedroom opened; Mrs. Sprague was emerging. In the few seconds before she appeared, his brain woke up again; realization came like jolts of black lightning. He saw that some failures, some cruelties, were irrevocable; some harm could never be undone. That he was nothing like the man he'd thought himself to be. That he would carry this knowledge for the rest of his life.

PART III

CHAPTER ONE

$\mathscr{H}$er daughter came every Saturday. All week she longed for these visits, as she had longed for the arrival of her first lover when she was young; every morning she told herself how many days it would be until Emma came. But as with her long-ago lover, whatever she was hoping for never happened; afterward she always felt bewildered, with a heavy sense of having failed. Sometimes she remembered her mother, twisting her hands helplessly in her lap, and thought she finally understood.

Weather permitting, they went walking in the scruffy park across from Mrs. Rafferty's house, where a row of benches overlooked the water. They headed for the farthest one, next to an abandoned boathouse, and sat looking out at the Palisades while Emma entertained her with little stories she had saved up during the week: the landlord's wife had shown up at her door again, to complain of her husband's stinginess (he had given her a can opener for her birthday); a fat man had chased a bald little dog back and forth across East Tenth Street, crying, "Come to me, my angel." Emma told her nothing about her real life, the things she reported were never what mattered to her. Louisa suspected there might be complicated troubles with a man. On one of those Saturdays in the park some months before, she had announced, in a brisk summary way, that she had quit the graduate program at Columbia and taken a job. Her boss was a Cambodian, a refugee, with slightly mysterious funding for publications about his country, which Emma was to edit. "You will detect many missing articles in these manuscripts, both definite and indefinite," he had told her at the interview, and said she must be firm with his authors, who would try to gain her sympathy by describing their sufferings. "They are lucky to be published at all," he'd said, adding, "Is good you are an American. They will behave in more civilized fashion, because of feeling intimidated." He had studied at the Sorbonne and wore extremely elegant ties. All these things Emma had told Louisa in the first few weeks, sounding amused, but now she never mentioned him.

When they reached their usual bench that day, there were two skinny young men in sunglasses standing in tense attitudes beneath the tree opposite, seeming to argue in low voices. They glanced briefly, contemptuously, at the women and went back to their conversation. "Dope dealers," Emma said, in the brittle voice she assumed for making such statements. Then she began adjusting Louisa's scarf, a plaid woolen square left behind by some former resident (all the residents were former now, except for Louisa). Mrs. Rafferty had given it to Louisa, as she gave her many things that nobody else wanted. Emma was trying to make it cover Louisa's ears without slipping down onto her forehead. The longer she fiddled with it, chiding Louisa to keep still, the surer Louisa was that something was wrong. Emma never fussed like that: she hated fuss almost as much as her father had. "Stop now," Louisa begged her. Emma's hands stopped moving.

"Listen," she said. "There's something I need to tell you."

. . .

He had waited too long.

The doctors told him this outright, to show their respect. They had served with him on the steering committee of the local hospital; at his urging—it was a nice irony—plans were under way for a state-of-the-art oncology unit. He knew all about Betatrons, cobalt-60 machines, orthovoltage. He knew too about the special, rarefied toxins they were using now at Johns Hopkins and Dana Farber. But it seemed that in his case the prospects for halting the disease were clouded. Already the cancer was in his lymph nodes. They would do what they could, they were ordering some of those very toxins to be shipped to the Connecticut suburbs in refrigerated cars, but they would be honest with him. He must not expect too much. He must be prepared for the worst.

What he never said was that he had to stop himself from hoping for the very thing they were warning him of. In that first moment he heard the news, he had felt a surge of relief, a lightening of the spirit such as he could hardly remember experiencing before. Of course he repressed this immediately.

And so he dutifully took up the job of staying alive.

For years Louisa had been tormented by thoughts of him, there was no room for anything else. Every morning, when she opened her eyes, the storm of grief and shame and disbelief began all over again, knocking her back with the same force. She imagined him at his desk, working his way methodically through stacks of papers, wholly absorbed in the world's business; at night, sitting in her airless room, with the

birdcage and the ancient dressing table and the window over-
looking the alley, she thought of him in their old bedroom,
six blocks away, waiting for Connie to come to bed. At least,
when they moved to Connecticut, she no longer had to know
what their bedroom looked like.

It was at about that time—when Emma too was removed
from her, to that house in the suburbs she had never seen—
that something had given way, she seemed to have shed the
self she knew, and other people became vivid to her again,
in a different way from before. The people themselves were
different from the ones she had known: the woman who came
with the mobile library van, whose daughter had spina bifida;
the wife of a former resident at Mrs. Rafferty's, who came
to tea sometimes, and told Louisa, in an anguished voice, of
wishing her husband would die. At about the same time, as
though to make up for the loss of Emma, who would hence-
forth come only on alternate weekends, Rolf had a television
installed in her room, word of its delivery having been sent her
by his secretary. The people on the screen, victims of earth-
quakes, tornadoes, racial hatred, came to fill her thoughts.
When she lay awake at night—since her operation she slept
badly—she grieved not for herself but for Korean orphans,
cerebral palsy victims, lepers in India. She adopted, through a
charity, an impoverished child in Peru; she shopped for toys
for her at the Woolworth's on Dyckman Street and used her
typing skills to write long encouraging letters when the little
girl began learning English in order to correspond with her.
She even volunteered to work at the charity once a week,
typing up envelopes with her good hand. Her sorrow had become vast, impersonal, and then she understood that in some
sense she had come through, though there was no point to it.

But since the news of his cancer she'd been remembering him again, the gruff child he had been, the early days in New York, his struggle not to look at her. And then when they were married, and she had brought him tea in bed on a Sunday morning, and sat there chatting to him in the green brocade dressing gown he had bought her: she had been heady with the weight of his desire, savoring it, until he had pulled her down beside him. Maybe she had loved him only for wanting her so much, maybe what had happened was a punishment for that. There was the Sunday she had coaxed him into going to Bear Mountain for a picnic, when he wanted to stay behind and work: she had dropped the lunch she'd brought for them into a muddy stream, and the mosquitoes had assaulted them, but instead of being angry with her he had found it charming, as he found everything about her charming then. She had believed she would always delight him like that.

In February, Emma told her that the poisons from Baltimore had failed to produce the desired results. It was too cold for the park, she announced, as soon as she arrived, and then asked if they could go to Louisa's room. Louisa knew that meant there was bad news. She could feel Mrs. Rafferty watching them as they went upstairs. Usually, if the weather kept them indoors, they sat in the parlor, and Mrs. Rafferty served them tea and biscuits while filling Emma in on the latest news about her niece, who worked for Hewlett Packard and was getting a divorce: her wicked husband had sold her jewelry to pay his gambling debts. When Emma was younger she had formed a dislike for Mrs. Rafferty, and sometimes been rude to her, but these days she only smiled tightly if Mrs. Rafferty told her how Louisa should get more fresh air or eat more vegetables, and she always remembered to ask about her niece.

Up in Louisa's room, Emma did not sit down when Louisa did, but remained standing, avoiding Louisa's eyes. She picked up a paperweight made of smoky glass from the top of the dresser and straightened out the embroidered cloth underneath, both the cloth and the paperweight being remnants of Jeannette's trousseau. Then she went to the pine bookshelf in the corner and blew on the photograph of herself, aged five, to remove the dust. After that she proceeded to straighten the pictures on the wall above the bookcase. Many of these too were framed photos of her as a child, taken by the school photographer in Connecticut: her third-, sixth-, eighth-grade pictures, for which Louisa had purchased frames at Woolworth's; Mrs. Rafferty had helped her slip the photos inside. Already, by age eight, Emma's eyes had been watchful, though when she was very young, back in the days when Mrs. Sprague had brought her to see Louisa, she had been full of laughter, hugging Louisa around the legs, singing merrily as she whirled around the room. When she was seven—shortly before the move to Connecticut—she had discovered Louisa's old photograph album at the bottom of the bookshelf, and hauled it out on every visit, making Louisa tell her about Julian, and the estate in Norfolk, the café in South Kensington, peering intently at each photo, looking from them to Louisa and back again. She had dissolved into giggles whenever she got to the last picture in the book, the one taken on the steps of city hall on Louisa's wedding day.

"The chemotherapy didn't work," she said now, and again straightened her third-grade photograph. "But they're going to try something new. Some new kind of radiation they've been experimenting with at Grace New Haven. High-voltage

Sagittarius something. One of the doctors gave him a bunch of articles about it, from the *New England Journal of Medicine* or something. You know how he loves shit like that." She turned around then, to look at Louisa. "You need a haircut," she said abruptly, and went into the bathroom to get the scissors and a towel. As she started to snip away, she told Louisa about a girl in the supermarket who'd been saying to her husband, "My daddy told me I was crazy to marry a poet." And then, when Louisa was silent, "What are you thinking?"

"Nothing," Louisa said, lifting her head. "I'm listening to you, that's all. I always like listening to you, you know that."

Emma removed the towel and flicked away the hairs from Louisa's neck. "I don't want you to worry, okay? He's going to be all right." But her voice was high and thin; for the first time Louisa understood how frightened she was. Poor Rolf, she thought, reaching up to squeeze Emma's hand. She almost felt he needed her now, to grieve for him. He would be no good at doing it for himself.

They could not keep the fevers down. There were the blisters on his skin, from the radiation, and then the burning inside his body. Even his eyes were hot, and his lungs, and his kidneys, and his brain. The doctors had faded out of the picture, replaced by nurses who dressed his burns and held his head while he threw up thin bile into metal basins; they checked his drips and adjusted his pillows and emptied his bedpan. Some of the younger ones, unfamiliar with the new treatment he was being given, seemed more distressed than he was. Once he heard two nurses talking in the hall outside his room.

"You want my opinion, it's sinful, what they're doing," one of them said.

"They spent so much money on that thing," the other told her, "they got to keep using it on everyone so they can justify the cost." It was strange how acute his hearing had become, when everything else seemed to be shutting down; they spoke in low voices, almost whispers, but he heard every word.

Here in New Haven he had many fewer visitors; it was too far for people to come. A Yale oncologist had dropped by once, to discuss Rolf's plans for a liaison between Grace and the local hospital's oncology unit, but it had been an especially bad day, a day when he could not finish his sentences or stop himself from grimacing. The man had not come again.

So there were only the two women. Connie came almost every day, keeping up a steady stream of jokes, mostly about his supposed malingering: how he was just trying to get out of work, or make people fuss over him. She liked to make this point in front of the nurses, who responded with varying degrees of warmth when she told them how he was really faking it, he just wanted all the pretty girls to pay attention to him. Once they had left the room, she would tell him triumphantly that she knew how to get around these people; what sourpusses the nurses in that place were, she said, but she lightened them up. Then she would report her comeback to the boy in the Pathmark that morning, when he told her they'd run out of the salami for which she had a coupon, or what she had said to the hairdresser, or the man at the gas station, all these remarks being of a jocular nature. It had been many, many years since she had shown him this convivial side of herself; it reminded him of those early mornings at the office off Union Square—the head-tossing, oddly childlike woman who had so bewildered and moved him. But after a while, offended by his lack of response, she always reverted to the bitter, aggrieved wife, full of sarcasm and wounded feeling. If he didn't appreciate her, at least other people did; if he didn't want her around, she'd be happy to go elsewhere, thank you very much. "If you want the truth, the smell in here is enough to make me sick."

Then there was Emma, who arrived, every time, like a messenger from the battlefield—charging in, shaking the snow from her boots, beginning at once to tell him about some encounter she'd had on the train, or some article she'd read in the *Times* during her journey—only to divest herself, seemingly, of her vehement energy along with her coat, until silence threatened. He could feel her waiting for something, some show of emotion, perhaps, that he could not make. And so he would summon out of his weariness carefully composed questions about the work she was doing, the situation in Cambodia, nodding gravely at her answers, feeling her watchfulness turn to resentment, the accusation always there just under the surface. At times he felt like a great white hunter, fending off an angry lion with only the power of his gaze.

He had told her she needn't come so often, she mustn't keep taking time off from her job, but she always protested, with a kind of strangled fierceness, that she wanted to be there, "unless you'd rather I didn't come." No, no, he said, as waves of fatigue washed over him, of course he was delighted to see her.

They exhausted him, both of them.

CHAPTER TWO

*O*n the first Saturday in April, they made a full circuit of the park; spring had come early that year, the maple tree had already lost its first young green and was settling into its summer color. As they reached their bench, there were two boys standing in front of it, shouting in Spanish; one of them gave the other a push in the chest, flinging him backward, but he recovered quickly and went chasing the first one over a flowerbed and across the grass. "Don't worry about them, they're just kids," Emma said. "Just young punks." It was the first time she had spoken since they left the house.

A minute later she launched into a story about a Jehovah's Witness who had knocked on her door and tried to give her some pamphlets about God's kingdom; when Emma, trying to get rid of her, had told her she didn't believe in heaven, the woman had said, "Face it, honey, if this is the only world we get, somebody has played a pretty mean trick on us." "The thing is," Emma said with a little laugh, "I sort of agreed with her." Then she fell silent again. The two boys came running back into view, in high spirits now, breaking stride to jump up and snatch at leaves on low branches. Emma stared after them.

"The radiation didn't work," she said. "They want to cut off his leg, they say if they amputate they can get all the cancer." The boys disappeared again, behind a clump of trees.

"Resorting to old-fashioned methods," Emma went on, trying, Louisa knew, for the wryly mocking voice they always used in discussing Louisa's own disasters. When she had fallen in the street that time, and the emergency room doctor had set her bad arm so that she could not lower it at all, Emma had said in just that voice that she certainly had a curious relationship with the medical profession. But now she could not bring it off.

Louisa stared blindly at the flowerbed, full of mangy daffodils, their leaves jagged where something had eaten away at them. She could feel the tears on her cheeks, and dreaded Emma demanding the Kleenex from her pocket and wiping them brusquely away. Instead, Emma took her good hand from her lap and held it. But she did not say he was going to be all right.

"So that one will be a rich widow," Mrs. Rafferty said that night. Louisa had told her about Rolf's illness as they were eating dinner. Once, Mrs. Rafferty had made stews and meatballs and apple brown Betty, but that was when the house was full. Now that it was only herself and Louisa, she prepared omelets for them, or they made do with Campbell's soup and fruit-flavored yogurt out of tubs. Tonight it was franks and beans. Mrs. Rafferty, radiating discontent, had cut Louisa's food into little pieces for her, and then urged her to eat up. Her niece had been expected to come the following day, but she had phoned earlier and claimed to have the flu—Mrs. Rafferty had known she was pretending, she said, from the phony way she coughed down the phone. "Your daughter had something private to discuss with you today, did she?" she asked, as she was sawing away at the hot dogs. It was then that Louisa told her about Rolf.

All those years ago, when Rolf had asked Louisa to go to Nevada and get a divorce (the only grounds acceptable in New York was adultery, and he did not want Emma to hear, some day, that he had been found in a hotel room with a prostitute), Mrs. Rafferty had told her she was a fool to go along with it. There must be another woman, she said, there was no other explanation for his wanting a divorce. Louisa had scorned this idea. "You don't know him, you can't understand what an honorable man he is."

And she had believed that all through the six nightmarish weeks in Reno, when for hours at a time she could do nothing but lie on her back in the boxy hotel room, with its garish purple walls, like someone with a broken spine. There had been a woman in the next room, younger than herself, a pretty little brunette, whose sobs came through the wall night after night, but she, Louisa, had made not a sound. And then Otto had come, poor Otto, and shouted about Rolf, while she stared at him, bewildered, because it hardly seemed by then that her present paralysis, the state of dumb suffering she had been reduced to, could be related to anything as specific as what Rolf had done or not done. It was more as though some final, irrefutable knowledge had been visited on her, of the bleakness that lay at the bottom of everything. Rolf was as remote to her as the traffic noises outside her window, as the fat waitress in the hotel coffee shop.

But of course Mrs. Rafferty had been right. Even after all this time, if she was feeling more than ordinarily dissatisfied with life, she sometimes reverted to the subject of Rolf's betrayal, while Louisa kept her eyes on her plate and chewed in silence.

Tonight, though, it was Connie Mrs. Rafferty wanted to talk about. She had met her when she accompanied Louisa to Sophie Joseftal's funeral, twelve years before, and Connie had come up to them, sighing, and reminisced about a visit Sophie had paid to the house in Connecticut, how she had admired the view from the living room and the Royal Worcester coffee service and said that was really gracious living. Nothing but trash, was Mrs. Rafferty's verdict, which she repeated now: never mind the airs Connie gave herself, and the fur coat and the diamonds. "I expect she'll be well looked after when he goes," she said darkly. "She'll have made sure of that. And what about you? What kind of provisions has he made for you? You'd better find out soon."

"I can't ask him about money right now."

"Suit yourself, then," Mrs. Rafferty said disagreeably. "I was only thinking of you."

In fact Louisa got a letter from him the following week, a typed one, as always, on office stationery, with his secretary's initials next to his own beneath his signature. He wanted her to know, he said, that whatever happened to him in the coming months—and he had the utmost confidence in his doctors, they were fine men as well as very able practitioners—she would be provided for. There was not only a small life insurance policy in her name, but a pension the company would provide. He did not expect that any of these arrangements would need to come into effect just yet, but he thought she should know that, should they be necessary, she would be taken care of. He hoped she was well, he said, and that she would have a pleasant summer.

She wished, as she so often had lately, that she could talk to Sophie. It had been unthinkable that Gustav would out-live her, with his weak heart, his bad color, the tremor in his hands. But it was Sophie who died, very suddenly, of a stroke.

She used to visit once a week, always on a Wednesday—Sophie never changed to the point where she ceased adhering to a schedule, even if she had softened in other ways—bearing a plain yellow cake and a small bag of sugared almonds. She would glue together a cup that Louisa had broken, or sew a button on Louisa's coat, biting off the thread with a satisfy-ing snap when she was done. Nothing in Sophie's manner, as she carried out these repairs, suggested that they were acts of charity. It seemed part of her pleasure in the visit to be stitch-ing away while they chatted about the day's news, or Emma, or what Sophie's children were up to, with music playing on the radio. Only on those Wednesdays when Sophie was there had listening to music felt safe to Louisa back then. Then So-phie had died, and Gustav had gone to live with their son and his family in Ohio, where he survived for another ten years.

If Sophie had been there Louisa could tell her the things she was remembering now, about Rolf. But maybe she wouldn't. Maybe they would only sit listening to Schubert or Brahms or Verdi's Requiem on QXR, and talk about their children. After Sophie died she had gradually trained herself to listen to music on her own again. But nowadays even Hindemith could bring her to the verge of tears.

In his private room, back in the local hospital, the little candy stripers came with their carts laden with candy bars and chewing gum and magazines, their shining hair tied in glossy ribbons for hygiene. The paintings on the wall were of sunsets over hayfields, or children building sand castles. But in the night, when he could not sleep, he seemed to smell the rot in his body; sometimes the stench made him drag himself out of bed to open a window. The night nurses came and scolded him for not having called them to do it.

There was one in particular he liked, a stocky diffident young woman with an air of gravity he found touching. Sharon was her name, and unlike the others she never joked with him or made perky small talk. She would listen to his breathing from the doorway, ready to move on if she judged him to be sleeping, but more often she found him wakeful, and entered to take his readings, with a surprising delicacy of touch. She was the one person whose presence he found soothing.

On the night before the operation, she came to his room at the start of her shift, to see if there was anything he wanted. He was fine, he told her; he had been very well looked after all day.

"You're sure?"

"Absolutely sure."

"Then I'd better go check on the others. Mrs. Michaels, that's the woman next door, she always wants to be turned over. And she weighs a lot."

The third time she appeared, she opened the curtains—so he could look at the moon, she said. "See? It's almost full." She stood there watching it for a minute. Then she asked, "Are you scared?"

"I don't think so. More squeamish than frightened."

"I'm sorry. I shouldn't have asked you that."

"Don't be sorry."

"It's just that I can't imagine it. Knowing I'd wake up and there'd be part of me missing. I'd almost rather it just happened, and I didn't have to know."

"You're a lot younger than I am. It would be different for you."

"I guess so. But I think it's because you're from Europe too. You are, aren't you?"

"Yes. From Germany."

"So you might be more used to terrible things happening, you know?"

Just then the buzzer sounded at the nurses' station. "I bet that's Mrs. Michaels again," she said. "I've already turned her over three times. She's got lumps everywhere. Do you think you could sleep a little?"

"I'll try."

"You really should. But if you can't, and you want anything, you'll ring the bell, won't you."

Of course, he said.

"No you won't. But I mean it. Even if you just felt like talking."

He supposed there must be people who poured out their secrets to her at such times, with the room half dark, and the time drawing near for the surgery. What could he tell her? How, when he was lying in that other hospital, sick from the radiation, falling in and out of fevers, he had started remembering things, remembering being something he had not done for years? The arrangements for sending oncology residents from Yale to do a rotation in the local facility had been turned over to someone else; he was no longer part of anyone's plans for the future, and though he still tried, as hard as he could, to keep his mind busy with thoughts of the projects he had set in motion, the past kept breaking into his dreams.

Sometimes the memories that returned to him—snow on mountains, disturbances of light—were not even his own. Those vast receding vistas of high peaks must be out west, yet he had never, after all, gotten to the Rockies. Those scenes that came to him at night were from his childhood fantasies, or else the ones Louisa had described, on the day they'd gone to Bear Mountain.

He had wanted to stay home and get through Mr. Starin's paperwork that day, but he had conceded, knowing that she had a right to his company, that all over the world husbands took their wives to the country on Sundays. And so they had taken the bus upstate, with their lunch in a picnic basket she'd bought specially for the occasion—a lunch that turned out not to contain any napkins, or salt for the hard-boiled eggs, or anything to drink. The bus had dropped them off in front of a drugstore with a CLOSED sign on the door, on a sunny Main Street deserted except for a little cluster of people on the church steps, the women with flowers or fruit on their hats, the men shifting impatiently from one foot to another as their more garrulous wives formed a little circle around the minister. But just a few streets away there were woods, as she had promised, and green hills, and the gurgle of a stream. When they reached its banks she took the picnic basket from him, spreading out a cloth on the grass, but as she was unpacking their lunch she stumbled on her impractical high-heeled sandals and dropped the cucumber sandwiches in the foamy water. She turned to him then with a look of pure dismay, her mouth a round tragic O, and suddenly laughter welled up in him; the wind was rustling the branches overhead, the sun was making patterns on the grass, and they both stood there helpless with laughter. The happiness he felt in that moment was almost like pain.

"Is this what the West looks like?" he had asked her later, lying with his head on her lap.

"Oh, no," she'd said, stroking his hair. "It's much more majestic. And it doesn't look like the Alps, either, though I thought it would. I thought it would be something like Oberaudorf. But nothing could have prepared me for that landscape. Even with everything that was going on, even knowing I was going to run away, I couldn't stop looking out the window."

"Then tell me what it was like," he'd said, with a sudden stab of envy.

"I can't. I can't describe it."

"Try."

Her fingers had stopped moving. "It felt like the cleanest place on earth. As though no other human had ever been there, as though nobody had ever put a foot on that ground, or even breathed the air. It felt as though you were looking at God. As though the world had just been born that day."

Another night he had a dream in which the other Louisa, the clumsy one from after the operation, sat on a lumpy bed in a room with red-flocked wallpaper; a dog was whining outside the door to be let in. This was not his own memory either. Otto had visited Louisa when she was staying in a rooming house in Reno, waiting for the divorce to come through, and written to him.

"She hasn't said a word against you," Otto wrote. "She hardly speaks at all. She just sits alone in that ugly little room.

I try to imagine what you say to yourself, how you justify this total destruction of a human life, and I can't come up with any answer."

He had just asked Connie to marry him when the letter came. It was spring, the time for new beginnings. Connie had told her family that his wife was crazy and had to be put away, that he was still deeply in debt for her care, which was why they'd decided to wait awhile to marry. (In fact, it was the loan for the surgeon's fee that he was paying off.) All her sisters and sisters-in-law were specially nice to him on that account, pressing food on him and asking solicitously after Emma, though the men of the family were sullen and watchful, addressing him only to ask for the pepper or the gravy and excusing themselves from the table to go smoke together on the stoop as soon as the meal was over. Probably they did not want their sister marrying a Jew, a divorcé, a foreigner. So he sat with the women among the coffee cups, embarrassed by their sympathy but unable to deflect it without telling them more than seemed advisable. He tore up Otto's letter without answering it.

When Sharon returned, and asked him once more if he was sure there was nothing he wanted, he tried to imagine telling her about Louisa, what he had done to Louisa. She would listen with all her young gravity; when he had finished, she would tell him, no doubt, that he was a good man, he must forgive himself, that being the only wisdom she knew. But he was not looking for absolution.

"You're going to have phantom pains," she said. "Have they told you about them? How you'll feel pain in the leg that isn't there any more?"

Yes, he said, they had explained all that.

"Okay then. You really ought to get some sleep."

He would try, he said. She probably thought his sleeplessness stemmed from simple dread: the next time he lost consciousness, on the operating table, he would awaken with one leg; the phantom pains would begin. But at least, as he'd told her, they'd warned him about those. Nobody had prepared him for the sort he was feeling now.

CHAPTER THREE

After Emma left on Mother's Day—it was the one time she switched her visit to Sunday—Mrs. Rafferty went on silently drinking the sherry she had pressed on them until, by the time she would usually have been making supper, her shoulders were heaving under her print housedress. Tears were running down her face, which she wiped away with the back of her hand.

Louisa had often seen her the worse for drink—since the other residents left, it had happened with some regularity—but usually she became argumentative, and then grew maddened by Louisa's failure to fight back. Louisa could not remember ever seeing her cry. She went and patted her awkwardly on the shoulder, feeling, as she did so, the muscle there. It had been years since she had been called upon to play the role of comforter.

She reached into her sleeve and pulled out the rumpled Kleenex she always kept there, which Emma was always telling her to throw away. But Mrs. Rafferty ignored this. "Oh, I'm a fool," she said, and then, as though the sound of it had satisfied her, "a fool." She took an identically crumpled tissue from the pocket of her housedress and blew her nose. "You don't know," she said in a thickened voice, "how much I loved that child. I used to be so happy when she'd come to stay. God forgive me, but after my sister's husband went off I had some of the happiest times of my life. She couldn't always look after Betsie, you see, she used to work those big parties, they went on half the night sometimes, over on Park Avenue, she'd come to pick her up in the mornings with such lovely food in her bag, you wouldn't believe how much those rich people just left on the tray, she told me. Little canapés with swirls of cheese and more shrimp than anyone could eat. And teensy petits fours with four layers in 'em, still sitting in their ruffled paper." She blew her nose again.

"Mr. Rafferty was alive then, of course, and he'd play cards with her after dinner, old maid and things like that, or chutes and ladders, I'd have to break it up and make her go to bed, she'd plead and plead to stay up later, and he was as bad as she was, he'd never say it was time she went off. 'This child needs her sleep,' I'd say, and he'd wink at her and say she could sleep at school. How she used to laugh at that. But finally she'd let me take her upstairs—she always slept in the room you have now—and after her bath I'd listen to her prayers and tuck her in. Those were the best times of all, after she'd gone to sleep, when I'd get on with the darning, or busy myself in the kitchen, with such a sense of richness, just thinking of her upstairs. Knowing she was there."

"You haven't heard from her?" Louisa asked gently.

"No. Not since that day she was supposed to come and she canceled."

"She's just young, that's all. Young and thoughtless. Or busy with her own life. I'm sure she'll call you soon."

"I don't want her to. I never want to speak to her again."

"You don't mean that."

"It's all very well for you," Mrs. Rafferty burst out. "You're lucky. Your daughter comes every week. How would you feel if there was nobody on earth who belonged to you? You think about it." Rising unsteadily from her chair, she seized her sherry glass and headed for the kitchen with a heavy tread, her retreating back eloquent with grievance. Meanwhile Louisa went on standing there, her own eyes prickly with tears. It wasn't the malice in Mrs. Rafferty's voice that had upset her; it was the glimpse of a loneliness so vast that even she could be regarded as lucky.

Two months after the surgery, when he was due to be fitted for a prosthesis, the surgeon phoned and asked him to come to his office. He knew what that signified: the last X-ray had revealed more cancer in the stump. So it was over.

"Is it really necessary that we do this in person?" he asked the man. "I've got my West Coast managers coming in this afternoon." He had returned to work only that week, hobbling around on crutches; it would be too onerous to haul himself downstairs and into a cab, then haul himself out again at the other end, only to hear his death sentence.

"It's just I'm afraid I've got bad news," the surgeon said, and told him what he already knew. After they'd hung up, Rolf sat staring at the phone for a minute, noting for the first time ever the exact contours of its plastic casing—noting also, dispassionately, that now his fate was certain he felt none of the elation that had been there when the idea first arose. What he felt was only fear. But a minute later he picked up his pen and made a note about the figures for the West Coast.

That evening he phoned Emma, while Connie slammed doors in the kitchen, all her anger now being turned on inanimate objects. When he'd told her the news, she had cursed at the Duncan Hines cake she'd been baking for the members of the hospital board, who still consulted him on matters pertaining to the new oncology unit, and had been due to arrive in a few hours. He did not tell them about the cancer; he concentrated on the linear accelerators instead, steadying his mind on the organizable facts. Number one, he said, number two, number three . . . Somebody has got to determine how many radiation physicists we will require.

How were things going at work? he asked Emma, and she told him, sounding wary, that it looked as though she'd have to find another job. Mr. Eath, she said, was running out of funding. But she had answered an ad for an editor's job at a college textbook publisher; she had an interview scheduled for the following week. He asked her the name of the publisher, and what sort of textbooks they published, and wished her luck. Then he told her.

As with Connie, the news seemed to enrage her. "But how could this happen?" she asked, her voice rising. "How could it?"

"There's no point asking why. It happened, that's all."

"But why did they put you through all that, why did they amputate your leg, if the cancer was only going to come back?"

"They couldn't know that. They did what they considered best."

She was almost shouting now. "You said that with the chemotherapy too. And the radiation. You always stick up for them."

"Are you suggesting that they deliberately deceived me?"

"I think they used you. I think they wanted to see if it

would work, but they didn't really know, and they pretended they did."

"That's very far from being the case. Nor is it very flattering to me. Nobody lied to me. They told me right from the beginning what the risks were."

"But they never told you it could come back so fast, did they? Not in eight weeks."

He could not remember any more, except that one of the doctors had said, "All I can tell you is, if it was me, I'd do it."

"It doesn't matter," he said, exhausted by all the passion being expended on his behalf. "It's just one more punishment."

"Punishment for what?" she asked, and now she really was shouting. "For what? What are you talking about?"

He cleared his throat; he was about to change the subject, to question her further about the textbook publisher. Where were the offices located? Would she be working with philosophy books? Instead, something else came out. "You know very well what I'm talking about," he said. After that she was the one who changed the subject.

CHAPTER FOUR

"Poor Emma," Khim had said once. "Poor Emma. She will be trying to understand death." He was lying on his back in bed, smoking one of his infrequent cigarettes, a Dunhill from a red-and-gold box.

"No I won't," she said, feeling accused. They had made love a few minutes before; now she sensed a shift in his mood. His upper lip, which curled over the filter each time he inhaled, looked cruel and taut.

"Nothing wrong if you do. Only I pity you." He swung his legs over the bed, stubbing out the cigarette in the bronze ashtray on the floor. "I go make us some tea and we can talk philosophy."

That was one of his recurring teases, that all she really liked him for was to argue philosophy with: "Such a serious girl. The first time you came to my office, about the job, I said to myself, this woman is much too high-minded for me, she will think I am a very frivolous person."

"You didn't really think that."

"Yes, I did. In your gray dress, like a Quaker. Then I looked at your résumé, I saw that you had been to graduate school in philosophy. Aha, I thought, she has a rich daddy, she has been trying to discover the nature of good."

"That's horrible."

"Not at all. Besides, you do have a rich daddy."

She had told him early on, when her father first got sick, that she might have to work irregular hours sometimes, so she could go to the hospital in Connecticut during the day; she would make up the time in the evenings, she said, if he didn't mind.

"Of course you can," he said, "goes without saying," watching her with that concentrated stillness that always unnerved her. Then he asked her what sort of man her father was.

"He's like a monument," she'd said flippantly. "Like an old-fashioned bank with pillars." Khim looked disapproving, as she'd known he would.

She used to go to the office directly from Grand Central, on those days she went to visit her father; she knew Khim's schedule, she knew when he was taking Mr. Seng out to dinner and would be safely gone by seven. Mr. Seng was the most demanding of the authors, he phoned almost daily to complain of something, but he was the only one Khim spoke of with respect. The others he called ungrateful, unrealistic: "They are lucky to be published at all. Where does money come from for these books?" She didn't know, she said. "Cultural agencies who finance press are certainly getting funding from CIA. Nobody else is caring about Cambodia now. Is miracle these writers being paid for such books no one is wanting." But Mr. Seng, he told her, was a true scholar, a man who had devoted his life to the study of the carvings at Angkor Wat. However frustrated he became at the stream of angry words issuing from the phone, however much he shook his fist in the air as Mr. Seng was berating him, he went on taking him to dinner week after week—in order, he said, to make sure the man got something decent to eat.

When she got to the office on those evenings she would begin conscientiously, sitting at her desk in the little alcove with her red pencil in hand. Sooner or later, though—unable to focus on the laws pertaining to agriculture in Cambodia in 1954, or defeated by the sheer impenetrability of the prose— she would get up and stand in the doorway to Khim's office, as though the polished desk with its brass drawer pulls and square crystal inkwell, the gray velvet couch, the carved chair, the lacquered cabinet, contained the answers to some urgent question she had not formulated yet.

A Giotto print hung behind the desk: a luminous angel standing with bowed head among the shepherds, against a sky so blue it seemed to eat up sunlight. It had disconcerted her the day she'd gone there for her interview, as Khim himself had disconcerted her—the fierce straightness of his back, his hands and mouth and gleaming hair, his very elegant tie that did not fit with her ideas, such as they were, about Cambodians. And then the furniture did not belong in that room; green paint was peeling off the walls of his office, and the radiators were chipped and rusty. She had felt clumsy, off balance, the whole time.

One night when she was alone in the office she went and opened the top drawer of his desk, very quickly, as though it were not herself but someone else who was doing it. She told herself she was only curious to know how old he was. It was so difficult to tell. There might be a passport in there, a visa application. In fact all she found were paper clips, some pencils with blunt ends, a cheap fountain pen, and an envelope containing a single, heavy sheet of paper covered with characters she could not read.

One day in February when her father was being irradiated with a new sort of machine at the New Haven hospital, she just caught him, as she entered, gripping the rails of the bed, his head thrown back, his teeth bared in a grimace of pain, but when he saw her he let his hands drop and said, "Well, well, look who's here," in that labored, hearty voice he adopted for her visits. He brushed aside her questions about the treatment and asked her instead what manuscript she was working on at the moment, what Mr. Eath thought of the latest news from Laos; he always inquired respectfully about Mr. Eath's views on the situation in Indochina.

It was not what she'd wanted to talk about with him. But there was no way in, there was never a way in. She found herself telling him, in phrases as stilted as his own, about the sixteen-year-old guerrilla fighters in the Cambodian countryside and the shockingly low rate of literacy among Cambodians under French rule. He nodded gravely, with seeming deep interest, gripping the rail of the bed again, until his knuckles were white; he shut his eyes and then opened them quickly, as though not to be caught out. She went into the white-tiled bathroom to refill the Styrofoam pitcher by his bed, and as she came out a spasm passed over his face.

"What happened to the prince's brother?" Sweat was pouring down his forehead.

"He went to France. Shouldn't I go ask someone to give you a painkiller?"

He shook his head. Without his glasses, his eyes looked soft and milky, the eyes of a ruminant animal. Until he got sick, she had never known that his eyelashes were longer than hers. It seemed the most intimate thing she had ever discovered about him.

"I don't see why you're torturing yourself like this."

"Don't you?" he said mildly. "Well, I'd like to cling to the remnants of my mind just a little longer." He had listened to a program on QXR that morning, he told her, his breath coming in gasps, about old people in the city whose rents were taking up most of their Social Security checks. The reporter said some of them were living on cat food. From there they got onto the subject of health insurance.

That same evening Khim arrived back unexpectedly at the office, very formal in a dark overcoat and a pale gray silk scarf. "Silly man did not show up," he said crossly.

"I'm almost at the last chapter of the Seng manuscript," she told him, but he ignored this.

"You have been crying."

"A little."

"More than a little. You visited your father today?"

"Yes."

"Come into my office. I give you something to drink." She followed him in, and he gestured toward the velvet couch. "Please be seated." He hung up his overcoat and scarf in the closet before going to the lacquered cabinet and taking out the Scotch. Even for him, the tie he wore was exceptionally beautiful: lush-looking white silk, with a pattern of deep pink peonies and dark leaves. Some woman gave him that, she thought.

He handed her a heavy crystal tumbler and sat in the carved chair opposite with an identical glass. She noticed how his upper lip curled over the rim, seeming to grip it, as he drank.

"Your father had the radiation?"

"Yes."

"And how is he now?"

"He's not very well."

"What did you speak about with him?"

"About the literacy rate in Cambodia in the fifties. And the prince's brother."

"Surely this is not his main interest."

She shrugged. "No. We talked about the homeless too, and old people eating cat food. He said it was tragic that the richest country in the world can't manage to provide health care for its citizens."

"And this is always how you talk?"

"Yes. We used to talk about Watergate a lot. He was fascinated by the hearings."

Khim gave a sharp nod of approval. "I too. To me they seemed the best of America, not only worst. Showing is true democracy after all."

"That's what my father said."

"Good. Americans must recognize this more. Not just the corruption, but that they expose it."

"My father isn't exactly an American. I mean, he is now, but he was born in Germany. He came in the thirties."

"Ah. An immigrant, like me." He laughed, a harsh cawing sound. "Maybe I could understand him better than you."

"Maybe," she said sullenly, looking down at her glass.

"You hardly drink anything."

"I don't really drink very much."

He nodded in satisfaction. "That seems to be true of many Jews, I have noticed. Correct?"

"I think so."

"You see, I did not know that you were Jewish, until you said your father was coming from Germany in thirties. Then I assume it. I did not think that Jews had this color of hair. Auburn, yes?"

"Yes. I inherited it from my mother."

"Is your mother as well Jewish?"

"Yes."

"So this must be why you hardly sip at your drink. Or maybe it is because you are alone here with me."

"Of course not," she said. "That's got nothing to do with it."

"No? It would be only natural, after all." He stood up. "Shall I take you to supper? Your crying will have made you hungry."

They went to a small French restaurant on Twelfth Street, where the headwaiter bowed and greeted him by name. "Are there no Cambodian restaurants?" she asked, when they were seated.

He gave her an ironic look. "Not enough of us here yet. In later years, maybe."

"All those things Mr. Nimol wrote in his book . . . the cadres of sixteen-year-olds marching into villages and killing the women and children, the training camps in the jungle . . . that's all true?"

"Yes. Too many eyewitnesses now to say it's lies. People who escaped."

"But you got out before all that?"

"I am like Mayflower immigrant, for Cambodian. Came five years ago." He took a sip of his water and leaned back, watching her closely. "When they kill my father." Then he snapped his fingers expertly at the waiter, who came hurrying over. After that he became very merry, teasing her for what he claimed was her air of noblesse oblige. "When you came to my office that day, I say to myself, this woman thinks of work as moral obligation, not for money. Something for the greater good."

"That's not fair," she said, stung. "I absolutely need the money."

"It is nonetheless how you appeared. Nothing wrong with that." He too had studied philosophy, he told her, when he was at the Sorbonne; he too had abandoned his graduate studies, and returned to Cambodia. Why had he quit? she asked him. "Because it was gobbledygook. I was like you, wanting to know the nature of good. I supposed my professors would be gods of enlightenment, showing me true path. Imagine!" He blew on his soup. "They were little monkeys, those men, only posturing. But real disillusionment was with myself, for thinking such questions were important. Good does not matter. Has no power."

"But it survives," she said. "It may not win, it may never win, but it can't be killed, either. Not completely."

He looked at her expressionlessly for a moment. "Maybe you are right. Maybe you are quite wise after all." Some giddiness of sorrow seemed to fill the space between them, that felt remarkably like happiness. Then he leaned across the table and brushed a crumb of coquilles St. Jacques from her upper lip.

Later he walked her back to her apartment. As they crossed Astor Place and headed east, he stopped, frowning around him at the sagging storefronts and the grimy-looking people on the pavement, vaguely Dickensian in their tattered clothing and long greasy hair. Two sunken-chested men in bright bell-bottomed trousers edged them out of the way, springing along on their skinny legs, laughing the high manic laugh of speed freaks. "Your father would not like you to live in such a neighborhood," Khim said sternly, the first of what would be many references, over the next few months, to her father's wishes as he divined them: her father would want her to wear pretty dresses, he wanted her to achieve something with her life, he would not approve of her swearing. When they turned onto her block, a bum who sometimes slept in the vestibule of her building, a grizzled man with many filthy scarves wound around his neck, veered toward them and asked her accusingly what she was doing with a Jap. She felt Khim stiffen by her side, and when she turned to look at him his face was stonier than ever. Then she pushed open the door to her building, and he followed her up the dingy stairs.

When he stepped toward her, inside the apartment, she had a moment of panic: she had never planned on this, never wanted it, she must not allow it to happen. The bed was right opposite the door, a few steps, which they took clumsily, in lockstep. He was squeezing her too hard. And then suddenly it was exactly what she wanted, the only thing, as though her body had been waiting for him all her life. They stood apart to shed their clothes, and when they lay down images tumbled through her head, of a river, trees, some place left behind a long time ago, long forgotten; the current gathered force; the sounds coming from her were not her own. By the end there was not a single bone in her body, only blind heat, and his breath moving through her.

Afterward she wanted to go on touching him, when she stroked his skin the pleasure was so acute she had to shut her eyes, but he moved away and lay silent, his arms folded under his head. She withdrew her hand as though he'd slapped her.

"Don't be expecting too much," he said after a minute.

"What do you mean?" But she knew very well what he meant.

"You must not rely on me too much." You might have mentioned that before, she wanted to say, in a sudden flare of anger. Or even, which he would mind more, you seem to have mastered the New York clichés. But she didn't trust her voice. A moment later the sound of his breathing told her he was asleep.

It was the only time he came to her apartment. After that they always went to the handsome, clean, boxlike room, high above the city, that he had furnished almost as a replica of his office: here again there was a carved chair, a gray velvet couch, a lacquered cabinet, a massive desk; but there was a table too, with two spindly French-looking chairs. The bed was a platform with a thin pad on it. The walls were painted a dull gold—the color, he told her, of the mud walls in the peasant villages of Cambodia. Windows ran all along one wall, but no sound entered from the junction of Broadway and Columbus below, the apartment was too high up for that.

Sometimes he would cook rice and dried fish for their supper and tell her stories of his childhood. His father had brought his mother a wristwatch from Phnom Penh, and Khim, never having seen such a thing before, had taken it apart to see how it worked and could not put it together again. It was the only time his father ever hit him. A young monk had fallen in love with his sister, and written her poems. Where is your sister now? she asked. The muscles of his face tightened; she thought he was going to say she was dead. But no. She was in Laos, he told her, and stood up from the table.

"Tell me about your father," she said.

"He was enlightened man, reformer, quite well known in region for this. So Communists try to get him on their side. When he refused, they kill him. End of story."

When he bit off his words like that, when his voice grew clipped and flat, she knew not to trespass further, she knew she was risking his anger. But it was at those times that his grief became a living presence to her; the whole atmosphere of the room seemed charged with it. It was as though he was carrying an overfull glass, holding it upright with immense vigilance, to keep its contents from spilling. Only she must not mention it, she must go on pretending not to notice, though she thought her heart would burst.

The other time he grew angry was when she criticized America. "This is merely the stupid fashion for your generation. You are only spoiled."

"For God's sake. Look at the horrors America has inflicted on your country. The illegal bombings. The destruction. The murders. How can you possibly defend it?"

All that had nothing to do with her, he said, over her protests. "You must be grateful for your own good fortune in being born here." He told her the story of a Latvian woman, newly arrived in New York, whom he had once taken to Macy's.

"But why you? How did you know her?" she interrupted, and he waved the question away. It seemed the woman from Riga, when she saw a dress she liked, meant to take it without trying it on; it had not occurred to her that the dress would come in more than one size.

"But that's just capitalism you're talking about," she said. "The glories of the capitalist system."

He scowled at her, folding his arms across his chest. "Is more than capitalism. More significant. Is choice, freedom."

And he reverted often to the subject of her father—his philanthropies, his plans for the liaison between the local hospital and Yale, his opinions on welfare reform and the missile defense—just as her father, on her visits to the hospital, went on inquiring respectfully about Mr. Eath's views on the situation in Southeast Asia or the latest debate in the UN.

Each of them nodded with evident satisfaction at what she told him, as though gratified to find his high opinion of the other confirmed. At such moments she felt a flush of pride at having brought them together, however incorporeally, however much she seemed to be excluded from their communion. On the train to Connecticut she sometimes imagined telling her father that she was in love with Mr. Eath, but when she got there he was so stately, so grave and majestic, that she could not drag the conversation down to the level of her personal life. Or her stepmother was cracking jokes with the nurse, or one of the doctors had dropped by with an article from the *New England Journal of Medicine*. In the end, through all her visits, she never told him about the room on Sixty-fifth Street, the gray velvet couch, the rice and dried fish. She never said that three, four, five times now Mr. Eath had called out in his sleep as she lay next to him, the same indecipherable words over and over, a hoarse cry that gave way to a scream.

She would seize him by the shoulders and shake him, terror making her rougher than she meant to be, and then he would turn to face the wall, lying rigid. A few minutes later, though, still without turning around, he might raise an objection to something she had said earlier in the evening: she was wrong about Fantastik, it had a very unpleasant odor. It wasn't strictly true that Wit of Silesia, back in the Middle Ages, had prefigured the ideas of the German transcendentalists. He would sit up in bed and point out some crucial distinction she had overlooked; she would sit up also, fighting back tears, longing to touch him but not daring to. He would speak about Fichte for a while, or Bishop Berkeley, until he turned grumpy and declared himself too tired to think—sounding accusing, as though she had woken him from a sound slumber to argue philosophical points.

One night when he had lain back down, and she was drifting off to sleep herself, he said, "Your father is not an American. You must not expect him always to speak out loud how he feels."

"I don't expect it."

"Yet you seem angry at him for speaking of homeless and Watergate. You are wanting confessions from him, like a sentimental film. You must arrive at forgiveness. He has suffered extremely."

"How do you know that?"

"I know. You should wear a dress when you visit him."

"Because of his suffering?"

"Because he will like it very much."

And she had done it, she had worn the gray Quaker dress on her very next visit, with a gauzy green scarf, and her father had told her how nice she looked, though she could not bring herself to report that to Khim. There were almost as many things she kept from Khim as from her father: that when she was alone in her apartment, for example, the thought of her father's death grew so huge that terror drove her into the streets in the middle of the night, to stride about crazily among the crazies until it was light; that the thought of Never was splitting open her skull.

She'd been going to tell him; she might have tried the night her father phoned to report the cancer in his stump. But by that time Khim was gone.

CHAPTER FIVE

*I*t was exactly a week since he'd disappeared. She had gone to the office as usual that Monday morning, having left his apartment at noon on Sunday to meet an old graduate school classmate at the Met, a sharp-faced Wittgensteinian now teaching at a college in Minnesota. As they wandered through the Impressionist collection Phyllis talked about the perfidy of her department chairman, who had urged her to propose a new multidisciplinary major and then, when the others objected, sided with them against her. "And wouldn't you know it, he teaches metaphysics. Metaphysicians never stick up for their principles. None of the analytical philosophers became Fascists; did you ever think of that?" She cocked her head at Cézanne's portrait of his wife. "So now of course everyone's against me, I'm going to have to fight like hell to get my contract renewed. The bastard. I could kill that bastard."

Her voice, made loud by agitation, echoed back from the marble walls; several people scowled at them. Emma suggested they walk in the park instead, it was such a nice day, and after they had stopped and bought pretzels and ice cream she told Phyllis about Khim. "You make him sound like Heathcliff or something," Phyllis said scornfully. Later they ate pizza on Bleecker Street and went to a Sibelius concert at NYU, for which Phyllis had complimentary tickets; when they parted, neither of them mentioned anything about staying in touch. She'd been intending to imitate Phyllis for Khim in the office the next day.

He'd never kept strictly regular hours, but he always arrived by ten. At ten past, Mr. Seng phoned and was outraged at not finding Khim there. She phoned him at home, and when there was no answer decided he must be on his way. By eleven, when she dialed his number for the sixth time, letting the phone ring and ring, she was imagining him felled by a knife, a gun, bound with rope, paralyzed by a stroke. At 11:05 she was driven to the expedient of phoning Mr. Seng, and asking him whether they had talked the day before. But Mr. Seng hadn't spoken to him since Saturday.

At 11:30, after letting the phone ring forty times, she concentrated on remembering—as though she were being interrogated by the police—if there had been anything unusual in his behavior the morning before. Had he seemed preoccupied, distressed, had he alluded to trouble of any kind? No, he had not. He had not even had a nightmare. He had made her tea, and they had listened to an Englishman on the radio who had written a book about the Second World War. He had told her how, when he first came to America, he had said *jolly good*, not knowing it was British.

At 11:52 she locked the office and headed for the subway. If he were simply ill, if he had unplugged the phone to get some sleep, then he would be angry at her for interfering, and angrier still because she would have to get the doorman, or the super, or the managing agent, to accompany her: he had never given her a key to his apartment. If they burst in to find him in his pajamas, throwing up, he would never forgive her. But surely if he had been ill, he would have phoned her.

When she got to his building, the doorman on duty was complaining about some unnamed person to a skinny, raddled-looking blonde with a dog under her arm; she waited until the woman had walked off before approaching him. This was the middle-aged man who had never acknowledged her in the months she had been going there— the younger ones said, hey, how ya doing, or winked at her as she went in and out. He let her deliver her whole prepared speech: how she worked for Mr. Eath, in 26D, who hadn't shown up at the office that morning, or called in, who wasn't answering his phone. "We're very concerned about him," she said primly, as though representing a whole army of Mr. Eath's employees. "We wondered if someone could go check on him."

"I know who you are," he said when she was finished, and then, his pale eyes full of malice, "Mr. Eath left for the airport early this morning. I got him a cab."

She backed away from him without a word; not until she was out on Sixty-fifth Street again, with the sun hot on her back, her jeans sticking to her legs—it was unseasonably warm, seventy-nine degrees and humid— did her brain begin catching up with what he had said. As she turned onto Broadway, she almost ran straight into a skinny boy wheeling a stroller, who yelled at her to watch where she was going. At Sixty-third Street a man on a scaffold shouted out, "How'd you like to sit on my face?" She kept going, kept going, noted green and red lights, stepped off curbs, crossed streets. Dimly, the sound of honking horns came through, and a man's angry voice; she was standing in the middle of Columbus Circle; she couldn't tell if the noises had been directed at her, but a middle-aged black man in a checked shirt took her arm and asked her if she was all right. "I'm fine," she said automatically.

"You sure?"

She nodded.

"No, you ain't," he said firmly, and guided her across the street.

In a third-floor window on the corner of Fifty-eighth Street was a large, dirty-looking sign that said Irving Samson, DDS. She could go and pay Dr. Samson to drill her teeth, to silence the screaming in her head. She had not asked the doorman which airport Khim had gone to; it might be that he was only on his way to Rochester, to Montreal.

Or he might be fleeing the agents of the Khmer Rouge, he might have gone to her apartment and be waiting for her, so that she could hide him. She began hurrying, faster, faster, sweat pouring from her. On Fifty-fifth Street she thought she saw him, ducking into a building, in a light-colored suit; on Forty-eighth he was there again, with gleaming hair; on Thirty-third a man with his shoulders and a flat brown face. But none of them had his stony grace.

None of them looked back at her, either. It was the others who kept looking, the pale mad-eyed man in Times Square shouting about Jesus, a man with a cigar and a fat hairy neck in the garment district, a Puerto Rican messenger boy: she could feel their gazes on her face, her breasts, her legs, her hair, and moved faster and faster, skimming the pavement. It seemed to her she had never been the object of so much male attention as she was on that walk, with everything sticking to her: her hair and the crotch of her jeans and her green silk top—grown dark, she knew, with the sweat that dripped from her breasts.

On her final sprint, heading east, she stopped in front of the Strand, where a book on the CIA was propped open in the window, and wondered if Khim could be a spy. If he was, she didn't know which side he was spying for. She still clung to the thought that he had sought refuge at her apartment; she clung to it even when she reached her building and he wasn't there, there was nothing in her mailbox, nobody in the vestibule. She wished the bum were hanging around, so she could ask him if anybody had rung her bell, but he had moved outside with the hot weather.

When she could no longer bear looking out the window of her bedroom she headed for the office again, where the phone rang several times, and she grabbed the receiver only to hear someone asking for Mr. Eath. She took three messages, forcing herself to attend, to write the numbers down correctly, so that he would have nothing to blame her for. She went through the Rolodex; she read half a paragraph of a manuscript about the departure of the French from Phnom Penh; finally she went and searched through Khim's entire desk, but there were only file folders, only contracts and printers' invoices and pamphlets about educational reform, except for that piece of heavy paper in the top drawer.

On Thursday, after lying on the floor all night with the radio next to her ear, arguing with herself about whether she existed, listening to people talk about their money problems and love problems and problems sleeping—she had discovered that she needed sound at all times—a letter arrived, not from Khim but from the offices of a foundation in Virginia whose name she could not remember hearing before. They regretted to inform her that the activities of the press would be suspended for the time being; she would be hearing from Mr. Eath himself shortly. In the meantime, they were prepared to give her a month's salary, with thanks for her services and best wishes for her future. They regretted any inconvenience this termination of employment might cause.

That was the first paragraph. The second one asked her to be at the office at ten on Monday, to meet with a Mr. Johnston, who would appreciate it if she could give him a list of authors to be notified and manuscripts to be returned. At that time, she could also give Mr. Johnston her key to the office. Once she had done so, the check would be sent to her within ten days.

After she had read it several times she dialed Khim's number again. Then she phoned Mr. Seng, whom she had not spoken to since Monday. She still thought he might know something she did not, that he might have some idea where Khim had gone. She had not considered that she would have to deal with Mr. Seng's own distress. What would become of him, he wanted to know, what would become of his manuscript, how would he pay the rent on his apartment in Queens?

Surely the Belling Foundation of Virginia would compensate him, she said, she would give him their address, so he could write them, but he was inconsolable. They might pay for the current manuscript, but what of his future, what was he to do, how to pay his rent, he would starve to death, what sort of work would anyone give him? He had been a professor, she remembered, he was an expert on the dancing Shiva, on the cult of Bhadeshvara. You must try the museums, she said desperately, you must try the Asia Society, but he hardly seemed to hear. Nor could she always understand what he was saying. It was true there were no very good job prospects for Mr. Seng, with his garbled English. He was sixty years old, he told her; he would wind up sweeping the floor in a grocery (at least she thought that was what he'd said). The small matter of a broken heart seemed minor in comparison, but she could not stop herself from asking him where he thought Khim might be. Immediately he broke into a fierce howl of outrage.

"No knowing, no caring. Couldn't caring less. I be there ten Monday morning."

On Saturday she went to her mother's. It was raining out, which cooled the air and would also keep them indoors; she would be spared from making a circuit of the park with Louisa, who tended to slow down, even to stop entirely, for no apparent reason, at various points along the way, as though she had forgotten they were meant to be moving. And then the air itself would seem to hang motionless, closing in.

Mrs. Rafferty ushered her into the front parlor, lowering her voice conspiratorially as she told her that Louisa had hardly been out that week, a recurring theme. But for once she was glad of Mrs. Rafferty's presence; it was easier, when Louisa had been summoned, to sit back and let Mrs. Rafferty's words roll over her. All that was demanded of her was an occasional nod, a murmur here and there. Mrs. Rafferty, growing expansive, harked back to her trip to Switzerland with her husband in 1938: how pure the air had been, how spanking clean the houses, and the lovely sound of the bells echoing in the valleys.

But finally, well satisfied, she stood. Goodness, how she had been going on, she said as she gathered up their cups; she guessed Emma hadn't come there to listen to her; she knew how precious their time together was.

"So what have you been reading?" Emma asked, in an unnatural voice, when Mrs. Rafferty had gone. She had forgotten to prepare any stories for her mother, those humorous little anecdotes, tinged with absurdity, with which she usually set the tone on these visits.

Louisa gave her an uneasy look. But she told Emma about her latest find at the Goodwill store, a historical novel about the mother of Richard III. "She was a very nice woman," she said firmly, as though Emma might argue with that. When she was a child, Emma used to read such novels herself, on her visits to her mother; sometimes they would sit next to each other in the room upstairs, both of them with fat, slightly mildewed hardbacks on their laps. Emma had found the look of those yellowing pages, covered in dense print, soothing in themselves, even when she couldn't keep track of who was intriguing against whom.

"Is there news of your father?" Louisa asked now, in a frightened voice. She must have interpreted Emma's odd demeanor as a sign that something bad had happened.

No, no, Emma told her, he was fine, doing very well; he was going to be fitted for a prosthesis that week. After that she rose and said they might as well go upstairs.

This was the room where Emma had been happiest as a child—where, in the days when Aunt May used to drop her off, she had sung at the top of her voice and whirled around and around and clutched her mother's knees to steady herself. Then, when she was three, came the next phase, the era of Connie, when Aunt May was sent packing (Emma was forbidden further contact with her, because, Connie said, she had been rude and disrespectful to her, and dirty besides). After that it was her grandfather who fetched her and brought her to Mrs.

Rafferty's. By the time of the move to Connecticut, some years later, Emma was deemed old enough to take the train into New York by herself to spend the day with her mother.

When she was ten, eleven, twelve, she used to plunder all Louisa's treasures—her old dresses, her bits of jewelry, her shoes—in the sure knowledge that however she behaved, however bossy or disobedient or willful she was, her mother would do whatever she wanted. She would take Louisa's green silk dress out of the closet and teeter around in the satin sandals she'd found in a box under the bed, while Louisa pleaded with her to be careful and she tossed her head to show she wasn't scared; she would go into the tiny bathroom and smear her mother's Woolworth's lipstick all over her cheeks. Then, having tied an old silk scarf around her waist, she would fetch the photograph album from the cupboard and demand that her mother tell her stories about the people in its pages: there was the frail little boy she had taught in England, and his distinguished-looking parents, sitting on a sloping lawn with statues, rimmed by thick hedges. On another, flatter lawn young men in baggy trousers and girls in sleek belted dresses lolled beneath a rose-covered trellis. All of them, in those black-and-white photos, looked startlingly pale, while the bushes were dark and luxuriant; she'd had a sense, when she was a child, that in England the foliage was more vibrant than the people.

But the stories she liked best were the ones from later on, when her father appeared, rescuing Louisa from mishaps involving overdrawn bank accounts, unwanted suitors, picnics drowned in muddy water. The man in those stories was ready to be coaxed into laughter, infinitely teasable, tolerant of others' mistakes. She had sensed that her mother had not been so powerless back then as she was to become, that she had not been afraid of him, not at all.

That afternoon she did not feel like mending the broken cup that stood on the little table, she did not feel like dusting the collection of objects on top of the dresser (despite her admiration for the Swiss, Mrs. Rafferty had never paid much attention to housekeeping). It was then that Emma remembered the photographs, which she hadn't seen in fifteen years. "Let's look at your pictures," she said in a sprightly voice, going to the rickety pine cupboard in the corner. The album was on the bottom shelf, still in its peeling white-and-gold box with one broken corner. Some of the glue had gone brittle, and the tiny snapshots on the first few pages were loose. But there they all were, the young man named Julian featuring in the first four pictures, her mother's blond, solemn young charge standing very upright next to a carved chair, in short pants and a sailor blouse. And there was Louisa herself, her hair tucked behind her ear on one side, her Botticelli mouth split wide into a tomboy's grin, holding up her glass to the camera. She seemed, in retrospect, to have been courting disaster with that smile of hers—flaunting herself heedlessly before fate, unmindful of the dangers ahead.

The pages that followed showed the apartment on Bogardus Place, some of its furniture familiar to her from her mother's room at Mrs. Rafferty's. Here there were more pictures of Louisa, less blurry than the English ones, as though they might have been taken with a better camera, and several of Otto, who still came from California once a year to visit her mother. But although the hallway of the apartment and the boxy kitchen and the cupboard from which she had just fetched the album

were all carefully recorded in black and white, as though someone had wanted to document them for posterity, her father was
absent, appearing only after several pages showing the living
room from various angles. It was her parents' wedding photograph; she could not remember ever seeing her father smile
like that, as though about to levitate from sheer giddy happiness. Quickly, she turned the page to see what came next, but
there was no next. The rest of the album was empty.

Mr. Seng was waiting for her outside the building on Monday
morning, a thickset, grizzled-looking man in a woman's pink
polyester blouse and baggy khaki trousers that didn't quite
cover his ankles. "I'm so sorry," she said, holding out her
hand. "Have you been waiting long?"

He glared and told her yes, he had. Together they went
upstairs, she in front, he following closely behind. This is the
last time I will climb these stairs, she thought. I'll never see
the Giotto print again, or the velvet sofa.

Then she remembered the piece of paper in the top drawer,
the one with the beautiful calligraphy. As soon as she opened
the door she went to fetch it from Khim's office. Meanwhile Mr.
Seng was standing by her desk in the alcove, scowling at the
bookshelves, with their neat rows of the press's English books,
all bound in blue and white. He took down a volume on the
Cambodian legal system, the first manuscript she had worked
on for the press, and made a disgusted face as he read the name
of the author. "Who getting this man write such book?"

"I really don't know. I suppose it was Mr. Eath." She
thrust the heavy sheet of paper at him. "Can you tell me what
this says?"

He took it from her and began reading. Then he looked up. "Where you find this?" he asked sternly.

"In Mr. Eath's desk. I thought maybe it would explain things."

Without a word, he carried it into Khim's office, replacing it in the top drawer and slamming it shut. Then he returned to the alcove. "Private. No should reading."

"But if it's private, mightn't it tell us something about where Mr. Eath has gone? That's why I wanted you to read it."

He shook his head decisively. "Nothing where gone. Private." Before she could stop herself, she seized him by the wrist, shouting at him that he had to tell her, she had to know.

He shook her off, and for one strangely intimate moment they stood glaring at each other, until understanding dawned in his face. She could feel herself blushing; it seemed the final humiliation that Mr. Seng should pity her. "I'd better check the files," she muttered, turning away and opening the cabinet in the corner. A little later Mr. Johnston arrived.

He was trim and tan and imperturbable, keeping up a constant flow of talk that allowed for no interruption: about his journey, about the heat, the government, what a pleasure it had been to read the press's publication. Of course he remembered Mr. Seng, he had read his work with great interest, and as for Emma, he had heard excellent reports of her, clearly she had been an invaluable contributor to the important work they were doing. But unfortunately he was in something of a rush; he would have liked to spend more time with them, but he had an eleven o'clock appointment uptown—"Fellow I'm going to see will chew my ear off, but he's a fine man, a little lonely, I'm afraid, retired now and not much to occupy him.

Used to be quite a muck-a-muck." So if she'd turn over the keys, he'd just lock up and be on his way.

Meanwhile he was looking around Khim's office, nodding to himself. Didn't he want the files? she asked, and he told her a colleague of his would probably be coming in the next week or so to clear things out. "I'm just what you might call the advance man," he said genially. He looked at his watch. "I'm afraid I really must get going."

But Mr. Seng was not so easily deterred. He blocked Mr. Johnston's path. "Must be paying me," he said. "I coming here to get what earned for books."

Mr. Johnston looked from him to Emma and back again. "Now, I'm really not the fellow you need to talk to," he said, slightly less genially. "I'm not the man who signs the checks." Mr. Seng began talking again, loudly and indignantly, and Mr. Johnston held up his hand. "If you'll just give me your details, I'll make sure you're paid whatever you're owed. The last thing we want to do is cheat anyone."

Mr. Seng looked at Emma, who told him, "He wants your address. He's going to send you money." She went to the battered Rolodex on her desk. "I've got it here," she said, and flipped through the cards until she found it. Then she removed it and handed it to Mr. Johnston, who put it in his pocket without looking at it. "How will you know how much he's owed, if you don't take the files?"

"I'll ask my colleague to look into it." He went to the door and stood back, waiting for them. Silently, they left the office and waited as he locked up. Only then did it occur to Emma that this was the one person who might know where Khim had gone.

When they reached the street door, he went ahead and opened it, stepping aside to let her go through. But she didn't move.

"Can you tell me where Mr. Eath is now?"

He shook his head, not as Mr. Seng had done, but lightly, dismissively.

"I'm afraid not."

"Because you won't? Or you don't know?"

"I really have no idea where he is at the moment."

"If you did know, would you tell me?"

Now he smiled at her, a richly good-humored smile. "I'm sure you'll be hearing from Mr. Eath yourself very soon." She went on standing in the doorway, blocking his path. "But right now, I really must be going."

Then they were all outside; he shook their hands again, more swiftly this time, and stepped into the back of a gray car that was parked at the curb. The driver pulled smoothly away into the traffic, leaving Mr. Seng and Emma standing forlornly on the pavement, staring after it.

CHAPTER SIX

$\mathcal{I}$n the hospital room, Connie kept up a frantic stream of wisecracks, hurling herself at the unbroken silence like an animal scrabbling at bare earth. Every day, when Emma arrived, her stepmother's chair was drawn up close to the bed, her voice shrill with fear. "Look, hon, look what came in the mail yesterday, it says you're a million-dollar winner. You don't want to miss out on your million dollars, do you? Come on, wake up . . . I saw your friend Dr. Pappas in the elevator this morning. You don't believe he takes the elevator like the rest of us, right? You probably think he sprouts wings when he needs to go upstairs. I'm going to say that to him, he'll probably bust a gut laughing. And then he'll have to operate on himself, right? Serve him right . . . You know what you should do, you should write a letter to the board complaining about the crappy flowers the Garden Club put in the lobby, you wouldn't believe it, those ugly orange lilies like on the roadside, and cheap crummy little pansies someone must have wanted to get rid of. They ought to be ashamed of themselves, I swear to God it's enough to make the people sicker than they are already . . . Come on, honey, say something to this nice nurse here. She probably thinks you're a son of a bitch, not even thanking her after everything she's done for you. Toiling away. Double bubble toil and trouble, right? And you thought I wasn't cultured." And then, when the nurse was gone, "I bet half these birdbrains think you're a Nazi. What do they know, it's the only time they ever heard a German accent, in some war film. *The Great Escape* was on TV the other night. I was going to stay up and watch it, but I fell asleep before it started, and then I woke up all stiff from sleeping on the couch and it'd been over for hours. Just my luck. But that's okay, you're going to get a million dollars, right?"

She read him the advice columns in the local paper, and the recipe for pumpkin cheesecake, and even the fine print on the coupons for Grandma's Apple Pie ice cream. She waved get-well cards from the people at the office under his nose and told him about the multifloor shopping mall planned for the site of the old fairgrounds. Some hippies had tried to disrupt the groundbreaking ceremony, would you believe it? "They're going to have a Macy's and a Caldor's and a luggage store and every other goddamn thing. If you start behaving your-a-self I even a-take you to the opening." Emma, her teeth clenched together, her eyes fixed on her father's face, thought she saw him grimace in protest.

"What the hell are *you* looking at?" Connie snapped at her. For just a moment, things were back to normal: this was the old, authentic note of venom, unnervingly absent for the past few weeks. It was almost a relief to have it back. It meant they knew where they stood, they could look each other in the face.

"Nothing," Emma answered, as she had a thousand times in her childhood. "What are *you* looking at?" "Nothing." "I'll give you something to look at. I'll give you a black eye if you don't watch out." But now Connie seemed to have forgotten her lines; she only snorted ambiguously and turned back to the bed.

"Did I tell you about the big fat slob I saw yesterday, hon? Eating doughnuts in the coffee shop? You'd think they'd be embarrassed, eating that kind of shit in front of people when they're fat as a horse already." But her voice trailed off uncertainly. Turning to Emma, she gave a long, quivering sigh. "Okay. That's it for now. I've got to go eat something. Why don't you take over for a while? You haven't exactly been the life of the party." She thrust the newspaper at her. "Here. In case you run out of inspiration. If it's not highbrow enough for you, too damn bad."

Emma stared down at the headlines: "Four Arrested on Drug Charges." "Factory Closure Expected." "Employees Rescue Injured Hawk." She listened to Connie's high heels tapping their way down the hall. Then she went and shut the door as noiselessly as she could. When she turned back into the room, she suddenly felt her father's presence as powerfully as a taste, a smell—just as, when she was a child, waking from a nap, she had always known, even in the dark, if he was there with her.

Some time in the past few days, his face had become another man's, a cardinal's in a Renaissance portrait, all hollows and sharp angles, the mouth a thin slash, the nose a waxy slice of bone. Yet there he was, filling the space around him with his presence. His hand too, when she touched it, was still his own: warm and fleshy, pouched around the knuckles, the same hand that had been her safety when she was a child. She raised it to her face in a sudden spasm of remorse, pressing it against her cheek. "Daddy," she said, the old word, feeling, like a tremor in the air, the ache of his sadness, a soundless vibration she had been listening to all her life.

She had thought that when he was dying all those words they had never spoken would be said at last, all that tangled freight of blame and rage and hurt that had pressed down for years would dissolve. Now it was too late. Only her mother, in all that time, had ever cried, had ever spoken of something as simple as love. "I saw Mother the other day," she said, too loudly. "I told her you were dying, Daddy, I had to tell her. She sends you her love."

His breathing shifted, caught on a rasp, lightened. For a moment, as his eyelids flickered open, she was hurled back to childhood, expecting the stern voice in which he had told her that the principal had phoned to complain about her misconduct at school, or Connie had reported that she'd slammed the door in her face. *Do you know what happens to girls who cannot control their tempers?*

But no. Instead he said faintly, "You have nice eyes." His own had a stricken, pleading look that made her feel, as so often, that she had failed him. But she was still holding his hand against her face. Stiffly now, self-consciously, she turned it over and kissed it, and then she was back in the orchard in Bucks Harbor, with the smell of grass and rotting apples, the sun beating down on her head.

She was three years old; she and Aunt May had gone to Aunt May's house in Maine for the summer, to escape the heat of the city. There was no electricity in the house, so they went to bed when it was dark and woke when the sun came in the round windows of the upstairs bedrooms. There was no plumbing, either; Emma never quite conquered her fear of the outhouse, with its cobwebs and old birds' nests and eternal clouds of flies, but she had her own little seat there, the smallest of the row of three; Aunt May's husband had built it for their children when they were boys. On Sundays Aunt May went to the Baptist church down in Bucks Harbor, and Emma attended the Sunday school upstairs; she sang "Jesus Is My Sunshine," holding hands with the minister's daughter, and "Jesus Loves Me" as she and Aunt May walked back home along the cliff road. Seagulls circled over their heads; sometimes a gull strayed into the orchard; she could hear it screeching from her bedroom.

Twice Aunt May's new boyfriend, Enoch, who never spoke much, took them out in his boat, where Emma was not allowed to speak either; it would disturb the fish. She liked it better when Enoch came to the house and Aunt May made blueberry pancakes for supper, or he brought a batch of jelly doughnuts he had purchased in Cherryfield. Once they all made molasses taffy together in the kitchen; another time he fed Emma sips of his whiskey and she got up and danced on the table; Aunt May laughed so much she said she like to've peed her pants.

Every morning, Aunt May told her how many days it was before her daddy came to see her. She told all the ladies at church about the long train ride he'd be making, overnight from the city, the hours he would spend in the bus from Cherryfield, just to see his precious little girl. What a good, kind daddy she had, Aunt May said, sending her away for the summer, to escape the heat of the city, and then traveling all that way to see her. They had blueberry jam ready for his breakfast toast, made from berries they'd picked themselves in the marshes. Enoch was going to provide them with a big fat lobster.

And finally the day came; she woke very early, she woke Aunt May and insisted she dress her in her checked red

Sunday school dress and put a ribbon in her hair. It was hours before he'd arrive, Aunt May told her; she would only get dirty before he could see her. But Emma clung to her arm and wailed until she gave in. Once she had gotten her way, though, and she was dressed in her finery, she almost forgot about him. The dog from the house down the road, a brown cocker spaniel named Major, was sniffing around the porch, and she made him follow her to the orchard. They roamed up and down the long rows of trees until her shoes and socks were damp; at one point, out of sheer exuberance, Major jumped up on her and smeared the front of her dress with mud. When she scolded him, he ran away, and she went and sat on the rotting bench at the far end of the orchard, where she often practiced her hymn singing, and fell asleep. When she woke up she was hot and cranky and thirsty; she brushed herself off guiltily and started back to the house, thinking not of her father but of apple juice and blueberry muffins.

But as she reached the orchard gate, there he was, in a brown suit and hat, coming to find her. She ran to him, screaming *Daddy*, *Daddy*, her heart beating wildly with excitement, but when he lifted her into his arms a shock went through her; she felt as though she was entering another force field, the waves of sadness washing over her, almost knocking her back. Kicking frantically at his stomach, she shrieked to be let down, though once she was back on the ground she clung to his hand, sobbing, turning it over and over, kissing it the way Aunt May kissed hers when she had shut the cupboard door on it. She didn't want him to think she loved him any less, because it wasn't true, she loved him more than ever.

That was when she had first seen he was separate from her, there was something in him that had nothing to do with herself. And now he was retreating from her for good, into some alien majesty; as she listened to the ragged sounds issuing from his throat, a crazy elation rose in her, a thought of heaven, which might be only this, release from pain. His breath came harder and harder, as though he were battling to push all the air from his body, to arrive at the end; the sweat poured down his face, and his hand, when she squeezed it, was clammy and limp. "Sleep now, Daddy," she whispered, laying it on the sheet. "You really want to sleep."

Outside the window, the sky was a magnificent pink, a waxy crescent moon was rising over the town. In the corridor, somebody laughed; somebody else walked by on heavy feet; a machine was trundled through a doorway down the hall. But her father's room was silent except for the ticking of the cheap alarm clock by his bed. The vacant space around her seemed to be expanding minute by minute. She thought about the silence there would be in her apartment that night, when she returned to the city, and in sudden panic reached for the buzzer draped over the bed's railing, pressing it for a long moment before allowing it to drop.

The minutes piled up, the silence and emptiness swelled larger and larger. There were streaks of silver in the sky, and a dark blue shape like a mountain, with the moon lying over it. But still nobody came. Then the door opened, and Connie walked in.

"What's going on?" She looked suspiciously from the figure in the bed to Emma and back again. "What's been happening here?" Emma could not think how to answer her. She stepped aside, and Connie took up her old position, peering down at the bed.

"Did you read to him, like I told you?" But the newspaper was lying on the floor, forgotten; Connie swooped down and picked it up. "You didn't, did you? I bet you stopped the minute my back was turned." She thrust her face within inches of his, waving the rolled paper like a fan over his head, then flapping it next to his ear, as though to clear a passage. "Can you hear me, honey? It's okay. I'm back now. I'm here. Seems like my sister's kid is going to be a priest, can you believe that? Vinny, you remember him, right? I went home just now and saw we got an invitation for when he's ordained. Over his mother's dead body, I bet. Come on, honey, can you hear me now?"

There was a knock on the door, which Connie had left open; a stolid-looking young nurse with mournful brown eyes, whom Emma remembered from previous visits, was standing there. "Did you want something?" she asked, just as Connie flung aside the paper and threw herself across the bed.

"What am I going to do?" she wailed. "How am I going to live without him?"

The young nurse rushed over and picked up his hand, which had been dislodged by Connie's assault and was dangling over the side of the bed.

"Can you still feel his pulse?" Emma asked her.

"Oh, yes. It's very weak, but . . . yes. Please try to stay calm, Mrs. Furchgott," she said firmly. "You wouldn't want him to hear you, it might upset him."

"I can't help it," Connie said, on a shriek. "I can't go on without him, I can't do it."

The nurse and Emma exchanged glances; a signal seemed to pass between them then, a flash of understanding that illuminated whole acres of her father's marriage. But the moment passed, they dropped their eyes at the same time.

"Do you really think he can hear us?" Emma asked, and the nurse shook her head regretfully.

"Probably not. But hearing is always the last thing to go. If there's anything you want to say to him . . ." She hesitated. "It won't be long now." She was looking at Emma as though they were alone in the room, as though she were about to tell her something momentous. But all she said was, "He never complained, he never even said he was in pain." Emma nodded, waiting. "Some people don't, especially men, but then they don't talk about anything. He wasn't like that, he always talked to me, he remembered what courses I was taking and stuff like that. But never anything personal, you know?"

"Yes," Emma said. "I know."

"I guess he was real old-fashioned that way."

Suddenly Connie gave a howl. "Oh my God," she screamed, jumping up. "Oh Jesus God."

The nurse hurried to the bed; she felt his pulse again. "He's gone," she said to Emma. "I'm so sorry, but he's gone. I'd better get a doctor."

"Oh God, oh God, help me God," Connie sobbed, and then, in something closer to her normal voice, "Fat lot of good a doctor will do him now."

"It's the law, ma'am. A doctor has to pronounce him dead."

Connie slumped in the pink plastic chair near the window, breathing loudly. "Well, then, go ahead. Go on, get out of here." After the nurse had left, she told Emma to bring her purse, which she'd left on the vestibule floor. She blew her nose loudly, took out a gold compact, powdered her nose, and applied lipstick. Then, having smacked her lips together, she snapped the compact shut and turned to Emma.

"Have you got a decent black dress for the funeral, madam? Or are you going to show up in some kind of hippie crap?"

"Please," Emma said, and it came out like a command. "I'd like to be alone with him for a minute."

Connie's shoulders twitched; she thrust her chin forward, ready to do battle—to ask Emma who the hell she thought she was, to remind her that she, Connie, was the widow here, thank you very much. But Emma kept staring at her, stony-faced, until she faltered. They were both registering the loss of Connie's power. Without a word, with only a little snort that failed to convey conviction, she turned and headed for the door.

Emma shut it behind her before approaching the bed.

She bent over swiftly and kissed his forehead—the flesh not cold yet, but faintly rubbery, making her shudder. She wiped his sunken face with a tissue that was lying there, carefully, as though she were performing some ancient rite, but already her mind was splitting in two: thoughts of Khim were flooding in again, those repetitive, consuming thoughts she had held at bay for the past few hours. She had to tell him that her father was dead, and then he would explain it to her, he would make her understand. If she picked up the phone by the bed and dialed his number—she had not tried it for forty-eight hours—he would have to answer.

Only when a sleepy-looking young doctor appeared, wielding a clipboard, and said, "I just spoke to your mother out in the hall," did she remember Louisa, who would be sitting in the dark, waiting to hear. "As you may know, your father donated his eyes to the eye bank," the doctor said, "which means we don't have much time. Somebody's on their way to take him downstairs." For a moment the old anger flared in her again. He had donated his eyes, he had done the correct, the virtuous thing, and yet in all that time, all those months he was dying, he had never mentioned her mother. Not once. He should at least have told her good-bye, she thought. He could have given me a message. She looked down at him for the last time—the doctor was walking toward the bed, there was the rumbling of a gurney in the hall—and felt as though she were falling off the edge of the world. She remembered his breathing, and his hand against her face, and the sun in the orchard. But his face had become something final, unreachable; in the draft that entered when the door was opened again, the room felt empty already.

CHAPTER SEVEN

*B*ack at the house, the head of the company's Brazilian subsidiary was asking Emma about her job, by which he meant her job with Khim. Her father had been most interested in the work she was doing, he said. It was hard to imagine her father discussing her with this man, who looked unnervingly like a flamenco dancer, with his beautifully smooth skin and tiny feet, and kept nodding encouragingly at her, as though pitying her for more than just her bereavement. She could tell that, not having seen her since she was twelve, he was judging her as a woman and finding her wanting: he would require of females that they be confident, alluring, that they carry off all situations, even this one, with poise. He could not know how valiantly she was lying.

Still, he seemed intent on sticking by her, afraid, perhaps, that the alternatives might be even worse. Just behind him, on the blue satin couch, Connie was sobbing into the shoulder of the mayor's suit, while the mayor patted her hand; two of Connie's brothers were leaning on the bar, arguing in low voices that occasionally rose on a single word. The director of development for the hospital was deep in conversation with the superintendant of schools; everyone else was milling around uncertainly, eating canapés with a slightly furtive air, as though ashamed of displaying a normal appetite. The small contingent of elderly German Jews who'd attended the funeral had not been invited to this gathering, and perhaps they were relieved. They had looked dazed by the sheer volume of human traffic in the synagogue vestibule, the mourners surging toward Connie in twos, crowding around her, pressing her hand.

"Of course the Orientals have a very different view of women," the Brazilian said genially, watching her. "You don't find that presents any problems, working with them?"

No, she said, startled, and then added lamely that her boss had been educated at the Sorbonne.

"Excellent. So he won't demand perfect deference." He laughed, flashing very white teeth. "I'm sure you're a great help to them all." Over his shoulder, she could see that another of Connie's brothers had joined the two at the bar and seemed to be acting out a scene involving a homosexual; he was running his fingers pettishly through his thinning hair and turning his head from side to side, batting his eyelashes. When one of the company's vice presidents crossed the room to ask the Brazilian how long he would be in town, she excused herself and left, turning right in the hallway and heading for her father's study. Stealthily, she opened the door, closing it as stealthily behind her; she turned the little knob that would lock her in.

This was the room where in her adolescence she had been summoned to be lectured; here judgment had been handed down, her probable future in a correctional institution laid out before her. This was where the bad reports from school were handed to her across the desk, her stepmother's version of their latest skirmish recounted to her; here she was warned what happened to children who did not do their homework, lied to their teachers about it, could not control their tempers.

Who lies will steal. Who steals will kill. She would sit there, heart pounding with rage at the unfairness of it: why should Connie not be told to control her temper? He, who cared so much about justice when it came to the NAACP and the rights of defendants, was condemning her without benefit of a trial. And yet she could hardly bear that he should be angry at her, she had to dig her nails into her palms to keep from bursting into tears.

But it was also the one place where, just possibly, she might feel her father's presence. There were so few objects she could associate with him, so little of himself was imprinted on that house; everything in it spoke of Connie. Even here, the mock-wood paneling, the red-and-green plaid curtains, the Barcalounger where nobody had ever lounged, had no connection to her memories of him. But there were two faded prints on the walls, of Nuremberg; there were two rows of green and brown and maroon leather books on the fake-veneer bookshelf. She used to sit there, on the upright chair opposite the desk, and keep her eyes fixed on those books while her father was cataloging her sins.

She went and pulled one of the green volumes from the shelf; the cramped German print, full of capitals and curlicues, looked dense and somber, like the forest in a German fairy tale. All the green volumes, numbered through XXI, were Goethe, the brown ones were Schiller. She slipped out a maroon volume—Heine—and as she was replacing it felt it meet with some resistance.

A small padded envelope stood upright on the shelf; when she withdrew it—the label, from a mail-order company, bore Connie's name—she saw inside it a jumble of letters and one small square envelope with scalloped edges, like the stationery her mother had given her for her birthday when she was a child. She spilled out the contents on the desk: photographs that had been made up like postcards, on stiff board. Haher and Kirchgang, they said on the back, Freytag und Sohn, Nürnberg; while on the front, stout, bald, bulging-eyed men in pince-nez and stiff collars looked out mournfully. She stared at their faces, all unknown to her, feeling how final the gulf was between herself and them. Not one of the pictures bore the sitter's name on the back. She wondered if her grandfather was among them; she wondered if her mother would know. There was no telling what her mother would remember and what she would not.

She riffled through the letters, looking for one in English, but there was nothing. Then she replaced them in the padded envelope, and as she did so saw that there was something at the bottom, something small and hard, wrapped in blue tissue paper. When she fished it out, her own name stared back at her, in faded blue-black ink; the handwriting was like her father's, but smaller, spikier; ancient, yellowed Scotch tape had been neatly wound around the back. She turned the thing over, about to open it, when someone rattled the doorknob.

"What are you doing in there?" Connie hissed through the crack.

She clutched the parcel in one hand and gripped the edge of the desk with the other.

"You come out of there right now, you hear me?"

"I'll be out in a minute."

For a moment there was silence; it seemed possible that Connie would start shouting, or go fetch the key and storm in. Instead, she only said, "You better be," trying to pack the old menace into her voice but failing. Already Emma had forgotten about her; she was tearing the tape carefully off the little package.

A small cameo, edged in dull gold, a woman carved in ivory on its surface. Her hair was piled on her head in elaborate swirls, with long ringlets trailing along her neck. Her expression was serene to the point of blankness, her nose curved a little at the tip, her mouth distended in a semismile. Emma stared at it, turned it over, tested the sharpness of the pin on the back; then she looked again at the writing on the tissue paper: just the one word, her name.

She put it carefully in the pocket of her black silk jacket, along with the photographs; the letters she stuffed in her other pocket, patting down the bulge as best as she could. Then she deposited the padded envelope in the empty wastepaper basket and unlocked the door.

The guests were thinning out; the mayor was gone, and the head of the hospital board, and the Brazilian. There was a place vacant on the plaid couch, next to Connie's unmarried sister Maria, who had hugged Emma at the synagogue. "How are you doing, baby?" she asked, as Emma sat down. "You know how sorry I am about your dad. He was a real gentleman. You should be proud to have a father like that."

"I know," Emma said, and Maria took her hand and squeezed it. One Christmas when Emma was young, Maria had gotten a little drunk and said to her, "I bet your life is no picnic, huh? She was a real devil to me when we were kids."

Now one of Connie's brothers approached them. He sat down heavily on the couch, where there wasn't room for him. Emma wriggled closer to Maria. "I'm real sorry about your dad," he said then, breathing whiskey in Emma's face. "Always treated me right. Never made me feel like I wasn't good enough." Emma tried to smile. He took a gulp of his drink. "Not like you."

"Leave the kid alone," Maria said. "She doesn't need that kind of talk right now."

But he ignored this. "You always thought you were better than us." It wasn't even true. When she was ten she had had a crush on him; he had a little black mustache then, and an air of dangerous maleness that her father lacked; he looked like the dashing heroes of the movies her mother took her to at the Loews on Dyckman Street, during her Saturday visits. Once Connie had mortified her by yanking up her pajama top to show him how skinny she was.

He put his arm around her. "That's okay. You've turned into a real pretty girl, you know that? And you was such an ugly little kid." He was squeezed up very close to her, pressing against the pocket with the photographs of the sad-eyed men. As she sat there, trying to smile, she suddenly remembered the portrait of her grandmother's brother that had hung in Jeannette's living room on Park Terrace West. What had happened to it when her grandmother died? It had vanished, along with the dark mahogany wardrobes, the embroidered dish towels, the pearl-handled fish knives and fish forks in their plush-lined leather cases. She had been at college then, and her mother had sold the whole contents of the apartment to a local junk dealer. The portrait must have been included; she hadn't thought of it until now. There had also been a painted photograph, in an oval frame, of Louisa as a child. She was wearing a cloche hat, a polka-dot dress with a lace collar, and a pin at the front—a cameo. Suddenly she sat up, and Charlie's hand was dislodged from her shoulder.

"What's up now?" he asked sharply.

"Sorry. I just remembered something."

More people were taking their leave, kissing Connie on both cheeks, hugging her, telling her she should phone them if there was anything she needed. She had begun crying again; she clung to them, sobbing. "Take some of this food . . . take the salami, go on, that was Rolf's favorite, just the sight of it makes me cry." Emma sat watching her, outside the circle of sympathy.

A fat man who had worked for her father for years, before going to Union Carbide, was walking toward the door in his raincoat, his wife in tow. "Excuse me," she said to Charlie, and stood to intercept them. The man pressed her hand, his wife said how very sorry they were, what a fine man her father had been.

"Do you think you could possibly give me a ride to the train station?" she asked. "I need to get back to the city, I have to work tomorrow."

He would be glad to, the man said, though his wife looked a little wary.

"I'll just get my bag."

When she returned, Connie, still surrounded by middle-aged women, glared at her accusingly, with that mix of belligerence and affronted neediness that had always been impossible to allay. Reluctantly, Emma walked toward her.

"So you're leaving us, are you?" Connie asked.

Emma nodded.

"You planning to leave without even kissing me good-bye?"

Emma felt the eyes of the other women upon her; she put her dry mouth against Connie's cheek, still damp from tears.

"I'll call you," she said, although until that moment she had meant never to talk to her again.

"You better, you little brat," Connie said. "You better, you hear me?"

Emma smiled stiffly. "Of course."

"Okay then." She gave Emma's shoulder a push, tantamount, in her private language of blows and slaps, to a caress. "Go on, get out of here before I sock you one."

Emma went to say good-bye to Maria, who told her not to be a stranger; she smiled apologetically at Charlie, who turned away. Then she followed the couple out the door and into their car, which was parked at the bottom of the hilly driveway.

Once she was safely in the back seat, she worked the fingers of her hand into her pocket, down past the photographs, to make sure the cameo was still there, bundled in its blue tissue paper, and the pin pricked her finger. When she drew her hand out, she saw a small bright spot of blood.

CHAPTER EIGHT

*T*here was a new bag lady in her neighborhood, tall and skinny, where the others had all been squat and misshapen. It was impossible to guess her age; she had large, milky-blue eyes in a bashed-in face and walked very upright, her shoulders thrown back, as though she might have been a model once, or a debutante; she shouted out commands in a hoarse, defiant voice—Right turn! Halt! March!—her clogs making hard decisive noises on the pavement.

"Pardon?" Emma said, when anyone spoke to her on the street. "Excuse me?" when the woman sitting next to her in the typing pool asked her if she wanted anything from downstairs. She had not gone to the interview at the textbook publisher. Instead she had signed up with a temp agency; she was typing lists of chassis numbers for a trucking company on Tenth Avenue and Thirty-ninth Street.

Her father's death seemed unfinished, something that was still happening to her. Her father himself was present at all times, a distillation in the air around her, the feel of his sorrow distinct from her own grief. Everywhere she went that week, she moved in a cloud of him. But it was Khim she thought about in the dark, remembering the smell of his skin, the curve of his mouth on a glass, the exact rough breath with which he'd said her name. He at least was still alive somewhere; in a year, or a hundred years, he might come back to her.

And then it was Saturday again, and she was mounting the steps of Mrs. Rafferty's orange brick house. The wind was surprisingly gusty; it blew grit in her face while she waited for Mrs. Rafferty to answer the door; it ruffled Louisa's gray hair when they headed out on their walk. Louisa's shoes—cracked brown leather with a bow at the front—had higher heels than usual, as though in tribute to her glamorous youth. Their progress through the park was slowed; at one point, on the uneven slope leading to the water's edge, Louisa stumbled and almost fell. Before Emma managed to haul her to her feet again, it seemed as though they might go down together.

But finally they reached their bench, and she lowered Louisa onto it. It was not clear to her whether her mother was crying. There seemed to be tears on her face, but maybe that was just the wind, maybe Louisa had a cold. She very often had colds, which was why her person seemed so hedged about with crumpled tissues; she had a habit of using not only her pockets and her handbag and her sleeve but her bad hand as a repository for them, closing her useless fingers around them with her other hand and then prying them open when she needed to blow her nose.

Still, Emma could not remember seeing tears on her cheeks before. Silently, she put her hand in Louisa's pocket and drew out the inevitable disintegrating Kleenex. But instead of using it on her mother, she dabbed at a spot of what looked like dried blood on the bench between them. On closer inspection, it proved to be ketchup, still wet, as though it had been spilled just a moment before. "Be careful not to sit in that," she said. Louisa nodded. There were definitely tears on her face.

"Are you crying for him?" She had meant to sound kind, but blood was rushing to her head; her voice came out harsh and angry. "You shouldn't cry for him. You shouldn't. He didn't cry for you." Louisa stared at her, her mouth a round O. "Never mind," Emma said. "Never mind." And then, squeezing shut her eyes, "He wasn't happy."

"No?" Louisa asked, bewildered. For a moment Emma hesitated. It was too late to tell her mother what had gone on for all those years in the house in Connecticut. Back when she used to phone Connie to make arrangements about Emma, Louisa had always spoken admiringly of Connie's energy, her efficiency, her outgoing nature. In the dream that was her mother's substitute for a life, other people were happy, other people were good.

"How could he be happy," she asked furiously, "after what he did to you? How could he?"

But Louisa only shook her head. "The poor man . . . the poor man."

The wind was rising on the water; papers rustled along the path. Emma's breath came faster and faster. "Why do you always see it from his side? What about you?"

"It was so long ago," her mother said mournfully, her head still turned away. "Years and years. You shouldn't think about it any more."

"He should have asked your forgiveness. He should have come to you and said he was sorry, he could have done that much, just once." She did not like the sound of her own voice, shrill and childish; she wished that her mother would stop her, but still she went on. "I hope he rots in hell," she said then, even as the image came to her of her father in the hospital, the sweat pouring down his face, trying to pretend for her sake that he wasn't in pain.

Her mother was struggling to stand, pushing herself up off the bench with her good hand; it took three tries, but then she was on her feet, walking away.

And in that moment Emma saw the two boys walking across the grass in their shiny orange jackets, their sunglasses pushed up onto their heads. One of them was carrying a radio and snapping the fingers of his free hand; the other was doing an exaggerated, mocking jive walk, almost a dance, as they veered toward Louisa, shambling along the path. Their eyes scanned the horizon briefly, as though to ensure there was nobody around.

Emma got to her feet, running, her shoulder bag knocking against her hip; she arrived, breathless, at her mother's side just as the two boys stepped onto the path. The radio was blaring out a harsh staccato music; they stood there grinning. "Leave her alone," Emma screamed, "you leave her alone." The boy with the radio reached into his pocket, laughing; the knife in his hand flashed in the sun as he cut the strap of Emma's bag, in one graceful slash; the other one caught it as gracefully, and off they ran, yodeling in triumph, leaping into the air. "Come back," Emma sobbed, racing after them but falling farther and farther behind. "Come back here, I'll get the police, you bring that back." The boy holding her bag turned for a moment and said without malice, almost kindly, "Fuck you, lady."

She stumbled back along the path, gasping, to where her mother stood, with that stricken look Emma knew so well. "It's all right," Emma said, out of long habit, "it doesn't matter," her breath coming in ragged sobs. "I'll just have to change the locks, that's all. It doesn't matter." For her mother had suffered enough; she had to pretend, for Louisa, that all was well. Only she could not seem to stop crying.

"I'm sorry," she said, on a shuddery breath, "I'm just tired, that's all. I haven't been sleeping." And then she felt her mother's hand on her arm. Her mother never took her arm, her mother never initiated any contact. Louisa's grip was tentative at first, and then stronger and stronger; somehow, in her impractical shoes, she was steering Emma down the path, out of the park, along the street, to the door of Mrs. Rafferty's house. And then, without the usual fumbling for her keys, the usual unearthing of wads of shredded Kleenex and old cash register receipts, she was opening the door.

"Come in now," she said soothingly, as though talking to a child. "Come on." And Emma followed her to the stairs, past the door to Mrs. Rafferty's parlor, up to Louisa's room.

"You need a cup of tea," Louisa said, disappearing, still in her coat, into the little alcove with the hot plate and the crooked shelf, covered in oilcloth, that held the row of pink plastic cups. Emma, meanwhile, circled the room, unable to sit. As she reached the bookcase for the third time, her eye was caught by a green leather volume on the bottom shelf that looked vaguely familiar. Squatting down, she saw that it was Goethe, volume XXII. It was then she remembered the scalloped envelope.

She had put it in her bag, along with the letters, on her way out that morning; she had wanted to show the photographs to Louisa, and leave the letters for her to look through on her own, so that the following week she could tell her what they said. The cameo too: she had placed it carefully, in its blue tissue paper, into the inside pocket of the bag. At that thought she began crying harder than ever, still kneeling by the bookshelf; she rocked on her heels, powerless to stop.

A shadow passed over her; she looked up to see her mother standing there, still in her nubby coat, a dish towel draped over her bad arm. She did not speak; she only bent down clumsily, gripping Emma's shoulder with her good hand.

"It's just . . . ," Emma said, and then more sobs came, horrible ragged breaths. "It's just . . ." She clenched her hands, digging her nails into her palms to steady herself, until she could speak. "I had some things in that bag I took from his study. That I brought to show you. Some letters in German, I think they might have been from the First World War, there was a postcard too, showing men in uniform. Sent to Trudl Furchgott on some street in Nuremberg that began with *N*. Do you know where that was?"

"Neutoragraben. Where your grandparents lived."

"I couldn't read them, I thought you could tell me what they said. Plus there was a whole bunch of photographs." She burst into tears again. Her mother released her grip to take the dish towel off her arm and hand it to Emma, but Emma waved it away, wiping her snotty face with her hand instead.

"There was a little pin. A cameo. I think it was the one you were wearing in that painted photograph Grandma had. Only I wasn't sure. And it was wrapped up in tissue paper, with my name on it. Someone had written it there a long time ago, the ink was all faded. I wanted to ask you"—she had to stop again, to gulp back the sobs—"who had written it. Whose handwriting it was." Louisa was silent; when Emma looked at her, she was staring out the window, from which the faint sounds of the announcer of the football game at Baker Field could be heard. "Do you know who it was?"

Her mother looked around helplessly, as though trying to pluck the answer from the air. "I think so."

"Who? Who was it?"

"Your grandfather," Louisa said. "He wanted you to have it."

"Because it had been yours."

"Yes. And there was a story behind it."

"What story?"

Louisa looked down, bewildered, at the towel she was still holding. "When the Nazis came, and took him away to Dachau, they ransacked the house, everything they didn't steal was smashed. But when he came back, he found the cameo on the floor of my old room. It must have rolled into a corner. It was his mother who had given it to me, right before she died."

"And he brought it with him to America?"

"Yes. He would have given it to your father to keep until you were older."

Emma stood up. "Then why didn't he give it to me? My father, I mean."

Her mother shook her head. "I don't know. Maybe he didn't want you to think about that time."

"But now it's lost," Emma said, on a fresh wave of tears. "They'll sell it on Broadway for two dollars, they'll throw all the letters and pictures away." She put her head in her hands, sobbing. "I'll never even know who those people in the photographs were."

"Never mind," her mother said, with unwonted firmness. She smiled faintly. "You would have found them very boring."

"How can you say that?" Emma wailed. "They were my relatives."

"That wouldn't have made them any less boring."

"And the letters . . . We'll never know what was in them now."

"I remember what the men used to write during the war. 'We have marched seven miles today, and it is very cold. I think of you and the child constantly, and pray for your safety. Don't forget to order the coal early, before the bitter weather sets in.' And then the women wrote back and said, 'Tante Lotte was here for tea, I'm afraid her digestion is still very poor. Margarethe's daughter Elise is engaged to a nice engineer who is with the army in the west; she came and played the piano for us on Tuesday, all the old songs, she plays so beautifully.' That was the kind of thing they wrote each other."

"Then what about the cameo? I would have kept it always, I would have given it to my daughter."

"It was only a thing," her mother said, with that firmness in her voice again, that Emma did not recognize. "There's no point crying about things, they come and go. You should cry for your father."

"I am crying for my father," Emma said, and realized it was true. She sank back down onto the floor, and her mother went away again. When she came back she handed Emma a clean tissue, which Emma took blindly; she buried her face in it, stifling her sobs, she rocked back and forth. A few minutes later, her mother returned, bending over her, holding out a cup of tea in its pink plastic cup. Emma stretched out her hand for it and set it down beside her as she wept and wept.

CHAPTER NINE

*T*he burial of the ashes took place after a week of thunderstorms, when the ground was pure mud. In the new Jewish cemetery, opened a few months before on a hilly slope above the interstate, there were only about a dozen gravesites, scattered, seemingly at random, on an irregular diagonal. Some decision must have been made, a plan drawn up, but its logic escaped her.

She stood on the tussocky grass with her stepmother and the rabbi and four members of the hospital's Committee for the Future. The rabbi's voice, as he read the psalm, was snatched away by the wind and almost obliterated by the roar from below; over and over, a car approached, grew louder, faded away in the direction of Hartford, then another came along, and another. On the other side of the highway was a row of squat metal buildings housing car repair shops, bargain outlets, fast food places.

He would have said it didn't matter where his ashes were laid to rest. After his eyes had been taken, and his kidneys, after the medical students had dissected his organs, he would not have cared what happened to the remains. But Emma was remembering the prints on the wall of his study, the spires and bell towers and ancient walls.

Three days before, she had finally heard from Khim. "Forgive me," he had written, "for what I am going to tell you."

He had been married back in Cambodia, he said; they had a child, a son. He had been told that the boy and his wife were both dead, but on the Sunday when he had last seen her in New York he had heard that his wife was alive; she had escaped from the detention camp and after a terrible journey arrived in Paris. That was why he had left so abruptly.

"She has suffered very much," he wrote, "but now we are together. Perhaps we will have another child. She is not sure it is possible, after what she has been through, but that is what she wants, more than anything. And so I too want it for her. Please try to understand. I am ashamed that I never told you these things, but I could not speak of them. Now I wanted to tell you I have loved you. But this is the center of my life."

She read the letter twice, three times, unable to envision him writing it, so that she almost thought his wife had done it for him. "I can't forgive you, I won't, don't ask me that," she wrote to him, on and on, a whole page of accusation, which she tore into tiny pieces.

An engine misfired on the road below, in a series of sharp staccato bursts. Her stepmother's black mantilla flapped in the wind, its corner blowing into her mouth, from which she kept brushing it away. "His name," the rabbi said, "means 'fear of God,' but it was through the mercy of God that he arrived in this country. He did not mourn for his past, he looked to the future instead, and he would want us to look to the future now, to go on working toward that future he believed in." But Emma was thinking of the future he had lost, back in that walled city; she was trying to see the man he would have been. And then there was his other future, the American one, taken from him when the knife had slipped in the surgeon's hand.

That was the final photograph in her mother's album, the one that would always be missing: a man, a woman, their child between them, seated at a table. Ordinary happiness: French windows, a garden beyond, the Sunday papers, daffodils in a blue-and-white jug, a pot of jam, orange juice in a glass pitcher. The mother in the photograph has two good hands, two good eyes, the father is reading aloud to her from the paper. The daughter goes into the kitchen, yawning, to fetch the coffee. For years, it seemed—until the day her father told her about the cancer—she had been carrying that other life inside her, waiting for it to begin.

Soon she would answer Khim's letter. She would tell him that her father was dead; she would tell him she hoped he'd have another child: perhaps this time it would be a daughter. She would imagine him, she'd say, with his wife and little girl, there in Paris. But he must not write to her any more. Please understand, she'd say, as he had done. Love, Emma.

ACKNOWLEDGMENTS

For the gift of time and (beautiful) space, I am grateful to the Spiti tis Logotechnias in Paros, to the Corporation of Yaddo, to the Château de Lavigny, and to the Writers' and Translators' Centre of Rhodes. Heartfelt thanks to my agent, Marly Rusoff, for bringing me onto her raft, and to Judith Gurewich and all the lovely people at Other Press for paying such close attention.

To smooth out my narrative, I have had to take some minor liberties with dates, bringing certain historical events forward in time and condensing others into a shorter period. I have also anglicized the spelling of some German names.